PERCEPTION

a novel

MAUREEN HARTMAN

PROBABLY A BEAR
PRESS

DEDICATION

This story is dedicated to my father, who passed away far too young, but whose love and support remain with me still.

PART ONE
Where Were You?

CHAPTER 1

Mia didn't see the patch of gravel until it was too late. She fought for control as her Honda Rebel skidded across the double yellow line with a cargo van headed right for her. Heart pounding, she downshifted and pulled onto the opposite shoulder beneath a thick canopy of trees that shaded her from the late afternoon sun.

Breathless, she eased her helmet free and shuddered as a breeze brushed across her face and short-cropped hair.

Then she felt her cell phone vibrate from her leather jacket. Maybe it was Moon Harvest calling to say the job was hers. The interview had run long, but she took that as a good sign. They were interested enough to look beyond her sexual identity, skin color, and the four-year gap since her last marketing job.

Still rattled from her near collision, Mia took a deep breath and removed her phone with a trembling hand.

It wasn't Moon Harvest. Far from it. It was TJ, her half-brother. They hadn't spoken in years.

Mia stared at the phone in her open palm, her thumb hovering over the keypad as she considered answering the call.

A dried maple leaf, cupped into a tiny fist, tumbled across the gravel toward her and stopped at her feet. She looked from the leaf to the incoming number and swiped.

"Yes?" she said, clenching her free hand. She'd lived nearly as many years in the US as she had in Haiti, yet her English still carried a heavy Creole accent.

"Mia?"

It took a moment for her to register his voice, so much deeper than when they spoke last.

"TJ. Hello," Mia said, her voice wavering. She still hadn't had time to recover from her near wipe-out. Now, hearing TJ's voice, it was all she could do to breathe.

TJ must have noticed something was off because the next thing he said was, "Are you okay?"

Mia looked up at the vibrant leaves overhead, fluttering in the cool breeze. "I'm fine."

"I have some bad news," TJ said. Mia's imagination splintered in a dozen directions. *Bad news* could mean poor grades, a lost wallet, a flat tire. Or it could mean something far worse. "It's Ellis. He's in the hospital. He had a massive stroke."

Their father. The man who'd abandoned Mia's mother when he learned she was carrying his child. A man Mia neither loved nor respected. She called him by his last name because he'd told her to, but she soon learned that everyone called him Ellis, even his mother.

"I don't know what to say." This was as frank as Mia ever got. No matter how deep her feelings, she couldn't articulate them. It was a point of friction between Mia and her girlfriend, Kali, whose *I love you* often went unanswered.

TJ sighed, exasperated. "How about, 'How is he?' Or, 'Is there anything I can do?'" He paused. "Ellis is in bad shape, Mia. He may not have long."

"Where are you?" Mia asked. "Where is . . . he?"

"He's in the hospital here in Meridian. I'm at the cottage. You should be here, too."

"TJ, I—"

"You'll regret not seeing him if anything happens."

"I'll add it to the list," Mia said. TJ didn't answer right away, but Mia sensed the gears turning as he, like her, recalled their last conversation.

"We all have regrets," he said, finally.

Mia wondered if he was letting her off the hook, letting bygones be bygones for Ellis's sake. *Ellis.*

She owed him nothing. It was Ellis's fault Mia turned her back on the family home. The incident with TJ only fanned the flames.

"So?" TJ said. "Are you coming?"

"I'll think about it," she said.

Mia cruised into Drake, recalling the night TJ was arrested for selling cocaine at a high school dance. He'd asked for her help, and she'd let him down, calling Ellis, their father, after TJ explicitly told her not to. But Mia was at an Occupy Chicago demonstration hours away with her college friends. Not only did she not have a car; she had class the next day. Calling Ellis was her only option.

They hadn't spoken since.

Now, she had an opportunity to patch things up with TJ. That alone should be a reason to go to Meridian. But seeing Ellis again—

She made a lap around the town square, passing a block of scaffolding across from Drake Park. Drake was still rebuilding after a massive fire months earlier, when a white supremacist group had converged on the small Iowa town and turned it on its head. The community had pushed back, but Mia still looked over her shoulder for anyone with menace in their eyes.

Mia parked her bike at the curb outside her apartment building, thinking of that look—that flash of evil that preceded trouble. Her heart clenched as she recalled her youth in Haiti and the man she'd believed was the devil himself.

The October wind kicked up, and Mia shivered as she climbed the stairs to her apartment, each step heavier than the last. Once inside, she tossed her keys on the shelf by the door and dropped her backpack and helmet on the floor.

Mia tuned out the muted sound of a car alarm down the street and an emotional argument from the apartment upstairs as she regarded her ghostly reflection in the picture window over the sofa.

The short hair was new—an impulsive decision made in the barber chair before the interview that morning. She'd long ago given up the braids she'd worn as a child. That had been another impulse, shedding her old self and her old life in Haiti. As a teenager, her hair had grown into a wild mass of curls, like a halo.

But now the halo was gone. An adult stared back at her. The spitting image of her mother.

Beyond her reflection in the window, Mia had a view of the Old Oak standing guard in the center of the town square. At its feet was a plaque proclaiming that spot as the Center of the World. A boast derived from the fact that the tree was in the center of the park in the center of town in the center of the United States. Like ripples on a pond.

In Drake, Mia was "that Black foreign lesbian who works in the toy shop." *Black. Foreign. Lesbian.* So many labels to wear. But there were many more her neighbors knew nothing about. "Poor thing," she'd heard Mrs. Gardner say. But Mrs. Gardner didn't know Mia's father was white, or that she'd lived with the heavy mantle of being "mulatta" in a black world, and then in a white world. Mia endured that Haitian slur as a child. "Don't let that trouble you," Mama would say. "You will always my Sunshine." But once a mulatta, always a mulatta—that hateful word lived just below the skin. One more label for her to wear, and though she hadn't heard it in years, she could still sense when someone was thinking it.

She had Kali, though. Mia grinned, thinking of how her Jewish girlfriend's persistence had won her heart. They'd met the night of TJ's desperate call seven years earlier. Both events had been equally life changing.

With a sigh, Mia picked her helmet off the floor and set it on the bookshelf separating the rest of her studio apartment from the kitchenette. She slipped off her jacket and draped it over a kitchen chair, then opened a bottle of Shiraz and poured herself a glass to ease her frayed nerves.

The day had taken a bizarre turn with TJ's call. When her alarm went off that morning, Mia had leaped out of bed with a fire in her belly. The job at Moon Harvest was better than she'd ever expected to find in this small town. It would come with more responsibility than she'd had back in Chicago, where she'd risen to Chief Marketing Analyst less than two years out of college.

Working in Drake's toy shop had its charm, but she'd only taken that job to be closer to Kali. And now she was ready to get her career back on track.

Her phone buzzed in her jacket pocket, and she jumped.

The interview.

She fumbled for the phone and answered before checking who the caller was. "Hello. Mia Ellis speaking." It was silly. Mia never answered the phone this way, but she was nervous and wanted to appear professional.

There was a soft laugh, then, "Why hello, Mia Ellis. This is Kalinda Moon." Mia could hear the playful tease in Kali's voice. "What's all the formality about?"

"Oh, hey," Mia said, leaning back against the counter. "I thought it was about the job. Have you heard anything?"

"No, but I wouldn't worry if I were you. You're a shoo-in," Kali said. "After all, it's who you know, right?"

Not what you know. Mia hated that expression. She wanted to be judged on her merits, not on her relationship to the family. Moon Harvest was a legacy family business that made its fortune in the canning industry under the stewardship of Kali's great grandfather, but now Kali's brother, Eli, was resurrecting it as a fresh produce distribution center. Mia hoped to be part of that success.

"If you say so." Mia sipped her wine, then reached for the open bottle to top off.

"We on for tomorrow?" Kali asked. "We have an appointment with the realtor."

Mia fell silent, thinking of her lucrative job in Chicago, her apartment with a panoramic view of Lake Michigan—and how she'd given up both for Kali. But even that hadn't been enough. Kali needed commitment, and Mia wasn't ready to let go of her last hold on independence.

As a psychologist, Kali loved getting to the root of any problem. But Mia resisted sharing her problems, emotional or otherwise. Like Hispaniola, the place of her birth, Mia was an island. When disaster struck, she held firm, standing strong and self-reliant.

"I get it," Kali said, breaking the silence, her voice suddenly strained. "You're a loner. I can't change that and don't want to. I love you the way you are, but—I need more. Something that says you need me. Anything."

Mia swirled the remaining wine in her glass, then finished it. *Or what? Was this an ultimatum?* No. Kali wasn't like that. And Mia's hesitance wasn't just about her independence.

"My brother called," she said. Kali knew about the rift with TJ. She'd been there when it happened, and even if Mia had never fully revealed how deeply it hurt her, she suspected Kali had some idea. "Ellis is in the hospital in Meridian," Mia continued. "He had a stroke."

"What? My God, Mia. Why didn't you say something sooner?"

Mia shrugged. She hadn't intended to say anything at all and immediately regretted her change of heart.

"You need to go to him," Kali said excitedly. "You need to—"

"Stop," Mia said. "Just—stop."

"He's your father, Mia."

"Ellis is not like other fathers. He's nothing like your dad was." There was a long pause. Kali's parents had drowned in a ferry accident six years earlier. It still weighed heavily on her and her brother. "Ellis and I were never close."

"He's your father," Kali said—as if repeating herself would change Mia's mind.

"You don't understand," Mia said. "You don't know."

"How could I? You shut me out! I don't even know how you feel about *me* half the time."

"I'm not like you."

"I'm not saying that you have to be," Kali said. "But maybe it would help if you could just let me in—let *anyone* in."

Mia shared a sliver of her past with Kali after the riots in town that summer, cracking open the door to her Haitian childhood. Corruption, threats of violence, and the mayhem following the fire had brought back vivid memories of catastrophic storms and poverty in her homeland, a single mother who worked tirelessly to give Mia a home and security while fending off street gangs and enduring the swinging door of Haitian leadership.

"I've seen it all before," she'd said thinking of the ugliness of her past, then buttoned up. But the memory of Uncle Jean's leering eyes amid a throng of angry protesters could not be silenced. Nor could the stain on her innocence. If Mia said anything to Kali, she'd have to say it all, and she was unready, perhaps unable to speak about any of it. That was the world Ellis left her to.

Kali wanted to dive deeper into how Mia's past inflicted indelible scars. She believed it was only by examining those scars that Mia could fully heal them and finally break out of her thick shell. After everything she'd been through, who wouldn't want to keep that shell intact?

Mia regretted ever opening that door. She didn't want Kali's help. She didn't want to remember all that—shit. And she especially didn't want to drag it out for Kali's examination. Kali had remarked early in their relationship that Mia was emotionally stunted.

Emotionally stunted? The words stung. Mia had never seen herself that way. She cared deeply about people and animals and supported every social cause. A bleeding-heart liberal to the core. Just because she struggled to open up with Kali didn't mean she couldn't, right?

"I love you, Mia," Kali said. There it was. Kali's secret weapon. That, and her disarming smile.

Mia stared into her empty wine glass, thinking of the magic words resting on the tip of her tongue. They should have been easy to say, but Mia couldn't—though she'd loved Kali since first setting eyes on her in college. Kali Moon was beautiful, intelligent, and patient to a fault.

"You too," Mia finally said.

After the call, Mia poured herself another glass of wine and cued up a recent playlist on her Bluetooth speaker. Joss Stone sang "Right To Be Wrong" while Mia sat at her kitchen table admiring her grandmother's hand-embroidered tablecloth and a pair of sapphire-blue salt and pepper shakers—the last vestiges of her life in Haiti. This was all that remained of Mia's childhood—before her mother's illness, before life in the United States, and before learning how to navigate the unfamiliar culture and family she'd been thrust into fourteen years ago.

The Ellis family estate in Meridian, Indiana was a six hour ride away, but as foreign to her as another planet. Light years from the little cinderblock on Rue Janvier.

Mia traced the coiled tendrils on the tablecloth with the tip of her finger until it rested on the words that followed: *L'union fait la force.* Unity Makes Strength—the Haitian credo.

Unity. Ellis. Hospital. *What should I do?*

CHAPTER 2

He's your father, Kali had said. Mia went to bed that night, haunted by those words. Though technically true, Mia had never had that connection with Ellis. Forget emotionally stunted. Theodore Ellis was altogether lacking.

TJ said she'd regret not seeing him. Would she? It didn't seem possible, though TJ had opened the door for reconciliation.

Sleep eventually came, but once Mia's room filled with the morning light, the push and pull resumed with the addition of a new anxiety. Moon Harvest and her interview.

She forced herself out of bed and padded into the kitchen, where her wine glass from the previous night sat beside the sink. She rinsed out the crusty garnet residue and filled the Bialetti coffee pot with freshly ground espresso. Then her phone pinged with a text from TJ.

Visiting hours til 8. Are you coming or not?

Still on the fence, Mia finished making her coffee, took a long shower, and scrolled through her newsfeed, all the while telling herself she was waiting to hear about her interview, knowing it was a convenient excuse. Cell phones are, by design, portable. If Moon Harvest called, it wouldn't matter where she was. Meridian was a six hour ride. It was two o'clock. She might still make visiting hours. Finally, she replied. *Just leaving.*

Mia tossed a few essentials into her backpack and grabbed her helmet, then bombed down the highway under a cloudless sky to whatever fate awaited her three hundred and eighty miles away.

The first few miles flew by—just two wheels on the pavement and the engine's purr as Mia rode past acres of farmland, bales of alfalfa and hay, and soybean fields being tilled under for the season. Then the gravity of the trip hit her. She felt ill suddenly, as bits of memory encroached from all sides, seeded by suffocating anxiety about returning to Meridian and the people she'd left behind.

Halfway there, Mia stopped to refuel, briefly considering whether to turn back before she mounted her bike with three hours to go in either direction. The prospect of house hunting with Kali sounded more appealing, stacked against seeing her father again after so long.

Had Ellis ever given Mama or me a second thought after abandoning us in Haiti? Mia wondered, convinced he'd never wanted her from the start.

Mia believed that she was nothing more to Ellis than the illegitimate child foisted on him after her mother died. A mistake that had come back to haunt him. He'd never said as much, but Mia saw it in his eyes when she met him at the port, fresh off the boat from Haiti on the heels of Hurricane Jeanne. Something in his stare that searched her face and found her wanting.

She'd resisted leaving the only home she'd known, but at the time, she had nowhere else to go. Neither of them, it seemed, had a choice in the matter.

Twilight had given way to darkness an hour before she spotted the clock tower and the steeple from St. Mark's up ahead.

Welcome to Meridian, Indiana—Population 15,158.

The sign was riddled with pop shots from gun-toting locals. *What is it with these people?* Mia wondered. *Don't they know how good they have it?*

She'd missed visiting hours. It was a strange relief. The idea of seeing Ellis felt like a hundred-pound weight on her shoulders. But now that weight was replaced by a new anxiety.

What awaited her at the Ellis estate. And who?

A flutter of guilt nested in Mia's belly, as she passed through the gates thinking of Rosa and Oscar, two undeserving souls she'd left behind with her life in Meridian. They'd been the housekeeper and groundsman when she'd first arrived. She'd thought they were old then, but they'd likely be in their seventies now. Mia had written Rosa after her move to Drake; a quick note to say she was well. Their correspondence was short lived, though. Something Mia felt responsible for.

The gravel beneath Mia's wheels popped and crunched as she rolled slowly down the dark drive past the big house she'd mistaken as a palace when she'd first arrived as a fifteen-year-old girl. A little further down the drive, she passed the stable and the tool shed.

Finally, she reached the little gray cottage her father called home. The porch light was on, meaning someone was there.

Mia hesitated at the front door—wondering if she should knock as a guest would. Instead, she turned the cold brass handle and let herself into the living room, where TJ sat poised in front of the television, clutching an X-Box controller.

In the television's glow, he looked much the same as when she'd seen him last with his shaggy blond hair and rumpled clothes. But he was stockier than she remembered, and the wire-rim glasses had been replaced by thick black frames.

Mia sat beside him on the ugly plaid sofa, which was stained and sagging under decades of wear. Despite having come from money, Ellis still lived on the meager wages he earned working for the same non-profit that had taken him to Haiti in the first place: Global Vision. An organization that researched poverty without ever ending it.

"You made it," TJ said, pulling his headphones from one ear but still staring ahead at the screen, busily working the controller as his dark-hooded game character stealthily darted through a thick forest, a hatchet in hand, intent on slaughter as he approached a band of thieves or some equal foe. Mia couldn't tell. She didn't really care. "Beer's in the fridge," he said. "Help yourself."

Mia reached beside her and flicked on the table lamp, then looked closer at the scene around her. A bong, half-filled with rank water, sat on the coffee table beside a family-size bag of corn chips and two empty beer bottles.

The kitchen reeked of spoiled milk from a tower of cereal bowls stacked in the sink among a pile of other unrinsed dishes. The refrigerator handle was so grimy Mia reconsidered the beer and returned to the living room empty-handed.

She glanced down the short hallway toward Ellis's bedroom behind the staircase. The door was open a crack and she imagined for a moment that he was in there, crouched over his roll-top desk, grumbling as he contemplated his mission to save the world from poverty while neglecting the people immediately around him.

TJ had warned her off the room in the early days. Once, left alone and to her own devices, she'd challenged that advice, getting as far as the threshold before Ellis's car pulled up out front. She remembered her heart-stopping panic as she hurried up to her room.

Another time, Ellis had invited her in. He was leaving for a trip and wanted to show her something important. "Just in case," he'd said without mentioning where he was going. It was safe to assume it was a dangerous place. Afghanistan or some other war-torn country. "Everything you need to know is there," he'd said, pointing to the waist-high antique file cabinet he used as a bedside table.

Now, Mia sighed and stretched, reaching high above her head and twisting side to side. Her back was killing her from the long trip.

"What are you playing?" she asked, returning to the sofa.

"Shh!" said TJ, furiously manipulating the controller, his eyes riveted to the television. "Fuck!" He glared at her as if it was her fault he'd lost. Then he threw down the controller and turned to her, breathing heavily through his nose, and she saw that his irritation went deeper than the game.

TJ grabbed a half-full beer from the table and cocked his head like a curious pup. "What'd you do to your hair?"

Mia reached into the open bag for a handful of chips. "Like it?"

"No," he said flatly. "You look like a guy." He sucked the beer dry and leaned back, his free arm draped across the back of the couch. "Did you see Ellis?"

Mia shook her head. "Just missed the deadline. I'll go in the morning."

TJ nodded and cleared his throat as if he was about to say something important, then focused on the empty bottle in his hand. They had so much to say to one another, but it seemed neither was ready to open that door. What would she say to him after seven years of silence? She wasn't about to apologize for something she'd had no control over. But she felt obligated to explain herself because, although their rift was ancient, she still felt guilty. She opened her mouth to bring up the difficult subject, then reconsidered.

"How is he?" she said.

"Ellis? He's . . ." TJ sighed, his face twisting into what Mia read as uncertainty. Was it uncertainty over whether to tell her the truth? Or uncertainty over what the truth even was?

"You said you didn't know how much longer he had," Mia said.

"I did?"

"You said it was bad and that I'd regret—"

"Right. Yeah. He won't eat. Can't speak. I don't know the details. You'll need to ask GG. Does she know you're here?"

"Not yet," Mia said, wondering why he'd implied Ellis's condition was terminal when he didn't even know. "I'll pop in on the big house tomorrow. It'll be nice to see Rosa." TJ nodded, then started collecting some of the mess around him. Tension, borne from years of absence, filled the space between them.

The big house was the main household on the estate. Only TJ and Mia called it the big house, something she'd learned from him when her English wasn't much better than baby talk. She hadn't known at the time that "big house" also meant prison. That interesting point made more sense later. She'd learned that GG had been TJ's name for their grandmother long before Mia arrived. They never said it to her face, however. They wouldn't dare.

"God, I'm tired," Mia said. "Mind if I just go up to bed?"

TJ glanced at the clock over the TV and shrugged, then picked up his controller. Mia grabbed her backpack and tramped up the worn wooden stairs that creaked and groaned beneath her feet.

She took a deep breath and opened the closed door at the end of the hall, exhaling as she flicked on the light.

Her old room looked smaller than she remembered. She noticed the gingham curtains missing from the wood-framed window overlooking the driveway. The plaster walls were flaking, and the blue-and-gold braided rug was missing.

A layer of dust covered the desk and matching dresser that was once cluttered with a rainbow of Post-it notes and hardcover schoolbooks. Mia opened the top desk drawer. Amid a jumble of dried-out markers, loose staples, and pencil shavings, she spied a heavily creased photo of her dog, Ezra, a German Shepard mix who'd been her constant companion and confidant. He was curled up beside her on her bed, his eyes locked on the person taking the photo. Natalie.

Sighing, Mia set the photo aside and felt around for the silver pen she had taken from Mama's dresser. It was missing. She waved away the loss. Ezra. Mama. The pen. All part of her past now, like so much of her life. Glancing at the unmade bed, she remembered the quilt Rosa had made that Mia took with her to college and now lay at the foot of her bed in Drake. An army jacket with a peace sign stenciled on the arm hung in the wardrobe beside a moth-eaten cardigan and a faded blue tote bag.

Mia tried the jacket on. It was hard to imagine a time when it had fit. But the sweater and jacket had been her odd uniform in high school, further distancing her from the other students—who'd rejected her before she'd arrived, based on her origins and the color of her skin. Mia wasn't *that* dark, but what was enough to mark her as *other* in Haiti made her untouchable in Meridian.

Mia unpacked what little she'd brought from Drake, two shirts, a pair of gray cargo pants, and the black cashmere sweater Kali had given her on her birthday a few years earlier. She retrieved some musty bedsheets and a down comforter from the hall closet, then shook them out before putting them on the bed, but the stale odor still lingered, and the elastic corners of the fitted sheet cracked beneath her fingers.

Mia's phone buzzed. It was Kali.

Where are you?

Meridian.

Why didn't you say? I'll pack tonight. Be there AM.

Don't.

????

I'm handling it.

Then Kali called. Mia let it go to voicemail and then played the message.

"What's happening, Mia? Is your dad going to be all right? Please call me. I need to hear that *you're* all right." There was a long pause, and then the message went on. "I'm worried about you. Don't you see? You're shutting me out again. Please don't shut me out." Mia turned off the overhead light and returned to the bed. "I'll leave first thing in the morning," the message said. "We need to talk."

Mia closed her eyes and took a deep breath, thinking of what lay ahead the next day. Adding Kali to the mix would only make things more complicated.

Mia texted her reply, *I said NO*, then turned off the phone, stripped off her clothes, and crawled under the sheets.

It was strange being in her old bed again. In her old room again. She gazed out the window at the stars, thinking of the four years she'd spent in Meridian, remembering Ezra, Rosa, and summer afternoons at the lake with Natalie.

Okay, she thought, *it wasn't* all *bad*. And she drifted off to sleep.

The next morning, while TJ slept, Mia put on her coat and hat and took a walk in the early morning sun.

Having arrived at night, she hadn't noticed how badly the estate had slipped into disrepair. But in the light of day, she couldn't help but see peeling paint on the cottage exterior and a door on the tool shed that hung cockeyed from its hinges. She walked around the fountain—defunct now, with the water turned off and crumbling cement along its edges.

Mia set off for the barn to see if Oscar was inside. When she got to the door, she tugged on the handle, anticipating the familiar scent of hay and manure. But it was dark and empty and smelled like dust and mold. A quick peek out the back—into the paddock and beyond to the overgrown pasture—painted a grim picture. When she'd first arrived at the estate, there were three horses. Her favorite was Freddy. He was calm and steady, making her feel at ease in her new surroundings.

With a heavy sigh, Mia left the barn to search for the trail from the house to the small private lake where she'd spent long days as a teenager swimming, reading, or hiding out. Sometimes alone. But her most treasured memories included her friend, Natalie.

The trail was easy to find back then, but the grass and shrubs had grown so high over the years that it eluded her now. She circled back to the cottage through the pasture veiled in a paper-thin layer of frost.

When she returned, Mia found TJ slouched at the kitchen table with a spoonful of Captain Crunch balanced before his open mouth.

"Do you know what happened to the horses?" she asked. "To Freddy?"

"Ellis sold Bitten and Liesel. Freddy's dead," TJ sputtered with a full mouth before bringing the bowl to his lips and slurping out the rest.

Freddy's dead. Mia felt a sharp stab deep in her heart.

TJ set down the empty bowl and bowed his head. "He was blind at the end," he said. "Kept wandering, so Ellis shot him."

The knife twisted, inflicting more pain. As if Mia didn't already have enough reasons to resent her father. Did he *have* to reach into his gun locker? Hadn't there been a more merciful way to deal with Freddy?

She picked up TJ's bowl and brought it to the sink, where she ran hot water over the mountain of dirty dishes.

"Are you going to the hospital today?" she asked.

"Yeah. Want a ride?" TJ said.

"No, I'll drive myself. I want to pop in on Rosa and check on Oscar."

"And GG?" he said.

"Ugh, yes. I should probably present myself to the almighty GG." She removed her jacket and laid it over a chair, then pushed up her sleeves. TJ eyed the growing dome of suds and grinned. "You knew I'd do this, didn't you?" Mia said, with a nod to the stack of dirty dishes.

"No, but I'm glad you are." He stood and joined her at the sink. "I'm glad you're here."

Where was the cold shoulder, the rage, and the accusations she'd braced for?

Mia felt her heart surge with love for her little brother. Growing up, he'd only been a part-time resident at the cottage, having spent most of his time with his mom, Francis, in Indianapolis. But he'd always tried to make Mia feel like she belonged.

"You still seeing that girl? What was her name? Chrissy? Christie?" he asked.

"Chrissy," she said, remembering her college roommate of four years. "We were never a couple."

TJ nodded. He'd known about Natalie, Mia's first girlfriend. Mia's only friend in high school, though they'd never discussed it.

"I'm seeing someone now, though." Mia stared down into the growing dome of suds filling and surrounding the bowls. "She wants to move in together."

"And you?" he asked. Mia shrugged one shoulder to indicate she didn't know, not that she didn't care.

She sank her hands into the warm, soapy water, thinking about Kali and the night they met. It was the same night TJ had called for help. She thought about how much she'd missed her brother. How on earth could she have let so much time pass? Was it pride? Was it shame? She remembered the early days when he taught her the ways of the household while providing her with an easy friendship she desperately needed. The five-year gap between them—irrelevant.

The cottage felt quiet after TJ left for the hospital—nothing but the sighs and groans of an old building and a funny wheeze from the refrigerator. A familiar feeling crept up on Mia, reminding her of days long ago while TJ was at Francis's and Ellis was out of town. How interesting that she preferred to live alone now, comfortable in the solitude she'd grown accustomed to under Ellis's roof.

Mia shook off the feeling and returned to her room. Her phone was plugged into the charger on her old desk. No new messages. No new texts. Not from Moon Harvest or Kali. She considered calling Kali to apologize or at least explain. But where would she start? She began to dial the number for Moon Harvest, then backtracked, not wanting to appear needy. "You're a shoo-in," Kali had said. But why hadn't they called? She checked her watch. Eleven already. She should be getting to the hospital, but first, she wanted to pop in on Rosa, who'd likely be in the warm kitchen at the big house—the only place on the estate where Mia ever felt at home.

After a quick shower and a change of clothes, Mia jogged down the drive, shaking off the cold morning. Then she looked up and saw Oscar coming toward her.

"Oh, Chica, where have you been?" he said, holding out his arms for her embrace. His face looked leathered, and his silver hair was overgrown and sticking out from beneath a ragged Chicago Cubs cap.

"I've missed you," she said, falling into his open arms while holding back the sting of tears and the sharp pang of regret for her absence.

Oscar stepped back and laid an arthritic hand on Mia's close-cut hair. "You're as beautiful as ever," he said.

She took his hand and held it. "You're teasing," she said with a wry smile. The feel of his cold, callused hand and swollen knuckles reminded her of someone she'd known back in Haiti. Someone she hadn't thought of in years.

Oscar gave her hand a squeeze. "So, you didn't come all this way to see old Oscar, did you?"

Mia felt a sharp pang in her chest. Although she had her reasons for staying away, they didn't include ignoring the couple who had treated her so kindly. Now, thinking of how she'd fallen out of touch with Rosa and Oscar, she felt ashamed.

"I'm sure your father will be glad to see you," Oscar said. But Ellis hadn't once been glad to see her. It was one of the reasons she'd been reluctant to return. Mia shivered as a chill went up her spine. "Go on inside, Chica. The kitchen is warm, and Rosa will want to know how you are." Oscar put a warm arm around her shoulders and gave her another embrace before setting her free.

Mia hurried to the kitchen door around the side of the big house. She ducked under a neglected wisteria arbor, its gnarled, woody tendrils woven up, over, around, and through. Mia recalled the clustered lavender-colored spring blossoms and reached down to run her hand across a clump of rosemary in the herb garden she'd helped tend with Rosa as a teenager. The piney scent reminded her of dirt-crusted fingernails and overflowing weed buckets, followed by the reward of Rosa's savory biscuits and a tall glass of milk.

The kitchen door stuck at first, then groaned open. Mia was overcome by the heavenly scent of cinnamon and baked apples. Her heart soared when she saw Rosa standing at the sink, her face glowing in the diffused light filtering through the window's lace curtains.

Rosa turned around and beamed. "Ah!" she shrieked playfully. "It must be a ghost I'm seeing!"

"Very funny," said Mia, amused but ashamed.

Rosa pulled her hands from the sink and gave Mia a warm hug, leaving wet imprints like angel wings on her back. Mia sank into the loving embrace. Rosa had always been an oasis of love in an otherwise loveless place. She'd been the housekeeper since Ellis was young, and her husband, Oscar, cared for the grounds just as long.

"Sit, dear girl," said Rosa. The oven timer rang, and Rosa removed a fresh apple pie with a pair of stained and tattered oven mitts. After a vigorous fanning, she cut a slice, placed it on a china plate dotted with tiny blue forget-me-nots, and laid it on the table, mumbling something about how thin Mia had gotten and how she was wasting away.

"I'm hardly wasting away," Mia said, ogling the sweet deliciousness of this unconventional breakfast. Or was it lunch already? The morning had flown by, and she still hadn't been to see Ellis. The word *procrastinator* might as well have been stamped across her forehead.

"It's been too long," Rosa said, placing two cups of hot coffee on the table and sitting across from her. "Tell me, how are you doing?" There was no hint of malice in Rosa's voice and no attempt to make Mia feel ashamed. As if Mia had been sitting at Rosa's table just yesterday.

Mia brought her fork to her lips wondering how much to share as the sweet pie filling tickled her tongue, but it had been too long since they'd sat across from one another like this, so she set the fork down and gave the moment the respect it deserved.

She talked about her life in Drake, glazing over the mayhem of the summer riots. It didn't come as a surprise to Rosa, the riots had been all over the news. But Mia didn't want to get caught up in that now with so much else to talk about, like her interview with Moon Harvest.

"You deserve every happiness," Rosa said. Mia winced. They were the kind of words Mama would have said. After so many years, that was still very difficult to think about. Grief was always standing by for a sneak attack.

Mia focused on the apple filling oozing across her plate. "You know about Ellis," she said.

Rosa nodded. "Yes, I know," she said. "It was pandemonium here that day. I heard he's struggling. That's why you're here? You want to say goodbye?"

"It's not like he's dying," Mia said, looking up. Rosa scowled, and for a moment, Mia panicked. Maybe TJ had been right. "He's *dying*?"

But before Rosa could answer, GG appeared at the door to the butler's pantry on the other side of the kitchen, her trademark French twist tightly in place. She wore a navy-blue cardigan over a starched white blouse and a pair of black slacks with patent leather mules shined to a mirror-like finish.

Years ago, GG had been tall and lean, with perfect posture and a piercing gaze. She was smaller now, thinner, her shoulders hunched protectively over a sinking chest. But the piercing gaze remained and fixed itself on Mia.

The sweet taste of apples and cinnamon turned sour in Mia's mouth as she set down her fork. "Hello, grand-mère," she said. It was GG who'd decided Mia would address her in French. At the time, speaking only Creole and the occasional French, Mia couldn't object.

GG pointed at Mia. "Come with me."

Mia took a deep breath, fighting the butterflies in her chest. "I should really be getting to the hospital," she said. But GG turned to go as if she hadn't heard.

Mia followed her down the narrow hall. There was a new cadence to GG's pace, slower, more careful than Mia remembered years ago. GG led Mia through the house and into the glassed-in sunporch stuffed with tropical plants. Mia had always enjoyed this room. Besides the kitchen, it was the only place in the grand house where she could breathe.

GG settled into a white wicker armchair. Mia opted for the sofa, using the glass coffee table as a buffer between them. From here, she had a view of the garden, the perennials brown with the latest freeze. The woods beyond were lit up in a spectacle of fall colors. Mia recalled TJ sharing the makeshift fort he'd created as his personal hideout. It hadn't occurred to her until now that he needed her company as much as she'd needed his.

"Well," GG said with a sigh, interrupting Mia's thoughts. "Here you are." The statement landed heavily in the space between them.

"Mm." Mia's phone buzzed from her back pocket. Kali? Moon Harvest?

GG leaned forward. "Is this what it takes to show your face around here after all this time?"

Mia had never talked back to the old woman, though she'd been pushed to her limit many times. "Excuse me, grand-mère?"

"You turned your back on us after your brother ended up in jail."

"That's not the whole story," Mia said, recalling that night and the days that followed. But the final straw came later.

Mia felt her phone vibrating again but didn't dare reach for it.

"So, TJ takes a wrong turn, and you turn your back on all of us. Even as your father paid for college. Even after he rescued you from that cesspool they call Haiti."

Mia shook her head but couldn't remain silent. "That was no rescue. He *had* to take me."

"Ellis didn't *have* to do anything. But he did. And where would you be without him?" GG locked her steely gaze on Mia. "Then, after all he did for you, you deserted him."

The man who deserted my mother and me to the perils of a country always on the verge of disaster. The man who later left me to my own devices in a foreign country, a foreign home.

I don't have a father, thought Mia, wishing she'd had the nerve to say the words out loud. But she knew where that would lead, and she wasn't here to fight, especially with a woman convinced of her own truth.

Mia wondered why her grandmother had requested her company. If it was merely to chastise her, then mission accomplished. But if she was fishing for an apology, Mia had none to offer.

Rosa entered with a steaming pot of tea and two china cups on a copper tray. "Grand-mère, I still need to get to the hospital." Mia said, making eye contact with Rosa. A silent thank you for her timely interruption. Rosa nodded, her eyes twinkling in understanding.

"You'll be at my table tonight. Francis will be joining us," GG said.

Mia remembered these affairs—a formal meal in the massive dining room, with china, crystal, and stilted conversation. The addition of TJ's mother, Francis, only made the invitation less inviting.

Mia did some quick calculations. How long would it take to pack her bag, check in on Ellis, and get on the road back to Drake? She'd planned for two days, three maybe, but one was more than enough. She felt no obligation toward GG, nothing at all for Francis. If it hadn't been for TJ, Mia wouldn't have made the trip at all.

"I'll be here," Mia said.

For TJ.

CHAPTER 3

Mia rolled cautiously into the hospital parking lot; her chest flooded with dread in anticipation of seeing Ellis again. Would he be angry? Disappointed? Or, less likely, glad to see her? She parked her motorcycle in an open spot between a shiny black Mazda and an old blue Toyota, psyching herself up for whatever awaited her.

Meridian Hospital wasn't more than two floors with an outpatient annex across the street. Nevertheless, it had ranked among the best in the state for the past six years. A record proudly displayed with a decal on the glass front doors.

Mia hugged her helmet to her chest as she reached for the handle. TJ stood just on the other side.

"Hey," he said, crossing his arms over a faded black sweatshirt. "What took you so long?"

Mia didn't feel like drilling down on the emotional gauntlet she'd cleared that morning just to get there.

"How is he?" she asked.

"He's asleep, but you should go up anyway. You need to see him. I'll meet you at home."

Home? Where was that, exactly? Not Haiti; not anymore. Not Meridian, certainly. She considered Kali's persistent plea to move in together. Would *that* be home?

But she knew what TJ meant—*their* home. The little gray cottage with white trim where they'd first set eyes on one another, and she'd learned she had a brother.

Inside, a middle-aged white woman in a pink sweater looked warily up at Mia from behind a crescent-shaped desk. Her nametag said *Marcie.*

"I'm here to see Theodore Ellis," Mia said.

Marcie narrowed her eyes and sized Mia up, as if thinking, *I'm not so sure about you.* Mia wondered if that had more to do with her foreign accent or her brown skin. "Visitor, then." Marcie peeled off the VISITOR sticker and handed it over. "Room 216. West End."

Mia applied the sticker and climbed the stairs to the second floor. She passed a wall of windows overlooking the parking lot and the hospital annex across the street. Once she reached the bustling nurse's station, she turned left down the first hallway. An orderly popped out of a door on her left, slinging a laundry bag over his shoulder. Mia entered a dimly lit room 216 across the hall.

A repetitive beep and wheeze of machines filled the air, and blinking lights and numbers flashed on several monitors. Mia stepped closer and glanced at the IV taped to the back of Ellis's black-and-blue hand.

As TJ had said, Ellis was asleep. Mia studied his face, something she hadn't done since stepping off that boat from Haiti. Back then, he'd been a big man with a thick beard, shaggy jet-black hair, bushy eyebrows, and a permanent scowl. Now he looked gaunt. He appeared far older than his sixty years. His hair was mostly silver and looked greasy, and it seemed his beard hadn't been groomed in weeks. Mia hated to acknowledge it, but she felt sorry for him. She looked closer and saw that his eyebrows were tightly knit together. Even sleeping, he didn't look at peace.

She sat on the vinyl chair beside the bed and checked her phone. Still nothing from Moon Harvest, but there was a string of texts from Kali.

> Call me
>
> We need to talk
>
> You're scaring me. Please call.

Mia tucked her phone into her back pocket and looked up at the whiteboard by the door. *Theodore Michael Ellis* was neatly printed across the top. The attending doctor, *Dr. SK Patel*, was printed below it, followed by *Becky*, the nurse on duty. Ellis's admission date was below that.

A week ago. TJ had waited a *week* to call?

The other side of the board read VISITORS: TJ Ellis, Francis Turner, and Jacob Sparks, Ellis's friend since childhood. They'd all checked in before Mia.

She heard Ellis cough and turned to see him gazing at her through glassy eyes.

"You," he whispered in Creole, his voice raspy with disuse. He'd used her name only twice in her life that she could remember. Mia scooted her chair closer, expecting him to say more. He didn't—or couldn't.

"Hey," she said.

A perky young nurse with rosy cheeks and strawberry blond hair entered the room in squeaky shoes and turned up the lights. Nurse Becky, Mia realized. She grinned at Mia, her big blue eyes taking in the scene. "More visitors, Mr. Ellis. Ain't you popular today?"

"Hmph," said Ellis, his left arm twitching as his right arm lay limp on the bed, held in by the side rail.

Nurse Becky busied herself with Ellis's chart, checked the drip on the IV, then turned to Mia. "Name?"

"Ellis," Mia said. "Mia Ellis. His daughter."

"Oh!" Nurse Becky sounded surprised. People usually were when they learned of her relationship to Ellis. It was like checking out a warbler's nest and finding a cowbird. *How did that one get in there?* Mia sighed and turned to her father, who still hadn't taken his eyes off her.

Becky turned to the board and added Mia's name in all caps, then walked out the door, the squeak of her shoes going with her. Mia glanced at the board and rolled her eyes. MIA. Missing In Action. Perfect.

Ellis raised his left arm in front of him, his hand turned up, and his fingers fanned out. He jerked his elbow back and tried again but gave up halfway through. Was he trying to wave? To point? Then his eyes focused on the top of Mia's head. She noticed a slight tug on the side of his mouth as if he was trying to smile.

"Oh, the hair?" Mia ran a hand across the back of her head. "It was kind of impulsive, but I'm getting used to it." She reached into her coat pocket and pulled out a black knit cap. "This helps."

"Mm," he said. Then he tried to speak. "*Eshed fa za . . .*" Scowling, he tried again. "*Eshed fos . . .*"

He stopped. It wasn't going the way he'd wanted. His frustration was transferred onto Mia with a look she interpreted as two parts irritation and one part embarrassment.

She could remember only twice since knowing Ellis that they'd shared anything resembling a conversation. It was strange on both occasions but not as awkward as this.

A quick tap at the door was immediately followed by a dark-skinned man wearing a white coat. He had a boyish face and beautiful doe-like eyes. Mia watched as his fingers toyed with either end of a stethoscope draped around his neck.

"Dr. Patel," he said, holding out a hand. "The nurse says you are family?"

"I'm Mia, his daughter."

There was an acknowledgment in his easy smile. *Namaste*, it said. Traditionally meaning, the divine in me sees the divine in you, but Mia guessed he was referring to their shared experience of being dark-skinned people in a predominantly white community. Perhaps he saw her as a fellow foreigner, though she felt more American than Haitian these days.

He stepped up to the bed and raised Ellis to a sitting position. Mia saw by the abrupt downturn of one of her father's bushy black eyebrows that he was irritated by this. Or maybe that was from the stroke.

"I heard about the feeding tube," said Dr. Patel, and Ellis grumbled. "It's just until you can swallow safely. Do you understand?"

One side of Ellis's face smirked while the other remained fixed in a pout. The doctor shook his head and pulled a digital tablet from his pocket. After jotting down a few notes, he turned to Mia.

"Do you have a moment?" he asked, clearing his throat and motioning for her to join him in the hall.

Two men walked by, the younger one speaking in whispers, the older one straining to hear him. Dr. Patel waited for them to pass before speaking.

"We identified a blocked artery in your father's preliminary tests. That's a common trigger for an ischemic stroke."

Mia raised an eyebrow. "What does that mean, exactly?"

"It's the type of stroke that happens when blood flow is restricted to the brain," said Doctor Patel. "We used a catheter to retrieve and remove the clot in emergency surgery. He's on blood thinners now to reduce the risk of another clot forming. The MRI didn't show any, but there's always the risk. Of course, there's a long way to go—physical and psychological therapy, for starters." He paused as if gauging how much she'd understood, then added, "I'll send you home with reading material." But he was wrong if he'd assumed she'd be his caregiver.

"He's thin," Mia said, remembering Ellis as a bear of a man.

The doctor cast his eyes down at the floor, his brows furrowed as he seemingly measured the distance between his feet and hers. "Yes, well, the stroke has temporarily affected his ability to swallow. We're doing our best to get him the nutrition he needs, but he's been uncooperative. Last night, he removed his feeding tube from his throat. Maybe it was uncomfortable, or maybe . . ."

"What?"

"Depression is common with stroke victims. They feel weak and powerless. Pulling out his tube might have been his way of saying, 'I quit.'"

Mia shook her head. "Not Ellis."

"A second stroke can change a person," said Dr. Patel.

Mia scowled. "A *second* stroke? This has happened before?"

"That's what his record says. Seven years ago—nearly eight. I can't remember the date exactly." Mia narrowed her eyes in confusion. "I'm sorry," the doctor said, swallowing hard. "You didn't know." Flustered, he stuffed his hands in the deep pockets of his white coat. "You're family. I believed you would . . ." He paused and then made a clumsy attempt to save the conversation. "Anyway, we'll try inserting a PEG later today."

"PEG?" Mia cocked her head.

"It's an implant that runs directly into the stomach."

"But if he rejected the other one, he'll probably—"

"Yes. Yes. I've considered that. Perhaps you could speak with him?" The doctor pulled his hands from his pockets and clasped either end of the stethoscope draped around his neck.

Mia nodded. "Thanks for the information. I'd better get back."

"Yes, of course. I'll leave the reading material at the desk. Very nice to meet you, Mia."

And with that, he rushed off.

Mia returned to Ellis, who waited expectantly.

"I saw Rosa this morning. She seems well," Mia said. "Oscar too, and GG—I mean, grand-mère." Her words tumbled out nervously. Ellis nodded. Mia thought he might be trying to smile again, which was unnerving. She'd never seen him smile before, yet he'd attempted it twice in this short visit.

"And TJ," she said, continuing with the small talk. "How old is he now, 24?"

"Mm." Ellis relaxed back into his pillows, still looking at her.

Mia's phone buzzed from the windowsill. She picked it up, saw Kali's name, and shut it off. Ellis grumbled from his hospital bed and pointed to the phone with his functioning hand.

"A friend," she said. "We've been texting." Ellis didn't know about Kali. Mia wasn't even sure if he knew she preferred women. She wondered briefly if she should tell him about Kali but didn't know him well enough to try. Since he'd collected her on the Florida dock the night she'd arrived from Haiti, he'd paid little attention to her. She'd been tired, frightened, and confused about the gruff man who called her "You." She'd wondered at the time if he even knew her name.

"I had a job interview a couple of days ago," she said, then went on about the company, the position, her current job, and so on. He seemed so . . . *engaged*, appearing to listen to every word, nodding and mm-hmming with each point she made. Then there was his stare. The penetrating eye contact that had always unnerved her now warmed.

She wondered if it was an act, a side effect from the stroke, or, more likely, some powerful drug Dr. Patel had prescribed. Ellis closed his eyes, opened them briefly, and shut them again. A moment later, he was snoring.

Where was the Ellis who'd callously left her and her mother to fend for themselves? That man was dark, mysterious, selfish, unfeeling, and incapable of love.

What the hell am I doing here? With her anger rekindled, Mia left the room. She had half a mind to leave Meridian again.

Dr. Patel stopped her in the hall outside Ellis's room with a half-dozen pamphlets on ischemic stroke, its causes, symptoms, temporary and lasting effects, and finally, recovery. Mia shuffled through the deck, then folded it up and tucked the bundle into her breast pocket.

"I'll read these tonight," she said.

"Sure, that's great. Also, I wonder if you have a copy of his health directive."

Mia shifted her weight from one foot to the other. "Health directive?" she asked.

"It's a—"

"I know what it is, but why would *I* have it?" She was more nervous now than when she'd arrived at the hospital.

"You're listed as his next of kin."

It was like a bomb went off in Mia's head. Next of kin? Health directive? She felt an unfamiliar concoction of panic and confusion; for the level of responsibility suddenly upon her shoulders, and for the realization that Ellis would put her in that position. Why not GG? Why not Francis?

Why *me?*

Mia left the hospital, reviewing what she'd learned. A blood clot caused the stroke. But what caused the clot? She should have asked. She should be more curious. She should care.

She parked her motorcycle beside the cottage and tramped

through a sea of black-eyed Susans gone to seed. Their naked stalks, tall and straight, like a hundred exclamation points standing on their heads, had been thoroughly picked over by goldfinches.

TJ wasn't at his post when Mia let herself in, though his game controller, headset, and paraphernalia were lined up on the coffee table.

She slipped her phone from her jacket and noticed Kali's texts had blossomed to nineteen. With a sigh, she texted back.

"I need a little time. Be patient." She noted the fundamental difference between Ellis, who cared too little, and Kali, who cared too much.

The refrigerator wheezed from the kitchen as Mia turned and walked down the short hallway to Ellis's room. It was a shambles—like a crime scene, compared to when she'd been there ten years earlier, like he'd been searching for something. The drawers of the roll-top desk lay open, and files were strewn across its surface. The bottom drawer of his dresser hadn't closed properly, obstructed by an unidentifiable garment. His bedding lay in a heap on the floor alongside soiled clothes. A suitcase, spread open like a shiny black butterfly sunning its wings, suggested he'd just returned from a trip—or maybe he'd been packing to go.

It looked as if Ellis had been struggling when he was last here. Was this where the stroke happened? Had a team of EMTs been scrambling to save his life?

The phone rang in the kitchen. Mia was too rattled to deal with it and set to straightening up, putting order to the room and her mind.

She opened the heavy curtains and released the spring-loaded shade, jarred briefly by the snap as it sprang to the top of the window. She closed the suitcase and set it aside, then collected the sheets and laundry and tossed them into the hall for washing. Finally, she approached the desk, not sure where to begin.

"What are you doing?" asked TJ from the door, a bottle of beer in his hand. Mia wanted to push him out the door, having laid her own claim to the room.

She fanned out her arms. "What happened here?"

"Fuck if I know," TJ said, stepping forward.

"You haven't seen this?" Mia asked.

"You crazy? I never come near this room." He tipped his beer to his mouth and smacked his lips. "GG called. She wants us for dinner at six. I said okay, okay?"

Mia checked her watch—five o'clock. "Fine," she said, taking one last look around the room before going upstairs for a shower and a change of clothes.

TJ looked up from the table as Mia stepped into GG's dining room, self-conscious of the nervous underarm perspiration seeping through her shirt. GG sat at the head of the enormous table, wearing an iridescent purple blouse, likely chosen for its attention-grabbing brightness. Francis sat across from her at the other end of the table. She looked up at Mia and flashed a Hollywood smile. Her blond hair was pulled back into a silver clip. Francis wasn't one for glitter or bright colors. She believed less was more when it came to fashion and was dressed simply in a gray V-neck sweater and pearl earrings.

"Ah, and the princess returns," she said, straightening her posture as if preparing to meet royalty.

"Sit down," GG said, nodding to the seat across from TJ. Mia pulled out a chair with a clammy hand and sat as Rosa entered the dining room with a mouth-watering platter of skewered kabobs. Then she filled their wine glasses with golden chardonnay and left the room as silently as she'd entered.

Mia waited for GG to serve herself before selecting a kabob under Francis's watchful gaze.

"It's been *years*, dear," Francis said. "How *are* you?" She sounded like some character from Downton Abby, though she was neither British nor aristocratic. "And how is your English coming along?"

"Well, thank you," Mia said, though her accent still bled through.

"Jesus, Mom, you're embarrassing," said TJ. Mia hadn't noticed before how much TJ took after his mother, physically. The blond hair. His jawline. The set of his nose. The cock of his head when he said something snarky. Like Mia, TJ hardly looked like Ellis's child at all.

GG sipped her wine. "A bit more respect, young man," she said, then turned to Mia. "You saw Ellis today. How did you find him?"

"He's thin," Mia said.

"Thin. Yes." Mia didn't recall seeing GG's name on the whiteboard.

"Dr. Patel asked about a health directive," Mia said. TJ looked up from his fork, eyes wide as silver dollars.

GG patted her mouth with the linen napkin. "Your father never discussed that with me," she said. "Perhaps Francis knows something."

"Afraid not," Francis said. "Can't help you."

"Tell us, Mia," GG said, clearing her throat. "What have you done with that expensive degree of yours?"

Mia hated this most about these dinners. GG holding court over everyone's failures.

"I interviewed for a marketing director position at Moon Harvest. It's a produce distributor in Drake."

"Ah, yes, I remember Moon Harvest from years ago," said GG, nearly toppling her wineglass as she set it down. "So old-fashioned. Is that the best you could do?"

"Moon Harvest is a respectable business."

"A bit far from the high-rise in Chicago, isn't it?" GG was baiting her. She'd never even seen the apartment or taken an interest in Mia's career, but now it served to belittle her.

"It is." Mia wasn't going to give her grandmother the satisfaction. She didn't need a high-rise apartment to feel important, or successful, or loved. She was about to say so when Rosa arrived to take their plates and serve the ham dinner.

Conversation switched to more mundane matters, the weather forecast, Francis's new apartment, and a local tax levy proposed for a new water filtration system, about which Mia had no opinion. Then dessert arrived, and GG focused her attention on TJ.

"And what about you?" TJ winced, and Francis rolled her eyes, suggesting this wouldn't be good.

The grandfather clock in the front hall struck eight.

"It's getting late, grand-mère," Mia said. "We should be going." She looked across the table and locked eyes with TJ, recognizing the gratitude in his stifled grin.

She had a long way to go before regaining his trust, but this was a start.

CHAPTER 4

Mia hoped she'd find Ellis sleeping again when she returned to the hospital the following day. That way, she could sign in, then slip out unnoticed.

But when she entered his room, he looked up excitedly from his bed and squirmed. Guttural sounds bubbled up from his throat. She noticed that same tug at his mouth as the day before. A smile? A sneer? The bushy eyebrows—one up, the other down—told an equally contradictory tale. When she moved to sit down, he motioned for her to come closer.

There was a nauseating smell coming off him. Ammonia mixed with something else. Mia was suddenly hit with a memory of her mother, who'd suffered a miserable death. She thought of the long days and nights, the rattled breathing, the stench. That's what she smelled now. Ellis smelled like death, and the thought moved her to speak her mind.

"Why?" she said, knowing he was unable to answer. "Why did you leave us? Why didn't you help us? Why did you have to be such a mystery for all those years?"

Ellis's face went blank. Then he shook his head vehemently.

"Mama said it was because you loved your job more than you

loved her—or me. Uncle Jean said you were a dangerous man, a giant, an ogre, a devil. I didn't *want* to believe him. I *hated* him. I remember hoping—praying you'd show up one day and prove him wrong. But nothing. Mama had been right all along.

"Then I saw you on the boat dock, so serious, so disgusted with me that you couldn't even use my name."

Ellis locked his gaze on her, his mouth contorted, his eyes glassy. Mia didn't care.

"I called you Papa, and you *yelled* at me. *You will call me Ellis,* you said, like there was no relation between us. I spent the next few days terrified of you, the next few years avoiding you as you'd avoided me." Mia backed away from the bed with her fists clenched, watching the tears tracking down the side of his face to his pillow. The tears unnerved her. She'd never seen him cry. Was it an involuntary reaction, or was she getting through to him? She crossed her arms and sighed, her throat clenched with emotion, on the verge of tears herself. "I'm grateful you took me in," she said. "I only wish it was because you *wanted* to, not because you *had* to."

He opened one side of his mouth and shut it again with a pitiful moan, then flailed his left arm toward the nightstand and slapped it. "*Der,*" he rasped. "*Aw der.*"

"*Ader?* What are you saying?"

He tried again, but the word didn't get any clearer. The nightstand was empty except for a small lamp and a call button fastened down with medical tape. "The button?" she asked. He shook his head and slapped the nightstand again—harder this time. She turned off the lamp, but that only made him more agitated.

"*Saw der,*" he gasped, his face twisted.

She'd intended to pop in, be seen, maybe say a few words about dinner at GG's, and leave again. But things had gone upside down. She hadn't meant to lose her cool. She hadn't expected the tears. And now this business with the nightstand and his struggle to speak. It seemed important. What was he trying to tell her?

A nurse stepped in. Not Nurse Becky. This one wore lipstick a shade too dark for her lily-white skin.

"I don't understand him," said Mia.

The nurse shook her head. "Can't help you there." She approached the table. "Are you looking for something, Mr. Ellis? What can I get for you?" He slapped the table again. The nurse took his bony wrist and checked his pulse with the watch pinned to her shirt. "You need to calm yourself, sir."

Ellis fumbled with the controller, trying to sit up, but it slipped off the bed and dangled from its cord. He dropped his arm, seeming to reach for it. But he snagged Mia's arm instead, pulling her close. His smell repulsed her. "*Aw—there*," he rasped.

"All there?" she said, glancing at the table. "What's all there?"

Mia looked at his face and stepped back. His breathing was tight, and his eyes glazed over. One of the monitors went haywire, with flashing red lights and a piercing alarm. The nurse called for Dr. Patel, and he arrived in seconds, barely acknowledging Mia as he examined the many monitors. Alarmed, she backed up, pushing her chair against the wall. Ellis wheezed, his eyes bulging as the line on the EKG bounced erratically up and down. Finally, another nurse arrived. The doctor murmured something. Then, as a team, they inserted a flexible tube down Ellis's throat. He looked around wildly, then locked his eyes on Mia.

Dr. Patel stood back with a deep sigh, then glanced at Mia with surprise "Take her down the hall," he said curtly to the nurse with the bright lipstick. A hand rested on her arm and spirited her out of the room. "I'll meet you there," the doctor called after her.

Mia was taken to a waiting room with beige walls and clusters of black plastic chairs. Four people sat together with their backs to the wall. Parents, Mia guessed, with their teenage sons hovering over their phones. Two men approached the nurse's station—one with gray hair, the other with a stringy ponytail. Both were distracted by Nurse Becky, giggling on the telephone. Mia sat by a post in the middle of the room and gazed out the window on the other side, thinking of Ellis and what she'd just witnessed.

A half hour later, Dr. Patel joined Mia and cleared his throat before settling into the chair beside her. "He's stable for now." He tried to sound reassuring, but Mia saw the doubt in his eyes.

She leaned forward. "What happened?"

Dr. Patel tugged at the cuff of his pristine white coat. "Another stroke. But there's a chance we can turn this around. I'll need to run more tests to see where we are."

"Worst case?"

"Permanent brain damage. We will do what we can to keep it at a minimum." He cleared his throat. "And the health directive? Have you found anything?" Mia shook her head. "It's a matter of life and death. We'll do everything we can, but his condition is fragile, Mia." He looked down at his hands on his lap. "In the meantime, I suggest that if you have something to say to him, you say it now." Mia rose unsteadily, her mind reeling, and returned to the room. She found Ellis placid. His eyes were dull and unfocused, looking toward the ceiling. They'd drugged him.

A flexible tube taped to his mouth led to a ventilator on a cart beside the bed. The tears were gone, but their memory clung to his dampened pillow. This was her fault.

She supposed an apology was in order. But for what? Speaking the truth? Venting her long-held resentments? Hadn't she held her tongue long enough? He'd abandoned her and deserted Mama. Mia listened to the ventilator's rhythmic whisper and gazed into his ghostly face thinking how helpless he looked. Her last words to him, and she couldn't think of a kind thing to say. She pulled herself together, approached his bed, and was hit by the stench that reminded her of Mama, the small cinderblock house on Rue Janvier, and, worst of all, Uncle Jean. Then she leaned down and whispered in his ear.

"I've always hated you."

Mia hurried out of the hospital feeling feverish, her heart thundering. She cruised through the small-town streets of Meridian on her motorcycle, eyes blurred by emotion. Confused feelings of hatred, disgust, and contempt merged with grief, compassion, and a profound regret.

I've always hated you. Where had that come from? She didn't *hate* him. She didn't love him either, but that didn't explain why she'd said what she said. The words were spoken before Mia knew it, leaving her grappling with long-buried emotions about her personal struggles in Haiti and her unceremonious thrust into American life.

Where were you when I needed you?

PART TWO
Bruised but Not Broken

CHAPTER 5

It was a hot afternoon when five-year-old Mia arrived at her Uncle Jean's corner shop in Port-au-Prince.

JC's was a small general store that stocked everything from propane to various grocery items and deep-fried delicacies like plantain and manioc. Best of all were the ribs Uncle Jean roasted all day on the firepit behind the shop.

Mama was a teacher's assistant at St. Michel's, where Mia attended pre-school, but wasn't allowed to have Mia underfoot until the older students were excused. Uncle Jean had volunteered to keep Mia at his shop until Mama got off work to pick her up.

They lived together in a tiny cinderblock house on Rue Janvier, where Mia and Mama shared one room, and Uncle Jean and Auntie Sis the other.

Mia stood chin-high at the counter, tugging at her new school uniform, a black jumper over a stiff cotton blouse with a Peter-Pan collar. Neither had been washed before she dressed that morning for her first day of school, and the itching was relentless. She wanted nothing more than to take it off.

Uncle Jean flipped the sign in the window to CLOSED and took her by the hand. "Back here," he said, leading her behind the counter and through the swinging doors to the storage room.

Firepit smoke seeped under the back door, and the smell of slow-roasting pork ribs tickled her nose as Uncle Jean pulled the shade down and slid the lock into place. Reaching for the shelf, he drew an extra-large T-shirt with the Haitian flag prominently featured on the front and held it out to her.

"Thank you, Uncle Jean," she said, shyly.

"Shall I help you with the dress?" He laid the T-shirt on the table behind them.

"No," she murmured.

"Here, let me." His breathing grew heavier as he eased the straps off each shoulder. The black jumper dropped to the floor, leaving her in nothing but the cotton blouse and her pink panties. Then he came around to face her and unbuttoned the top button of her blouse, his eyes glazing over as if possessed by a Vodou spirit.

She'd heard the stories told proudly among adults. Snippets describing a friend or relative consumed by one loa or another that was responsible for their actions, be it love, rage, lust, or power. In such cases, there was no stopping them. The worst loa was Kalfu—the devil. A loa so evil, he could evoke curses merely by meeting your eyes.

"No, Uncle Jean," she said, nervously. "I can dress myself." She tried to pull away, but grinning, he continued to the next button.

"You're a big girl, eh?" His laugh was deep and raspy. "A giant like your father. But he'd eat children like you." Mia pulled the T-shirt from the table and brought it to her face. He took the shirt from her hand and dropped it and her blouse to the floor beside the jumper. Then he kicked them aside and lifted her onto the table, wearing nothing but her panties. "But your mama couldn't resist his special friend." Uncle Jean unzipped his pants. "Would you like to meet my special friend?" Mia shook her head, her heart beating wildly, terrified by Uncle Jean's strange behavior. "He's a *secret*. Do you understand?"

"I want to go home," Mia whispered, wiping warm tears from her eyes while wondering how long it would be before her mother arrived. The corner of Uncle Jean's mouth twitched as he ran his rough hand up her leg. Mia was more convinced than ever that he'd been possessed.

She looked up at him with tears streaming down her cheeks. "Uncle—please no." She tried to pull away.

"No!" he said, moving closer, his breathing heavier. "A secret. Tell no one, or the people you love the most will suffer."

That was it, thought Mia, horrified. *The devil's curse.* He met her terrified eyes directly as his face contorted into an ugly and unfamiliar expression. Then the curse took hold with a blinding jolt as he baptized her in his sin.

Mia looked away at her uniform lying in a heap on the floor. The itch only a distant memory.

"How was your first day of school, Sunshine?" asked Mama when she arrived to pick Mia up later that afternoon. "And why are you wearing that ridiculous shirt?" Mia looked up into her mother's golden-brown eyes, unable to answer.

Uncle Jean stepped in with a to-go box of ribs in one hand and Mia's uniform neatly folded in the other, telling his sister the uniform needed a good washing.

It would take more than soap and water to remove his stain, however.

Later that year, Mama clenched Mia's tiny hand in her own and dragged her from St. Michel's school past neighbors and friends rushing for shelter from the oncoming hurricane as the heavy rain soaked the streets.

The midday sky loomed dark as night, and the palm trees bent low, overpowered by the intense wind slamming the island.

A trash can tumbled violently across the street as the warm wind whipped plastic bags, empty pop cans, and food scraps into Mia's path, causing her to trip and fall, breaking free of Mama's grip. She flailed for her mother's outstretched hand, but Mama was swept into the crowd and vanished from sight. Mia screamed.

"Mama!"

She looked into the surrounding chaos, from one panicked face to another. No one seemed to see her as raindrops spattered her face and dampened the ground beneath her sandals.

"*Mama!*"

Mia's dress flapped wildly. Rain slashed against her bare legs. A young man pushed past her, chasing after a dog who looked as terrified as Mia felt. She staggered back, breaking the strap to one sandal that was soon kicked away and lost to the crowd. Then the other sandal slid out from under her, and she stumbled barefoot through the mud into a small open area on the side of the road, where a white man with bushy eyebrows and a face blanketed in a thick dark beard snatched her up and held her tight to his chest. She wriggled, trying to free herself, but he tossed her over his shoulder, her legs pinned beneath his arms.

Terrified, she screamed again. A shrill, desperate cry.

"*MAMA!*"

"Quiet," said the man, holding her legs against him as she bounced against his back. "You're safe." Then her mother appeared at their side and grabbed for Mia, her fingers digging into Mia's arms, pulling frantically to free her.

"You can't have her!" she screamed in Creole. "You can't!"

"Stop!" the man said. "I only want to help." He spoke Creole, too, but it was difficult to understand.

Mia felt her mother pull and pull again, leaving deep scratches where her fingernails broke the skin.

Reluctantly, the man handed Mia over. Her hot tears mingled with the rain as she wrapped her arms and legs around her mother and fixed her gaze on the man whose tangled black hair whipped about, lashing his face.

"Let me explain," he said.

But her mother tightened her hold and they fled from the stranger. They vanished into the crowd and hurried home through torrential rain.

Within sight of the little cinderblock, Mia spotted Jonas—her best friend and the closest thing she had to a brother. Their houses were separated only by old Mr. Desante's tin-roof shack. Jonas looked at her from his open door, nervously biting his lower lip. Then his mother yanked him inside.

Mama did the same with Mia, slamming the door behind them

and securing the wooden handle Uncle Jean used to brace the door.

"Quick!" said Auntie Sis, rushing into the front room. "The sandbags!" Uncle Jean appeared and chucked three half-filled sandbags on the door sill.

"Water!" shouted Uncle Jean. Mama disappeared into the kitchen to fill their largest cooking pots with water. Mia heard her gasp with relief, thankful the plumbing was working. But Mia knew it wouldn't last. It never did.

"Mia!" Uncle Jean swept her up and carried her to her bedroom, then dumped her on the bed she shared with Mama. "Don't move!" he commanded.

She hugged her pillow tightly to her chest, pressing her back against the wall while waiting for Mama. Then the adults stacked pots of clean water and sealed tubs of food on the dresser, only joining her after they'd collected their other valuables on the bed.

They huddled together, straining to hear Junior Jadotte's weather report on Radio Caribe` through the heavy static on Uncle Jean's transistor radio. "Hurricane Gordon . . . level 1 . . . flood warning . . . take shelter."

Though only five years old, Mia was no stranger to tropical storms and knew the drill. But for some reason—maybe the energy she felt from her family—she was more afraid this time.

Uncle Jean focused on the ceiling.

"Don't worry, brother," said Mama. "The roof is easy enough to repair."

Uncle Jean fixed his gaze on her. "Easy enough for that American devil, you mean."

"The Old Dog," said Auntie Sis. Mia felt Mama flinch.

The winds howled eerily through the boarded-up windows. Soon, the tin roof rattled overhead with a loud *radabadat*. Whimpering, Mia pressed herself tighter against her mother.

"Hush, baby," said her mother in a voice soft as talcum powder. "Think of something nice. Tell me about that new game at school." She pressed closer. "What was it called again?"

Mia shut her eyes tight, doing her best to block out the storm's relentless moaning. "Jacks," she said in her tiny voice. "A counting game."

"Tell us how it's played," said Auntie Sis, squeezing Uncle Jean's hand so tight the pain showed on his face.

A heavy object struck the side of the house with a deafening thud, and they all jumped. Mia reached her tiny fingers into her dress pocket and removed three sharp jacks and a small red rubber ball, though her eyes remained fixed on the front door and the water oozing under the sandbags and creeping across the cement floor. She took a deep breath through her nose. "First . . ." she said through gritted teeth. "First, you throw the jacks." She held out the silver asterisks for them to see. "Then . . ." She paused to take another breath.

"You're doing fine, baby," said Mama, wiping a tear from Mia's cheek.

Mia held the ball out in her other hand. "Then you bounce the ball and grab one of the jacks." She glanced around, looking for something to bounce the ball on. Uncle Jean reached across the bed for a box lid that he set on his lap. A subtle grin tugged at his mouth.

"You can play here, Sweet Thing," he said. *Tell no one.*

Suddenly no longer interested in the game, Mia turned away

and buried herself in her mother's arms, where she was soon lulled to sleep.

The winds subsided by morning, but the water seeping into the house progressed steadily into the kitchen, and Mia's bed stood like an island hovering over six inches of muck. A pair of white plastic sandals floated in the mire like two water lilies in a filthy pond.

Radio Caribe` announced the first reported deaths. The toll rose to over a thousand Haitian lives lost. The mood was somber as Uncle Jean left their nest to assess the damage.

Mia waded across the sitting room and looked out at the street from the open door. "Touch nothing," Mama said before she and Auntie Sis stepped tentatively into the street to check on vulnerable neighbors like Mr. Desante.

The old man was considered a hero among the neighbors for fighting the Tonton Macoutes, a volunteer army that took no prisoners. He fought hard beside Mia's grandfather, who'd lost his life trying to save him. The Tonton Macoutes left Mr. Desante with one arm and a prominent scar on his cheek.

Hurricane Gordon had shattered his ramshackle home to smithereens. All that remained now was a heartbreaking gap between Mia's and her friend Jonas's houses on either side.

Mia stood on her battered front porch, transfixed by that empty space while her neighbors waded through thick muck in the streets, searching for loved ones and treasured belongings. Though the rain had passed, thick dark clouds remained overhead, casting an ominous gloom over the scene. Across the street, a dead body was hauled out of the mud and onto a blanket. From what Mia could tell, it was no one anyone knew, but the adults mourned the stranger anyway, wrapping the blanket around them.

Mr. Desante wiped the mud from a dead chicken that could have belonged to anyone in the city, blown there by the hurricane's force. Garbage, debris, and death loomed all along the flooded streets. But Uncle Jean stood tall in front of their cinderblock home with a hand over his mouth to obscure his proud grin. His family had remained unscathed. His tin roof had held up in the storm, while others were much less fortunate.

Jonas's mother stood alone in her open doorway, looking tired and disheveled. Jonas's father had died years ago. His fishing boat was swallowed whole by Hurricane Gilbert six months before Jonas was born. He'd been a deacon at St. Cecilia's, where Mia and her mother went to Mass. He'd owned a thrift store where he gave most things away to those in need.

Mia saw Jonas standing ankle-deep in mud in front of his house while his mother joined the others in the street. He ran to her. The five-year-old friends embraced fervently, and when they finally parted, Jonas pointed at a dog half-buried in the mud beside Mia's house. Its head was smashed in. One eye remained tethered, hanging off to the side. The other stared skyward.

"Is it dead?" Jonas asked, reaching down.

Mia pulled him back. "Touch nothing!" she said, repeating her mother's warning.

In the days that followed, the body count rose. Debris from whatever cleanup could be managed piled along Rue Janvier, the dirt road outside Mia's house. Neighbors pitched in, stacking towers of trash and rubble.

Two days later, a bulldozer leveled the street, pushing aside anything in its path and creating a thoroughfare where massive, mud-caked dump trucks filled with trash and debris rumbled past on their way out of town. Mia's quiet little street was now unrecognizable.

There was little that Mia's family could do for the neighborhood, but they focused their efforts on helping Mr. Desante rebuild, using random scrap wood and metal. Mia helped with what she could as the sun shone brightly overhead, slowly drying the swampy mess.

Their lives had been twisted into a new normal.

Four days after the storm, as Mia stood in the relative shade of her porch, Jonas ran over to tell her about the American soldiers marching through the city. Mia begged her mother to take her to see the excitement.

Uncle Jean stepped in. "Nothing is exciting about occupiers," he said, sternly.

"Occupiers?" said Jonas. "What's that?"

"No better than the street gangs that extort us for protection. Filthy, greedy bastards." The gangs, like the Tonton Macoutes, operated openly without fear.

"But these men are here to keep us safe, brother," Mama said. "We all want our dear Aristide to succeed, but that's impossible without help from our friends."

"Ha! Friends?" Uncle Jean pulled his dingy shirt collar up to wipe sweat off his face.

Mia looked from her mother to her uncle, trying to figure out if the Americans were good or bad. More importantly: when could she see them?

She didn't have to wait long. That afternoon, after Uncle Jean added a fresh coat of white paint to the windowsill, Mia peeked through the open window and spied a group of soldiers patrolling the dirt road in front of her house, dressed in military green and heavy boots.

One man followed behind, catching Mia's attention. She recognized his thick beard and bushy black eyebrows that cast a shadow over deep-set eyes as he looked from one side of the street to the other—and then, to her horror, directly at her. He wasn't wearing a soldier's uniform but rather a soiled linen shirt and a camera hanging from a red leather strap across his chest.

He stepped cautiously from the group when he noticed Uncle Jean standing in front of the house. His forced smile unnerved Mia as he approached her uncle like an old friend. But Uncle Jean refused to shake his hand, so the man turned his attention to the window, shielding his eyes for a better look, and moved forward. Mia gasped.

Uncle Jean held him back.

"I have a right to see her!" the man shouted in Creole.

"You're not welcome," Uncle Jean said. "Go now before there's trouble."

The stranger shook his head. "Luisa—the girl. I have a right."

"My sister has no interest in you. You have no rights here," Uncle Jean said.

"Just tell her I'm here. Please!" the man said. "You know what happened, so why—"

Uncle Jean turned, suddenly aware of Mia watching from the window. Then, in one swift motion, the man snatched up his camera and snapped a photo of the house, then another and another until Uncle Jean pushed him away. The man took hold of Uncle Jean's collar and said something Mia couldn't hear, then looked up at her again. Then it struck her; he wasn't taking pictures of the house. He was taking pictures of *her*.

Mia jumped away from the window; out of his view. White paint, wet and sticky, coated her fingertips. Uncle Jean burst into the house.

"Who is he?" Mia called over her shoulder.

"No one important," said Uncle Jean, slamming the shutters closed. "Stay away from that window. And . . ." He grabbed her by the face. She stared into his crazed eyes, terrified. "Listen to me, child. Never speak with him. Do you understand? That man is the devil."

But Mia knew the devil. She was looking at him.

CHAPTER 6

Four years later, Mia sat in her third-grade classroom at St. Michel's, between Jonas and the sweet-faced Annabelle Roun, waiting for the final bell to ring. Annabelle had given Mia a small plastic frog the previous week and Mia kept the gift in her pocket, affectionately handling it from time to time.

"Homework!" said Madame Bernard, Mia's teacher. "Vocabulary test tomorrow!" The teacher wrote each word on the chalkboard for the class to copy. *Surtout. Bonheur. La tragédie.* Etcetera.

Jonas smirked. "What are we supposed to do with all these words?"

"Your nine-year-old ignorance can be excused today," Madame Bernard said, "but be careful, young man, or you'll be ignorant forever. A fate worse than death."

"That would be *une tragédie*," Jonas whispered to Mia.

Mia looked in Jonas's twinkling eyes, remembering the other day, when he'd kissed her behind Uncle Jean's shop in town. A horrifying, spit-laden experience—even the memory made her queasy.

That kiss came to mean more when, a week later, a half dozen boys from her school surrounded Mia in a dusty treeless lot on the way home from school.

"How 'bout some sugar, Sugar?" said one.

"Forget him. My lips are the sweetest!" said another, pushing the first boy out of the way. Still another swiped at her shoulder-length braids, and a fifth tugged at her shirt and asked to see her "mulatta tits."

"Stop it!" Mia screamed, holding her shirt in place.

"Saving it all for Jonas?" said Flossie, a boy in the next grade who wore Kanaval beads to school every day. "Go away!" Mia pushed Flossie to the ground and started to run, but the boys chased her.

"Maybe it's not *boys* you want," Flossie called after her. "Lezbo!"

"Leave her alone!" Everyone looked toward Jonas, barreling toward them. "She's mine!"

He was only a few months older than Mia, but exuded confidence beyond his years.

Flossie scrambled to his feet and threw his hands up in surrender—but the gesture was insincere, and when Jonas got close enough, fists flew. The other boys joined in, slugging and jeering, a cloud of dirt and dust churning around them. Mia was embarrassed to see Annabelle watching the scene from across the street, either too stunned or too afraid to approach and pulled Jonas from the fracas, hoping to stop the fight. She spat at Flossie before throwing a punch of her own. When he fell, she jumped on him, arms swinging like windmill blades, her fists striking his face, chest, and shoulders.

Finally, he twisted away, his friends laughing, his beads freed from their string and scattered in the dirt around them.

Mia turned to Jonas with her fists still clenched. "Let's go," she said, breathing heavily and turning away from the group.

Jonas jogged after her. "You're angry?" he said, mouth agape in indignation.

Mia picked up her pace. "What did you tell them?"

"Nothing. I said nothing!" Jonas said as he caught up to her.

"You told them about that kiss. Did you mention how disgusting it was? Did you?"

"It was beautiful. *You're* beautiful."

They were a block away from the skirmish, and she stopped to slap him. She didn't care what Jonas thought. She'd gotten enough unwanted attention from Uncle Jean, she didn't need it from him too.

"Don't try it again," Mia said. "Hear me?"

Jonas stepped back, pouting like a dejected puppy. "I love you, *Ti-Quitta*."

"Ugh!" Mia stomped off toward home, leaving Jonas alone by the side of the road. The *vodou* loa of sexuality was a common ploy among the boys at school. They'd boast that Ti-Quitta slipped into their beds at night and fondled them beneath the sheets, as if their own hands hadn't gone in search of self-pleasure. Kalfu and Ti-Quitta were often used as scapegoats.

Mia went to church with Mama, where they disavowed the Haitian loas. Nevertheless, Mia had her favorites. Loa Damballah, the loving father figure, and Loa Erzulie, goddess of love and beauty, who was called upon to heal the sick and aid the hopeless. Knowingly or not, by calling her Ti-Quitta, Jonas had disrespected Mia as harshly as Flossie and his boys.

"Mia," called Jonas. "Wait up."

After that first introduction to Uncle Jean's "special friend," the encounters in the back room had grown bolder. She hated him for it and hated herself for keeping his secret. Which was the greater sin, the act she was helpless to stop or her long-held silence?

As Mia began to doubt her belief in the curse, another fear emerged. Mama loved her brother, and without him, they'd have no roof over their heads. Mia's only choice was to make it more difficult for Uncle Jean to get her alone. This was why she'd waited for Jonas.

Mia looked over her shoulder, still angry but knowing she couldn't take another step without him.

That September, shortly before Mia's ninth birthday, she and Jonas sat on stools at the counter of her uncle's corner shop, dredging fried plantains through ketchup. The television mounted to the wall behind the register announced the onset of Hurricane Georges. Mia peered out the window at the overcast sky. Across the street, the branches of the locust tree danced playfully in the wind.

"Category 4," the announcer said, "Seek shelter."

"Here we go again," Uncle Jean said, laughing. State radio had already told them the storm was far from Haiti, and they had nothing to worry about.

"What's the truth?" asked a patron standing at the register with a six-pack of beer.

"Look at the sky, you idiot!" shouted another.

"Out, all of you. I'm boarding up," said Uncle Jean, pushing them out the door. Mia prayed Auntie would make it to the shelter in time, as her pregnancy would undoubtedly slow her down.

Uncle Jean put Jonas to work boarding the windows while he went to get everything off the floor in the back room.

"Mia, come help me back here, Sweet Thing," called Uncle Jean.

Mia's stomach lurched to hear the pet name that always preceded his unwanted attention.

There was no way she was going back there with him. "I'm busy helping Jonas," she called back, already on her way outside, where the sky was blackening. "I'll hold the nails," she said to Jonas when she got there. He cocked his head; he didn't need her help with this.

"Now!" shouted Uncle Jean. Mia looked at Jonas, pleading with her eyes for his help. He looked concerned and confused by her reluctance to be alone with her uncle.

"We'll help you out as soon as we can," called Jonas through the open door as Mia handed him another nail.

Uncle Jean stormed out, lugging a filthy half-full sandbag that he dropped outside the door. He placed a hand on Jonas's shoulder. "That'll do. I'll finish up here. Maybe you should be off. Your mother will be looking for you."

A sudden gust of wind knocked Mia off balance. The storm was coming in fast. Jonas caught her arm and sputtered, "She's p-probably already at the shelter."

"That's where we're going," Mia said. "Come with us." She looked from Jonas to Uncle Jean, who glowered at her, his plans foiled.

"Let's get those last boards in," Uncle Jean snapped. "Then we'll go." The minute Jonas turned his back, Uncle Jean slipped a hand around Mia's waist. She winced as he whispered in her ear.

"You think you're clever, don't you?" he hissed. Jonas appeared at her side. Her unwavering protector.

They met Mia's mother at St. Michel's. The school had recently been designated as the local storm shelter. It was packed. Babies wailed inconsolably, and women shrieked, as if this was where they'd meet their end. They settled into one of the interior classrooms on the second floor—safe presumably, from the inevitable flooding. They sat with Jonas's mother, propped against the inside wall of the windowless classroom with warped alphabet cards tacked above their heads and rows of desks pushed against the opposite wall.

Auntie Sis joined them soon after. Her pregnant belly was large, looming, and ready to pop any day. Mia wasn't the only one afraid today would be the day.

Mia looked on as Auntie Sis smiled nervously, palming her belly like a basketball and nodding at Mia as if to say they'd all be fine.

The storm lasted the rest of that day and into the next. Mia clung to Jonas through the long hours of roaring wind and rain. Several men, including Uncle Jean, stood watch together in the hall, calling out weather updates as they heard them from the transistor radio. Eventually, Uncle Jean gave up his post and joined the crowded classroom. When he tried to sit beside Mia, Jonas pulled her closer as if sensing Mia's discomfort. Mia glanced at Mama, who seemed unconcerned.

There was a time when Mia considered telling her mother about Uncle Jean's unwanted attention. Once, when she was seven, she'd run away to Jonas's house when Uncle Jean had volunteered to bathe her. Mother chased after her and asked what the matter was. But before Mia got the words out, she saw her uncle glaring at her from the porch and was reminded of the curse.

"Luisa, are you seriously going to let that boy manhandle your daughter right here in front of everyone?" Uncle Jean shouted now, over the thunderous gusts thrashing the walls of their classroom sanctuary. Jonas's mother glared at him. Mama scooted closer to Mia and draped a protective arm around her. She felt safe sandwiched between her mother and Jonas. Safe from the storm and safe from her uncle.

"You know she doesn't handle storms well, Jean," Mia's mother said. "She needs all the support she can get." She turned to Mia with a wink. "I've got you, Sunshine. Me and Jonas. We've got you."

Mia handled storms just as well as anyone in that room, but it made her proud to hear her mother stand up to Uncle Jean, and she dreamed of the day she could be so strong.

The aftermath of Hurricane Georges was catastrophic. Ten times worse than Gilbert four years earlier. Death and destruction prevailed, with no foreign aid to help keep the peace.

The house was a disaster when they returned from the shelter. Looters had run off with their best radio, their microwave oven, and Mia's grandmother's jewelry. The jewelry wasn't worth much to anyone but Mama, but there wasn't time to mourn. The dressers had been emptied, and the clothes that had been left behind in the silty mud were unrecognizable.

Mia was crushed to find the bed she'd shared with Mama toppled against the wall. The mattress was drenched and filthy, the frame splintered like kindling.

Auntie Sis stood paralyzed in the kitchen, surrounded by trash and what remained of the tin roof.

Even after they'd been home for a week, the streets were still flooded. Cars and corpses, too many to count, remained buried in the mud.

The destruction of Mr. Desante's shack left him homeless again. But even with his handicap, he pushed a broom with his one arm to help clear the street.

"You are the embodiment of Damballah himself," Mama told him. "If we all could be so good."

"Like your Ellis?" He winked at her, the scar on his cheek pinched at either end.

"Ellis?" asked Mia, her head twisting at the unfamiliar name.

"Your father," said Mr. Desante. "Such a good man."

"My father?" She looked at Mama with such confusion it made Mr. Desante laugh. He hobbled back into the street with his broom, whistling through his teeth.

Mia knew four things about her father. He was an American, a liar, a thief, and a coward—nothing like the benevolent, innocent, and loving Damballah.

"Get inside, Mia," Mama said, taking her by the shoulders and turning her toward the house. "Auntie needs your help."

"But I want to stay out here," Mia said, then saw the scowl on Mama's face and instantly regretted her defiance.

Mama gave her a push. "Go!"

"You should go in as well, sister," Uncle Jean said, climbing down from the roof he'd patched together from whatever materials he could drum up. "I'm off to open the shop, and I don't want you all in the street while I'm gone."

Mama huffed and turned to him, hands planted firmly on her

hips. "The shop? Are you joking? We need you here."

"People need food, fuel, water. I'm an important man." He looked at Mia and grinned that phony smile he'd used with her in the shop's back room. *Don't you trust me?* he'd say. "Now, go inside and lock the door. I won't be here to protect you if the gangs roll through." The gangs were just as scary as the Macoutes. At least the Macoutes didn't show up at the door demanding payment for protection.

With that, Uncle Jean turned to speak with Mr. Desante. Mia wondered what he wanted. Was it because the old man knew her father?

It seemed *everyone* knew her father—everyone but Mia. But no one spoke of him the way Mr. Desante had. With no photographs and little information about the American who'd come and gone, leaving an offspring in his wake, Mia naturally felt curious.

If her father was indeed kind and loving like Damballah, then surely he would come for her. Is that why Uncle Jean hated him so? Was he afraid her father would take Mama and her away?

Mama closed the door and secured it with the flimsy wooden handle Uncle Jean had fashioned. Then she and Mia began cleaning up the house while heavily pregnant Auntie Sis sat on one of two mismatched armchairs Uncle Jean had salvaged in town.

As Mia helped her mother, she wondered how to ask about her father—the mysterious man called "Ellis." She considered saying, "He's my father. I have a right to know." Or, "Do I remind you of him?" Or, "Did you love him?"

That was it. She would ask her mother if she loved this Ellis.

But just as she was about to open her mouth, there was a knock on the front door.

"Don't open it," Mama whispered. The three of them stared at the door. Auntie Sis speculated that it could be the gangs, there to demand payment for "security." The gangs, Mia knew, demanded money for protecting the neighborhood. If you don't pay, they'll beat you. In Mia's memory, they'd never done anything helpful, ever. Mia wondered if it was the man with the bushy eyebrows who had shown up after the last hurricane.

"My name is Billy Krieger," said the man at the door, in terrible French. "Is everything all right?" His words tumbled out in a nervous rush. When there was no answer, he knocked again. Mia looked from Auntie to Mama, who held a finger to her lips. "I heard there was a pregnant woman here. I have food and clean water." That last promise must have been too tempting for Mia's mother to ignore, and she came forward to peek out the window.

Mia rushed to join her mother. Billy, she saw, was a small, scrawny man with wispy blond hair and a clean-shaven face. He wore a white button-down shirt that he'd sweated through and cradled a large brown box. Mia watched and waited, curious if Mama would open the door to this stranger. Uncle Jean could always bring food from the shop, though it would cut into his profits. Still, the cupboards were nearly bare, and their little icebox held nothing since the power had gone out.

Mama looked at Auntie Sis, who nodded, massaging the side of her enormous belly, apparently just as curious and hungry as Mia.

Cautiously, Mama lifted the wooden lever from the door and opened it. "Come in."

Billy stepped into the house and set the heavy box on the table with a grunt.

"*Merci*," he said, sighing with relief.

"What is all this?" asked Auntie Sis, rising from the chair with a grunt of her own.

Billy opened the box with hands as bent and inflamed as if they belonged to an old man, though Mia guessed he was younger than Mama. Mia peered into the box as Mama ran her fingers across cans of powdered baby formula, bottled water, disposable diapers, dry beans, and rice, and things she'd only dreamed of—like dehydrated potatoes and strawberry jam that made her mouth water. Billy began unpacking the goods. He nodded shyly at Mia, then looked away quickly. Mia was so focused on his misshapen fingers that she hardly noticed.

"I am Luisa Bacri," Mama said. "This is my daughter, Mia, and my sister-in-law, Sissy Bacri."

Billy glanced at Auntie's belly. "When are you due?"

"Yesterday," she said, hovering over the loot as if it were a pile of gold.

"You don't say! I'm here just in time." Billy's infectious smile was broad enough to expose a dimple on one cheek and a slight overbite. "The hospital is crowded after the storm. Do you have a midwife?"

"I'll be her midwife," said Mama.

Billy looked at Auntie Sis, who nodded. The crease in his brow deepened as he intertwined his gnarled fingers. "I see."

"I've helped others," said Mama.

He raised an eyebrow. "Do you have a telephone?" All three shook their heads. "Hmm. Is it all right if I check back with you over the next few days?"

Mama folded her arms. "What organization did you say you're with?"

Billy blushed and turned to go as if he hadn't heard her, then said shyly, "Global Healing, ma'am."

Mama gasped. After a moment's hesitation, she placed a hand on Mia's shoulder and said, "Stay here."

Mama followed Billy out the door, closing it behind her. Mia nodded, surprised by her mother's odd behavior. Mia didn't know why her mother wouldn't allow her to join them, but suspected it was because she didn't want to be overheard. So, she waited for Auntie Sis to waddle into the kitchen, then crouched beneath the open window to listen in.

Billy spoke in his terrible French, but Mama's wasn't much better.

"Global Healing?" Mama said.

"*Oui, madame.*"

"Not Global Vision?"

"It's a new branch on the same tree, madame. I play a very small role."

Mia rose to her tiptoes to look out the open window, clinging to the bottom sill as she spied on them through the shutters.

"Same tree?" said Mama. "Please, sir, can you tell me, do you know a man named Ellis?"

Ellis? Her father? Mia gripped the sill tighter.

Billy looked away as if considering his answer, then cleared his throat and looked Mama in the eye. "I do not."

Before her mother could respond, the sill creaked under Mia's weight. Mama froze and looked toward the window. Mia took off running to her bedroom, her heart hammering. It was the second time that day she'd heard her father's name.

The second time ever.

That night, Mia lay beside her mother on their mattress that had been drying on the porch. It smelled like rot and mildew, but Mia had other things on her mind.

"Mama?"

"Mm?" She was already half asleep, exhausted after the unrelenting clean-up.

"Did you love my father?"

There was a long pause before her mother propped herself on her elbows and sighed. Her breath smelled like sweet milk.

"How old are you, my Sunshine?"

"You know how old I am. I'm nine."

"It has been that long since I laid eyes on your father. Any love that may have existed is long gone now."

"Jonas says that love is forever."

"Jonas says this?" Mama laughed. "The boy has romantic notions. People fall in love, my dear. They fall out of love, too, when they have a good reason."

"What if he came back? What if—"

"That's enough. I'm tired." Mama lay back down. "I understand you have questions, but you are too young to understand." She wrapped Mia in her arms. "I will always love you, though. You are my sunshine."

"How can a person love one person forever but not another?"

Mama kissed Mia on the back of her neck. "Hush. Go to sleep."

Mia closed her eyes, wondering what her father had done to

lose her mother's love. It must have been something terrible.

While Uncle Jean attended the shop the following day, Billy returned to the house amid Auntie's moans and cries, jumping right into action as if he helped deliver babies every day. Everyone was surprised, though his timing couldn't have been better.

"How did you know?" Mama asked.

"I didn't," he said. "But I promised to come back and—well, here I am." Mama was annoyed at first. She'd have been happy to deliver the child with only Mia's help. But she let down her guard when Billy rushed to the kitchen to unload a stack of clean towels and other supplies.

Mia enjoyed playing nurse's aide to her mother and Billy. When the yowling newborn came, Billy wrapped her in a thin cotton blanket with his crippled hands and handed her off into Mia's arms.

"*Félicitations*, Mia," said Billy, smiling with a firm nod. "You're a cousin now."

Mia gazed tenderly into the infant's cloudy black eyes.

CHAPTER 7

The day Mia was invited to dance in the annual Kanaval parade for the first time was the proudest day in her life. At twelve, she was finally old enough to participate in this rite of passage. She'd been waiting to do so since first attending the spectacle when she was just a few years old.

In the weeks leading up to this year's festival, Mama brought Mia to the lot behind Uncle Jean's shop, where the women practiced the group dance for the big event in the shade of a giant Catalpa tree. Uncle Jean remained close by, often standing just outside the back door as he sucked on a cigarette. They also worked on costumes with Nadine, Yasmin, and Annabelle Roun's mother, Deseret. Since Mia couldn't sew, she'd entertain Cousin Sasha while Auntie Sis worked with the others. Finally, they gathered with neighbors to plan festive dishes, like Yasmin's signature corn fritters and mouth-watering manioc cakes, and stockpile rice and beans for Auntie's famous rice pot that would serve hundreds after the parade. Mia felt proud to be part of the preparations, and prouder still of Mama, whose leadership was respected among the women.

"You're just like her, you know," Deseret said, pulling her long braids into a bright red scrunchie behind her neck. Mia gazed up at her, wondering what she meant. "Your mother. You have her grit and her beauty."

Mia felt the heat rise in her face. Grit and beauty were not qualities she would have chosen. She was content to be quiet and ordinary. Was that a trait she shared with her father?

"The spitting image," added Nadine with a firm nod.

One week before Kanaval, dance practice ran late. By the time Mama turned off the music and gathered her things, it had grown dark behind Uncle Jean's shop. The only sounds were the women's hushed voices and the crickets chirping from a hedge of shrubs behind them.

"Deseret needs us to help her finish the costumes," said Mama, speaking for Auntie Sis and herself. The vibrant, flowing skirts and halter tops were a huge undertaking.

"I'll come with you," said Mia, excited by the prospect of spending more time with the women but more concerned about being left alone with Uncle Jean. "I can look after Sasha." The drowsy three-year-old, resting her head against her mother's shoulder, lifted her gaze to Mia.

"It's late, Sunshine," said Mama, thinking. "You still have schoolwork."

"I don't care. I'll finish it in the morning." Mia's pleading eyes were met with Mama's shaking head.

"Don't fight me on this," Mama said, glaring at her. "I'm in no mood for it."

"I'll walk her home, Luisa," said Uncle Jean, stomping out the stub of his cigarette, "then come for you at Deseret's."

"No!" Mia grabbed her mother's arm and pulled, trying to catch her eye. "Please, let me go with you." Being left behind was one thing. But being left behind with Uncle Jean was far worse.

"Nonsense. We'll be late. You'll go with your uncle." It was settled.

Mia broke out into a full-body sweat, her mind working out worst-case scenarios as rapidly as the crickets' incessant chirps, wishing she could disappear into the shrubs' cool green leaves and be taken in by the harmless insects.

Mama turned to leave with Auntie Sis, while Sasha tried to wriggle out from her mother's grasp. They didn't know Uncle Jean the way Mia did. They couldn't if she remained silent about his abuse. Up to this point, she hadn't risked Uncle Jean's wrath or his curse. She wasn't sure the curse was real but did not want to take the chance that it was, for that would ruin Mama's life. Up to now, her family had been safe because of her silence.

Uncle Jean took Mia's arm and led her away.

"The practices are going well, Mia," he said as the two walked home under widely spaced streetlights—some working, some not. "I'm looking forward to seeing you dance in the parade." He draped an arm across her shoulder, his hand swinging against her small breast with each step. His fingertips flicked across her nipple as he gazed down at her.

Mia cringed, recalling the first time Uncle Jean lured her into the back room of his shop to meet his "special friend." The day he asked to meet hers was as vivid on this night as if it had happened yesterday. He hadn't touched her in years, though—she'd gotten more adept at avoiding moments like the one she found herself in now.

Near their house, the streets were darker. Uncle Jean drew

her closer to him, and she stumbled, her bare feet wanting to run. Because of the darkness, he didn't have to hide behind the pretense of incidental touching, and his hand slipped down her shirt and groped her budding breast.

"Do you like that?" he asked.

"No," said Mia, trying to break away.

"Where do you think you're going?" He pulled her onto a darker path that led to another neighborhood.

In the pitch black of this enclave, Mia was terrified when Uncle Jean threw her up against a fence and pulled up her shirt while violently kissing her on the lips. She writhed, trying with all her might to pull away. But he was stronger and more powerful.

She felt his heat against her and smelled the bitter tang of cigarette breath.

"No, Uncle Jean," she begged. "Please stop." He growled something she couldn't understand. Mia was about to scream when she heard the shuffle of footsteps approaching.

The gang?

"Is everything all right here?" the man said in French.

"Go away," grumbled Uncle Jean, holding a hand over Mia's mouth. "This doesn't concern you."

"Young lady?"

Mia bit her uncle's hand and broke away. Now, with her eyes adapted to the dark, she noticed a blond man in a white button-down shirt. It was Billy Krieger, the man who brought them food from time to time when Uncle Jean wasn't home. The same man who helped deliver Sasha.

"Who the fuck are you?" asked Uncle Jean, adjusting his pants and stepping closer as if daring Billy to stop him. Though Billy was the smaller of the two, he took Uncle Jean by the shoulders and thrust him into the fence. It seemed to take everything he had. Uncle Jean grabbed Billy by the throat, his grin as evil as Mia had ever seen it. She lunged at her uncle, grappling with his arm as his hand squeezed tighter around Billy's neck. Uncle Jean released Billy and turned on her.

"*Bouzine!*" he shouted as he pushed her into the dirt.

Coughing and rubbing his throat, Billy staggered toward Mia, but Uncle Jean hit him, knocking him to the ground, then began kicking him repeatedly.

Billy curled into a ball, his hands over his face, knees to his chest. Uncle Jean kept kicking, as if intent on killing him.

"Stop it!" Mia cried, scrambling to her knees. "Help! Someone! Anyone!"

"Who is it?" called a man on the other side of the fence. There was a clink and a rattle. Then a gate opened, and the speaker appeared with two giant dogs at his side.

Billy labored to get to his feet. He looked from Jean to the man and his growling dogs.

"Get out of here," the man said, pointing at Billy. "And take the girl." Billy grabbed Mia and ran with her back to the cinderblock house, leaving Uncle to fend for himself.

They didn't stop until they reached the door at home. They were panting. Billy clutched his gut, visibly hurting. Mia noticed that his shirt was torn and dirty, and his lip bled. "Go on to bed, Mia," Billy said. "I'll stay and wait out here for your mother." He kept a safe distance as if knowing that standing closer would scare her.

"Don't tell her," she said, wide-eyed. Tell no one, Uncle Jean had said the first time, or the people you love most will suffer. The ramifications for breaking her silence were as real to her today as it had been back then.

"Mia, she should know about this. She should know about your uncle. It's not safe for you here."

She wrapped her arms around herself in a failed attempt to stop her trembling. "Don't. I'll handle it." The words sounded so final, so mature for her twelve years, she almost didn't recognize her own voice.

Billy removed his wallet and drew out a small white card. "Take this," he said, handing it to her. *Global Healing International*, it read in bold print, with Billy's name. He pointed to the phone number and address. "If ever you need me."

Mia looked into his downcast eyes and nodded, thinking of Billy's bravery. He'd fought for her. Would her father have done the same? Unrealistic as that thought was, she tucked away the small fantasy that he would. That if he knew what hell she'd endured, that he'd sweep in and take her away from it all.

Three days before Kanaval, Jonas strutted into Mia's house wearing a homemade mask that was big and clumsy and wobbled like an upturned basket on his head, exaggerating his already lanky body. He was a puma with a pink tongue, wide eyes, and unusually long fangs. Mia touched a fang and shrieked as if she'd been punctured, then doubled over in laughter.

"Very funny, silly girl. Let's see your costume." Removing the mask, he placed it on the table full of ingredients intended for the last few street-party dishes.

Mia slipped into her room and returned wearing a bright pink, red, and green skirt with a matching halter top fastened around her neck. She held the strings that bound the rest of the top behind her back.

Jonas stepped up and tied the loose ends together. "*Magnifique*," he said.

"Oh, Jonas, it's going to be such a day!" she said, excitedly. This was his first time in the parade as well.

"Our group goes out behind yours," he said. "I'll be able to watch you."

"Me too," said Uncle Jean, emerging from his bedroom.

Mia jumped back, knocking Jonas's mask and a bowlful of shelled peas off the table.

"Careful there, Sweet Thing," said Uncle Jean, making a show of grabbing her before she fell. Mia looked at Jonas with desperate eyes as her uncle held her around the waist. Finally the grown man slowly released her and sauntered out the front door.

Mia was struck by the sound of his voice, the feel of his touch on her waist, and the vivid memory of being thrust against a fence on a dark street.

"What was *that* all about?" Jonas said as he and Mia collected the peas strewn across the floor.

"I can't tell you." She knelt beside the table and reached for a sapphire blue saltshaker that had fallen along with the peas. It had a chip at the bottom but was otherwise all right.

"You have secrets from *me?*" Jonas knelt alongside her and pouted playfully while corralling the fallen peas.

Mia frowned and looked around the room to make sure Uncle Jean was really gone. She wondered what or how much she could say. Or whether she should say anything at all.

"Is it your uncle?" Jonas asked, his tone more serious. Mia's head snapped up at his guess. Jonas continued. "Oh, God! Is he hurting you?" He glanced over his shoulder, as if expecting Uncle Jean to reappear.

They abandoned the peas and sat huddled together beneath the table.

"I—I can't say," Mia said. "It's too dangerous."

Jonas moved closer. Mia shook her head and eased away, her heart racing. She wanted to tell him. She wanted to start from the beginning. But again, she thought of the curse. That vile curse. She'd only been five years old and would have believed anything. She knew better, though. Why was she letting it get in the way of doing what was right?

Had she kept her silence too long already? Was that it? She could have said something sooner, but after so much time, an element of shame and embarrassment had seeped in. Plus, Uncle Jean would deny it, and she'd end up looking like a liar.

Mia's mouth went dry. "He—" Unable to make eye contact, she focused on the saltshaker, running her thumb over the chipped edge. Then she told Jonas about that first time in the back room of Uncle Jean's shop. How he'd stripped her, then exposed himself. She glossed over the graphic details, cutting to the curse. "Tell no one or the people you love most will suffer."

Even now, the threat sent shivers up her spine.

"A curse," Jonas said. "Like, an *actual* curse?"

"It's not like he said, 'I curse you and your loved ones,' or anything," Mia said. "But Kalfu . . . you know what they say." Jonas shook his head, so she added, "He just has to look into your eyes, and you're cursed."

"No one says that," Jonas said. She'd only been five. She could have been wrong. She had no idea how curses worked. But why risk the lives of the people she loved most? "Some people say my father was cursed, but I know it's a lie," Jonas added.

"He died at sea," Mia said, recalling the story.

"Yes, but it was the storm that killed him. Not a curse. There's no such thing as a curse, Mia. My mother will tell you that."

"Mama says your father was a great man," Mia said.

Jonas sighed. He'd never known his father either, but at least he had the stories. "Does your uncle still—you know?" he said, clenching a fist.

"I do my best to stay out of his reach." Mia turned the saltshaker over in her hands. It and the matching pepper shaker were two of her mother's greatest treasures, having been handmade by Mia's grandmother. The tablecloth was her grandmother's, too, intertwining vines and delicate blue flowers embroidered with the Creole inscription, *Inite se Fòs*, stitched on one end. "Unity Makes Strength." The French translation was stitched on the other. It was the national credo, printed on the Haitian flag.

"I remember you acting weird before Hurricane George," Jonas said. His eyes darted from Mia to the door Uncle Jean had left through. "So, this was why."

Mia sighed. "Yes." She felt a small sense of relief at having shared her secret.

"That steaming pile of shit. Have you told your mother?"

Mia shook her head, wondering how she could have kept Uncle Jean's "special friend" secret for so many years. But real or not, the curse had become a part of her. Even when she wasn't thinking of it directly, the risk of telling was ever-present.

Now Jonas knew, and Mia braced herself for retribution.

Two days before the parade, Mia noticed the streets filling with painted faces, bright costumes, loud music, and riotous dancing as the community celebrated. It was a joyful time.

Cakes, pies, and candied fruit were sold along the street. Locals paid next to nothing, while tourists paid outrageous prices. Mia knew it was wrong, but that's how it had always been. And the profits benefited everyone around her. Even St. Cecilia's. The plate was passed from parishioner to parishioner and into the hands of generous visitors hoping to make a difference in the little church.

Amen.

One day before the parade, Mama took Mia behind Uncle Jean's shop, where the other dancers were waiting for one more practice run. It was difficult to concentrate with all the partying going on.

Mia ignored the ogling boys. Uncle Jean watched from the shop's back door as he tended the ribs on the firepit.

When the group took a break, Jonas waved her over.

"Have you told her?" he asked. He had one eye on Uncle Jean, still standing in the doorway. Mia shook her head. "Say something soon," Jonas said. "Before he hurts you."

"Before he hurts me," she repeated, recalling the night in the alley.

CHAPTER 8

The morning of the Kanaval parade, Mia was in the front room while her mother fussed over her, making sure the costume fit and her braids were tight before they joined the other women for the big event.

"Hold still," Mama said.

"I can't. I'm too excited," Mia said as Auntie Sis stepped in from her bedroom.

"So am I," Auntie Sis said with an impish grin and a hand on her belly. "I'm expecting."

"That's wonderful!" Mama said. She released Mia and threw her arms around Auntie Sis, her smile bright enough to light up the world.

Mia was thrilled for her aunt and happier still for little Sasha, who would soon have a baby sister or brother.

"This is truly a day for celebration, no?" Uncle Jean cried, approaching the women. He threw an unwelcome arm around Mia. Mia winced and pulled free to embrace her auntie, then darted outside to meet Jonas for their first foray into Kanaval.

"Everything all right?" Jonas asked.

"Let's get out of here," Mia said, leaving Mama and Auntie Sis to catch up with them.

Mia fanned herself as she entered Rue Merced at the heart of their neighborhood alongside Mama and the twenty other women in their group.

Her heart thumped in time to the drums as her nerves abandoned her to the thrill of dancing. Surrounded by music, laughter, and friends, Mia was enchanted by the festive spirit and happier than she'd been in her entire life. Was Kanaval always this wonderful?

Mia watched, enthralled by the number of tourists who were pushed this way and that as they took photos; souvenirs of their holiday among the revelers. People of every color and walk of life, speaking languages she'd never heard before. In the past, she'd been sheltered from foreigners. She recalled the man who'd snatched her up when she was very young. It was a hurricane. She remembered shrieking and Mama coming to free her. His bearded face and bushy eyebrows still haunted her dreams some nights.

As Mia looked around at the many tourists surrounding her, praying he wasn't among them, she noticed Billy in the crowd. He smiled at her with a nod, then snapped a photo when she smiled back and laughed at his corny thumbs-up.

The hodgepodge of black, brown, and white revelers, all celebrating together, left Mia feeling less conspicuous in her lighter skin.

The parade route was only a mile long, but Mia was so exhausted when they reached the end it felt like it had been twenty. Her legs trembled with fatigue. Mama quickly led Auntie Sis and her to the first refreshment table they saw and handed Mia a bottle of water, which she drank gratefully as they waited for Jonas and his group of masked dancers to reach the end of the parade route.

Jonas broke away from the others and ran up to Mia, taking her hands and spinning her gleefully.

"Come," Mama said excitedly, leading them past crowded food booths and game stalls to the refreshment table at the end of the block where Uncle Jean met up with them, struggling to keep hold of three-year-old Sasha, who leaped from his arms and ran to Auntie Sis.

Mama laughed wildly as she took Mia aside and handed her a brown glass bottle of something bubbly and refreshing.

Beer? Had Mama handed her a beer?

She gave one to Jonas, too, and he was just as surprised. Though it was not illegal for minors to drink in Haiti, Port-au-Prince had an established drinking age of eighteen. Was this a test? No, it was a celebration.

Sasha reached for the bottle in Mia's hand. "Mimi," Sasha squealed using the special name she had for Mia. Mia held the bottle back with a wide grin. She was hot and thirsty, and the beer was delicious. Her initial sip quickly turned to gulping. Jonas laughed and drank his down without coming up for air.

Mia was still a little wobbly from the parade, but the beer made her feel downright dizzy. She stumbled forward, then overcorrected, and fell back into Jonas, who laughed as he caught her. The world was upside down, and Mia's head reeled.

"Easy does it," said Auntie Sis, balancing Sasha on her hip. "Here, eat something." She handed Mia a pork-filled hand pie. "It will keep you from feeling sick in the morning."

"Thank you," said Mia. But she remembered what it had been like during Auntie's first pregnancy, and assumed it was *she* who would be sick in the morning—and probably for the next few months.

"Look, there's Deseret!" said Auntie Sis, waving at her friend. The moment her back was turned, Uncle Jean tugged the tie around Mia's neck, and her halter flopped over, exposing her small breasts. "Oops," he said, chuckling.

Embarrassed, Mia quickly pulled it up, fuming at his impudence.

"Hey, old man. Back off!" Jonas said, shoving Uncle Jean hard in the chest. But Uncle Jean laughed it off.

"One beer, and he's already drunk. Such a lightweight!" He gripped Jonas by the arm and pulled him aside as if to strike him. Mia watched, horrified. She looked around for another ally. Auntie Sis had gone to meet Deseret. Mama was busy heaping a spoonful of something onto her paper plate but turned just in time to see Uncle Jean release his grip.

"Jean," she said, stepping up to him. "What's happening here?" Mia wondered what, if anything, Mama had seen.

"That boy is untrustworthy. Keep him away from your daughter." Uncle Jean leered at Jonas, then looked at Mia with a contemptuous grin. Mama must have missed it because she just stood there, her brow furrowed as if puzzling out the scene.

"No, Uncle Jean, *you* cannot be trusted," said Mia before running off into the crowded street with Jonas.

"That wasn't what I meant when I said you should tell your mother," said Jonas. "She's just confused now."

"He's disgusting," said Mia, reaching behind her neck to ensure the halter was fastened.

"The way he looks at you. How is it your mother doesn't see?"

"Well, you didn't see either until I told you."

"I knew something was off. I just didn't know what."

Later that day, as sunset colored the sky, Uncle Jean reached down to pick up his daughter, but Sasha screamed for her mother, who was helping Mama clear the tables.

"Mother is busy, Sweet Thing," he said. "Papa has you."

Sweet Thing? Mia felt her skin crawl. "I'll take her, Uncle Jean," she said, quickly reaching out for Sasha.

"Mimi," Sasha cried as Mia held her tight, glaring at Uncle Jean.

Over the next couple of days, Mia agonized over how to tell Mama of her suspicions regarding Uncle Jean and Sasha. It meant revealing the abuse she'd kept secret for years.

There was the chance Mama wouldn't believe her and would side with her brother. And Auntie Sis might disregard the accusation rather than accept the horrible possibility.

Mia would put them both in a difficult situation but decided it would be worth the risk. Maybe this is what Uncle Jean had meant when he'd said "the people you love most will suffer." She would have to tell the whole story and to hell with the consequences.

Late one evening, after Auntie Sis had gone to bed early. Mia pulled her mother into their bedroom and shut the door.

"I have something terrible to tell you," she said, feeling a stir of nausea as she spoke.

"Mia? Sunshine? What is it?" She looked into Mia's face with such worry that Mia almost lost her nerve. "Is it your auntie? Are you worried? It's a difficult pregnancy, but—"

"It's—" Mia's sweaty hands were trembling, so she clasped them in front of her, then released them again as she searched for her next words. "It's Uncle Jean."

"Is something wrong with Uncle Jean?"

Mia's legs felt as shaky as they had after the parade. She eased over to the side of the bed and sat. Mama joined her, curiosity and concern in her eyes.

It wasn't too late to back out, but Mia thought of Sasha, and took a deep breath.

"I think he's touching Sasha—you know, down there."

Mama immediately shook her head. "Don't be ridiculous," she said, frowning. "Your uncle would never . . ." Then she went silent. Did she have her own suspicions?

Mia took a deep breath. "I know because he touched me when I was small, and . . ." Mia felt the sting of tears welling in her eyes. Her vision blurred, making it impossible to read Mama's face. Does she believe me? Is she angry with me?

Tiny rivulets of tears began flowing down Mia's cheeks. She heard voices outside their room. Indiscernible chit-chat between Auntie Sis and little Sasha.

"I cannot be alone with him, Mama," Mia finally said. "And neither should she."

Mama leaned back and stared into Mia's face, then put an arm around her, sighing heavily. A thinking sigh that Mia recognized whenever she'd asked a difficult question. Mia wiped the tears from her face with the back of her hand and leaned into her mother. "Remember that day you picked me up at Uncle Jean's shop, and I was wearing an oversized T-shirt?"

Mia told her mother everything, from the "secret friend" to the rape attempt that had been foiled by Billy two weeks earlier.

A look of understanding washed over Mama's face. "That's why Billy was here?" she said, her voice trembling. "He told me to keep an eye on your Uncle Jean. I didn't understand what he meant then, but—" Mama shook her head as if doing so would help her thoughts fall into place.

"I'm sorry, Mama," Mia said, looking into her lap. But sorry for what? For not telling sooner? For allowing it to go on for so long? Or for shattering her mother's ideal of Uncle Jean?

"Mia. My darling girl." Mama's worried face deepened now. "This was not your fault. You have nothing to be sorry for. But why didn't you say something sooner?"

"Kalfu," Mia said. The short answer. Then she elaborated on the nightmares she'd had as a five-year-old girl that still clung to her.

The following day, Mama waited for Uncle Jean to leave for his corner shop before approaching Auntie Sis with Mia's dreadful news. The

prospect weighed on Mia so heavily she could hardly breathe. And the dark rings under Mama's eyes suggested she hadn't slept a wink.

"Sister," Mama began. Her voice was low as she sat down beside Auntie Sis resting on the sofa and reached for her hand.

Auntie Sis cocked her head to the side and sat up strait with a soft groan. "I love it when you call me Sister," she said, clasping Mama's outstretched hand.

Mama glanced at Mia, watching them from her bedroom door. It had been hard enough telling Mama what Uncle Jean was capable of, but Mia dreaded what was coming next. She swallowed hard and crossed the room to sit in the stuffed chair beside the sofa.

"What's wrong, you two?" Auntie Sis asked, pulling her hand back and looking from Mia to Mama. She winced and rubbed her stomach, her eyes narrowed on Mama's solemn face.

"Where is Sasha?" Mama asked, looking around. Auntie Sis motioned to her closed bedroom door.

Mama did the talking, to Mia's great relief. But it didn't appear Auntie understood the extent of abuse Mia had endured. She leaned back, staring at the ceiling with her arms folded across her chest.

"Why do you say this?" Auntie Sis said, her voice quivering. "Are you trying to ruin my happiness? Jean has been good to you. He's like a father to Mia." When Mama suggested that Sasha may be in danger, Auntie Sis stood up and slapped Mama's face. Mama didn't budge.

"It's all true," Mia said. "Every word. And I see the way Sasha runs from him. Something is wrong, Auntie. I know it."

Auntie Sis stormed from the room and slammed the bathroom door. Seconds later, Sasha's door opened a crack. Mia saw the little girl spying out and went to her, unsure how much of the conversation she'd heard or understood.

They went to the kitchen to fix breakfast. Mama followed and made scrambled eggs while Mia spread guava jelly on brown bread. It seemed oddly routine except for the sobs coming from behind the bathroom door. They seemed to get louder and more anguished each minute.

"Mama's sad," Sasha said.

"Yes," Mia said, placing the bread on the table.

Sasha reached for the bread, getting jelly on her fingers, then licked it off. "I want her to be happy."

"We all want her to be happy, Baby," Mama said as she placed four plates on the table.

Mia felt sick. She felt responsible for Auntie's misery. She loved Auntie Sis and never wanted to hurt her. Maybe it would have been better to keep quiet. But when Sasha gazed up at her with jelly dripping from her chin, she remembered that she'd broken her silence for the little girl. As badly as she felt for Auntie, she would have felt ten times worse if anything had happened to her cousin.

Auntie Sis finally emerged from the bathroom with puffy, bloodshot eyes and tear-stained cheeks.

"I lost the baby," she murmured.

Mama's shoulders slumped as she set a plate of eggs in front of Sasha. "Oh, Sissy," she said with a heartfelt sigh.

Mia's stomach roiled with guilt. She ran outside and looked along her street, where it was business as usual while her world was falling apart.

As dusk fell on Rue Janvier that evening, Uncle Jean came home to a locked door. "Sissy!"

Auntie Sis took Sasha into their bedroom and shut the door. Mama stood up from the kitchen table and carried two black plastic garbage bags filled with Uncle Jean's things into the sitting room. She stood at the door and took a deep breath while Mia locked herself in her own room. Mama would handle Uncle Jean. That was the plan.

Mia listened as the brace was lifted and the front door creaked open. She imagined her uncle catching sight of the bags, the look in Mama's eyes, and putting two and two together.

Mama kept her voice low and calm. "You're a monster," she began. "How dare you lay a finger on them."

"What the hell are you talking about? Let me in."

"Stop right there."

"Luisa."

"I know everything," Mama said.

"The little slut is lying," hissed Uncle Jean. Mia wanted to scream.

"I'll keep the house," Mama said. "You are no longer welcome here."

"It's my house," Uncle Jean said.

"Mama left it to both of us, remember? But that will change unless you want me to go to the police." There was a long pause where Mia imagined a stare-down in the open front door. Mama wouldn't want a scene, not with the neighbors nearby. But Uncle Jean wouldn't care.

"They'll never believe you—or her," Uncle Jean said.

"You're willing to risk that? End up in jail again?"

Mia wondered if she'd heard that right. Jail? When had he been in jail?

Uncle Jean answered with a low growl. "That's where this whole mess started," he grumbled. "You and that *Ameriken*." Then Mia heard the crinkle of plastic and stomping feet on the porch. She rushed to her window and peeked out just as Mama slammed the front door in Uncle Jean's face.

"You need me, Luisa," he shouted at the door. "Admit it! That damned American, that beast of a man, left you pregnant and alone. *I'm* the one who picked up the pieces. *I'm* the one who supported you and that bastard child."

Mama held her ground. "The child has a name. And any support you may have offered is nothing after what you've done to her." Mia had never heard her mother speak this passionately. But the image of her father was coming into focus. He'd left her mother. He'd abandoned his daughter. What if he hadn't, though? What if he'd stayed? Mia paused to consider how different her life would be. But he hadn't stayed, and now here she was.

"You'll regret this, Luisa. Don't think for a moment that this is over. You think you can strip me of my home? My family? *You're* the loser here. You and that mulatta spawn."

Mia cringed.

"Out!" Mama said. "If you show your face around here again or come anywhere near us, I swear I'll turn you in."

"Dammit to hell and back, Luisa!" he shouted, loud enough to be heard a block away. Mr. Desante was talking with two boys in the street. All three turned to see what was happening. And just as Uncle Jean turned to go, he took one last look at the house and locked eyes with Mia, watching from the window.

A week after Mama kicked Uncle Jean out, Auntie Sis began acting strangely. When Mama asked about it, Auntie Sis said she was afraid that Mama would kick her out, too.

"Absolutely not. You belong with us, Sister."

"But I'm not blood. I have no claim to this house."

"We need to stand together," Mama said. "You, me, Mia, and—our little Sasha, here. We are all the family we need."

Part of Mia wondered about the strength it took for Mama to reject her own brother so completely. She was grateful but felt responsible for splitting up both families. *Tell no one, or the people you love the most will suffer.* She wasn't five anymore. She didn't believe in the curse, but Uncle Jean's words had come true anyway.

"But the house," Auntie said. "It's still his, isn't it?

"Technically, yes," Mama said. "It was left to both of us when my mother died."

Mia's mother traced her finger along the words stitched into the tablecloth. Unity Makes Strength.

Mia knew the story well. Mama was only fifteen when her mother died from cancer. Just a few years after her papa died in the same skirmish in which Mr. Desante lost his arm.

How devastating it would be to lose Mama in such a horrific way.

Auntie Sis handed Sasha a biscuit, hoping to stop the fussy three-year-old from squirming out of her chair.

"Jean knows that if he bothers any of us again, I'd turn him in." She looked from Mia to Sasha. "In that case, he loses any claim to the deed."

"You're sure?" Auntie Sis said. "He's been to jail before, and nothing happened. My father was beside himself—his future son-in-law hadn't made a very good impression—but in the end, he handed the shop over to Jean when we were married, anyway."

Mia leaned in. "What was Uncle Jean in jail for?" She wondered if he'd been violating some other girl.

"He never told us, but whatever it was, it cost him six weeks behind bars."

"Well," Auntie chimed in, grinning, "he brought you a nice surprise when released, didn't he?"

"Hush now, Sissy," said Mama.

"What did he bring you?" asked Mia.

"Nothing," said her mother.

"Not what," Auntie Sis said. "*Who.*"

Mama stood abruptly, inadvertently knocking her chair to the floor. "No more of this," she said. "Time to clean up and get your homework done."

Mia leaned in closer to Auntie Sis. "My father was in jail with Uncle Jean?"

"They say he was taken in as a vagabond. Imagine that. When they released him, he had nowhere to go, so Jean brought him home like a stray dog."

"Not a vagabond," Mama said under her breath.

Mia glanced at her. "He stayed here?" How could Mama have kept such information from her?

"You should have seen him, Mia. The *Ameriken*—"

"Am I like him?" Despite Mia's mixed feelings, she couldn't help her curiosity.

Auntie Sis placed her fork on her empty plate, glancing at Mama, who looked ready to strangle her, willing her to be silent. Auntie Sis shrugged. "No, Mia, but he did leave his mark."

Mulatta, thought Mia. Bastard child.

Sasha slipped from her seat and skipped to her toy basket in the middle of the room, oblivious to the adult's conversation.

"Mia. Homework. Now," said Mama, hastily collecting the plates from the table.

Later, as Mia sat quietly at the table with her books sprawled before her, she overheard Mama and Auntie Sis in the kitchen.

"You should tell her about him," Auntie Sis said.

"Tell her what? That Ellis loved his job more than he loved me—or her? He left us, Sissy, and never looked back."

CHAPTER 9

"Good morning, Sunshine," said Mama, gently nudging Mia.

Mia sat upright in her cot. "I'm up," she groaned, rubbing her bleary eyes.

Mama was already dressed and ready for a long day at St. Michel's school, where Mia had recently begun ninth grade. "That's my girl," Mama said, opening the shutters to the golden sunlight that failed to disguise her ashen skin. "Have you considered what you'd like to do for your birthday?"

Mia yawned. "That's not for six weeks." She swung her legs around and sat on the edge of the cot, her sleeping shirt still twisted around her waist.

"Fifteen," Mama turned away from the window and cast her weary eyes on Mia. "Are you really that old?"

The family had given up exchanging gifts. There wasn't enough money to pay for the things they needed, much less what they wanted. So, Mama and Auntie Sis made birthdays and holidays an event—like a picnic, a day in the local park, or a bus ride to Lake Azuéi to swim and lounge on the beach.

In times like those, Mama would say life was like picking flowers in the dark. The old Haitian expression meant you must take the good with the bad, and you never know what you've got til the light of day. Mia preferred to look for the good. Like Billy's occasional food boxes and the mysterious scholarship granted to her from St. Michel's after Uncle Jean moved out, though it didn't include funds for a new uniform.

Mia looked closely at the dark rings under Mama's eyes and the deep creases on her brow and around her mouth. She looked older than she was. She hadn't been sleeping well. She tossed and turned at night, talking nonsense in her sleep. Life was hard for single mothers working full time, the primary breadwinners for their households.

Now that Sasha was old enough for school, Auntie Sis helped by working several hours a week in the thrift shop with Jonas's mother. But Mama still bore the brunt of the family's financial burden; she was the principal source of income in the little cinderblock house on Rue Janvier.

Fifteen was the minimum age to apply for a worker's permit. Mia decided to apply early, since her birthday was right around the corner, so she scrounged up the bus fare to sneak into town after school. She could be there and back before Mama or Auntie Sis noticed she was missing. She felt confident she could manage both school and work. And she knew how much the added income would help the family.

Her mother reached for the door, her thin wrist bent awkwardly as she twisted the knob.

"Mama?"

"Mm?" She must have heard the concern in Mia's voice because she turned to Mia with a weak smile. "I'll be fine, my love. Just need rest, is all."

Reluctantly, Mia climbed from her bed. It wasn't even seven o'clock, but the heat was already oppressive. She felt like she'd melt as she threw on her school uniform, a frayed navy blue skirt, and a rumpled linen blouse with buttons down the back. The uniform was too small and too tight, but it would have to do.

When the final bell rang at the end of the school day, Mia slipped out the side door and jogged three blocks to the bus that pulled up as she arrived. The bus downtown was crowded. Mia stood between two men—one in a Bob Marley T-shirt and the other in a filthy tank top. The latter leaned into her every time the bus turned a corner.

"Pardon," he grunted. "Just trying to steady myself." Mia hugged her bookbag to her chest and inched away, relieved when the bus finally arrived at her stop. She kicked herself for not asking Jonas to go with her. Her pride had fooled her into thinking she could do this alone.

Outside the courthouse, a swarm of passionate demonstrators was gathered with placards held high, proclaiming Jean-Bertrand Aristide as Haiti's true president, and calling with full-throated chants for the removal of Boniface Alexandre, who'd taken over as provisional president in March after a coup d'etat. A group supporting Boniface shouted back angrily.

Mia noticed men resembling the gangs who patrolled and bullied citizens into paying for security. Uncle Jean always accommodated their demands when they marched down Rue Janvier. Mia appreciated their unusual absence over the past few years, but wondered how long that would last. These gangs were different from the Tonton Macoutes who dressed in mismatched uniforms and carried out their own form of justice on the streets of Port-au-Prince. Both groups, however, operated with impunity.

She put her head down and pushed through the crowd, entering the courthouse—a whitewashed two-story Georgian-style structure with high ceilings and gleaming dark wood floors. The racket from outside filtered through the thick walls, its drumbeat reverberating throughout the building.

A sign above the employment office rattled as she pushed open the door. She was immediately hit with the reek of body odor and the sharp smell of wood polish. The room was spacious, with wooden chairs along the back wall and a counter with four clerks at the other end. Beads of sweat trickled down Mia's neck in the stifling August heat while she waited her turn in the long line of applicants, who were quickly growing irritable. She was by far the youngest person in the room, but she wasn't going to let that dissuade her.

Finally, she reached the front of the line.

"Next!"

Mia straightened her skirt and stepped up with her shoulders back and chin high. The clerk looked her in the eye. Her glossy pink lips parted, revealing a flash of straight white teeth. Despite the stench in the room, Mia could smell the honeysuckle oil from the woman's dark, slender neck.

Mia nervously straightened her skirt. "I would like an application," she said, surprised by her quivering voice. "Worker's permit."

"Identification?"

Mia reached into her bookbag for her student card and slid it toward the clerk.

"Is this all you have? No birth certificate? No national identification card?"

Mia shrugged, suddenly flush with embarrassment.

"I'll need to find you in the system," the clerk said impatiently, typing into her computer. "Date of birth?"

Mia collected herself, though her heart still pounded uncontrollably. "September 23, 1989."

The clerk stared at the screen, then back at Mia. "Bacri? You're sure?"

Mia nodded.

After a few more questions about her level of education, interests, and possible skills, the clerk plucked a sheet of paper from the printer behind her and handed Mia the official-looking document.

"This won't be valid until your birthday," she said. Mia blushed, embarrassed by her youth. "Remember to present it whenever you apply for a job. No one will hire you without it." Then she looked over Mia's head, calling for the next person in line.

Mia hurried out of the building, permit in hand. The crowd outside had doubled. Their tenor had grown angrier and so loud her ears rang. She sought a way through while clinging to the railing along the right side of the steps. There were a hundred yards between her and the bus stop across the street. It seemed an impossible divide, but Mia gritted her teeth, put her head down, and forged ahead, being turned around and pushed this way and that—until she found herself face to face with Uncle Jean.

Her whole body went numb.

He clutched Mia's arm and pulled her aside. It had been three years since she'd seen him last, and he looked rough. Not even forty, deep-set crow's feet fanned from his eyes, and his whiskers revealed a graying beard.

"What are you doing here?" he demanded. Mia wondered the same.

The mob pushed ahead. Their chants grew louder. A surge of adrenaline emboldened her as she fought to tug her arm free. "Let me *go!*" she hollered, looking for a friendly face.

Uncle Jean wrapped an arm tightly around her waist and pulled her against him. "No one can hear you, Sweet Thing," he said, lips pressed to her ear. His sour breath and body odor enveloped her.

"Get away from me!" Mia cried out, working at freeing herself. "Help!"

"You're wasting your breath. Come with me. I'll take you someplace . . . safe."

Mia winced. There was no getting away. "Help me!" she called again. But the protesters drowned out her screams. She knew it was useless, but she had to try.

With his arm firmly around her waist, Uncle Jean led her down the city street. She fought, wriggling this way and that, her permit still clutched in her hand, her bookbag hanging limp from her shoulder and slamming against her leg with every step.

Most of the shops in the area were closed because of the demonstrations, so Mia wasn't surprised that Uncle Jean's shop had been locked and shuttered when they arrived. The air felt stifling in the heat. Uncle Jean pushed Mia against the counter and secured the door behind him.

"Not—one—word." He appeared intent on one thing as he pressed himself against her, pinning her to the counter. Mia turned away from the evil grin that had haunted her dreams since she was a young child. Her book bag dropped to the floor, and his large hands gripped her wrists.

"What's this?" he said, noticing the worker's permit, balled up and damp with sweat, still held in Mia's hand. The harder he tried to pry it away, the tighter she clenched her fist.

A fat vein throbbed at his temple. "Don't play games with me," he said through gritted teeth.

Mia hoped if she could hold her ground, he'd release her so he could see the document, though she had no intention of letting go. He grimaced and grabbed a fistful of her braids as he wrestled her, kicking wildly, to the sticky floor.

"Stay still!" he commanded, laying a foot on her chest. Mia twisted, and he pressed harder, his heel digging into her ribs as he loosened his pants.

"Yes, yes," he said. "Remember this fellow? He's missed you." His demonic grin stopped her cold. "If you fight me, you will pay the price—understand?"

Mia nodded, trembling and terrified, staring at him while tears streamed down her face. By the time he'd lifted her skirt and wrestled her panties off, he was ready and wasted no time.

He spread her knees and knelt between them, sneering, and reeking of stale cigarette smoke and peppermint antacids.

The few blows she'd managed were thwarted when he took hold of her wrists. Then she felt him enter her—the pinch, the sting, the unrelenting thrusts pushing her across the filthy tile. The buttons down her back ripped into her flesh. She yelped in pain.

His hold on her relaxed, but she was too frightened to fight. Instead, she flung her arms out in surrender, and her hand hit something that clattered to the floor. She turned her head to see.

A mop. And right behind it, a bucket.

Mia gripped the mop handle, praying it was enough, then raised it and clubbed him across his back. He lifted his head in surprise, and she brought the handle down on his thick skull. He was furious but didn't relent. Neither did she. With one great gasp, she pushed him with all her might and reached for the bucket, then swung it at his face.

He howled in pain as he rose to his feet to confront her. She got to her knees, still holding the mop and bucket in either hand as he pulled up his pants and removed the belt, ready to strike.

She stumbled to her feet, staring at the belt. He stood between her and the door, his lips curled in a menacing smile.

"Get out of my way," she said.

Uncle Jean lunged at her. She swung again with the mop, but he grabbed it away. She sprang for the door, stumbling over her bookbag, then noticed her work permit under Uncle Jean's shoe and stopped. "Give it to me," she hissed.

"For a price." He smirked. Mia feared he'd want her to yield to him again and again—like she was his. Or was her silence the price she'd have to pay?

"I'm not five anymore, Uncle Jean," she said, dropping the mop and hoisting her bookbag over her shoulder. "Your threats don't scare me."

Her words rang empty in her head. She was petrified.

Mia straightened her shirt, opened the door, and ran.

She ran past the mission school. She ran past the small tavern outside her neighborhood. She ran past Jonas's house to her own, where she found Auntie Sis on the big chair with five-year-old Sasha playing on the floor by her feet.

Mia slammed the door, panting—the sweat, dirt, and humiliation clinging to her as Auntie looked up and gasped.

Auntie Sis rushed to Mia with open arms. "What is it? Tell me." She stood back and took Mia in with a new awareness. "Who did this to you?" Mia stood trembling, motionless, unable to speak. The words were not there. "Was it Jonas? Did he hurt you?"

Mia wanted to scream at her aunt's ignorance. Jonas would never hurt her. But still, the words did not come.

Auntie gave Mia a cold glass of water and took her to the bathroom to clean her up. Then she put her to bed and closed the shutters, saying, "Your Mama will be home soon."

But Mia didn't want to see Mama. She didn't want to see anyone. She wanted to close her eyes and make it all go away.

Hours later, Mia was holed up deep under her bedsheet, preferring the dark solitude over the bright sunlight seeping through the shutters. When she heard approaching footsteps, she held her breath. The voice in her head chanted, *Go away, go away.* But then she heard Mama's reassuring voice.

"Please, Sunshine, tell me what happened," her mother said.

"Go," Mia groaned, doing her best to block the relentless vision of her uncle's contorted face and the pain from bruising between her legs. "Leave me be."

"The police have arrested Jonas. He is unable to hurt you anymore."

"Not—Jonas," said Mia, curling herself into a tighter ball. "Uncle Jean."

Mama gasped. "Oh, my darling girl. I am so sorry." The cot gave way under Mama's weight. Mia could feel her heat. "That monster should have been locked up years ago. This is my fault for not turning him in sooner."

"Don't blame yourself," Mia heard Auntie Sis say. "You did what you needed to do at the time to keep a roof over your head. There was no other way."

"There's always another way," Mama said.

"And poor Jonas," Auntie Sis said. "I should have known better. That sweet boy."

"The police have the wrong man," Mama cried. "We need to clear this up."

"It should be me," Auntie Sis said, her voice quivering. "I'll make this right." Mia closed her eyes and wept. She wanted to die for causing so much pain. As tears dampened her pillow, she silently prayed for Jonas, Mama, Auntie Sis, and Sasha. Had she come forward about Uncle Jean sooner, none of this would have happened.

Mia refused to eat or drink in the following days, regardless of her mother and aunt's coaxing. She heard their concerned whispers. She heard Sasha's innocent questions. She heard the front door open and close as neighbors stopped in to bring food and comfort. It wasn't until she heard Jonas's voice that she came around.

He stood in her open door, his eyes red from crying, his hands clasped behind him. It broke her heart to see the agony on his face.

"I'm sorry," she said.

"No, Mia. It's me who should be sorry. I swore I would protect you, and I wasn't there."

"You went to jail."

"I knew the truth would come out. I knew you wouldn't let it stand." Jonas sat down on the side of the bed, and she leaned into him.

"Did you see him?" Mia asked, imagining Jonas's release as Uncle Jean was taken in and locked up.

"No, but I overheard the guards," Jonas said. "They don't think the charges will hold."

Mia turned sharply toward him, her eyes burning with hatred for her uncle, whose old threat still held power over her, and the legal system that would tolerate his behavior.

She looked Jonas in the eye and said, "He's the devil."

Billy knocked softly on her open bedroom door. She'd seen him only twice since Kanaval. Once when she was in town with Mama and Auntie Sis, and again when he came by the house with a box of toys for Sasha the previous Christmas when there hadn't been enough money for gifts. If Mia didn't know better, she would have believed Billy was the Messiah himself. It left her to wonder whether he'd singled them out, or if his organization was responsible for his charity?

Seeing Mia, Billy cast down his eyes, then stepped slowly toward her, shaking his head.

Jonas backed away to make room for him. He looked beleaguered. What was left of his fine, blond hair was disheveled, and his hands were red and raw with arthritis. Mia had always believed he was close to Mama's age, but he looked decades older today.

"How did you know?" Mia asked, horrified. She'd wanted to keep the rape secret. As if denying knowledge of it could wipe it away.

Billy glanced over his shoulder toward the door. "Your mother sent for me."

Mama peeked into the room at the mention of her name, her brow creased, and a hand pressed against her lower back.

"Did I hear you right, Jonas? The charges won't stick?" Billy said. "It can't be true!"

"Just something I overheard," Jonas said. "I could be wrong."

"I pray you are," Mama said.

CHAPTER 10

While Mia's appetite returned over the next few weeks, her mother's waned. "Cramps," she'd say. She'd sip water and nibble at the brown bread Auntie Sis made but couldn't keep anything down. Finally, Auntie Sis and Mia took her to the clinic.

During the examination, Mia, Auntie Sis, and Sasha waited outside under the shade of a scraggly bayawonn tree, its branches fanning wide overhead, its long ominous thorns portending pain and suffering. An hour passed before a nurse led them into a small office where a middle-aged white doctor in a white coat and thick, black-rimmed glasses sat behind a stainless-steel desk. His nameplate read Dr. Martin Craig.

Dr. Craig motioned for them to sit, indicating the two folding chairs across from him.

A box fan in the corner of the room hummed. Its cooling breeze brushed across Mia's skin and fluttered the pages of a calendar tacked to the wall.

Auntie Sis sat, trying to lift Sasha onto her lap—but the five-year-old rebuffed her mother. Dr. Craig removed a sleeve of paper cups from a desk drawer and passed them to the girl, who promptly settled on the floor and began stacking them.

"Where is my mother?" Mia asked, sitting down beside Auntie Sis.

"She's resting." Dr. Craig looked from Mia to Auntie Sis with eyes half-mast, his hands knitted together in front of him on his desk.

"Will she be all right?" Auntie Sis said.

Dr. Craig sighed and adjusted his glasses. "We're looking at pancreatic cancer." Auntie Sis glanced at Sasha, who was deeply engrossed in building a cup pyramid. "I'll have to order more extensive tests to confirm how advanced it is, but my exam tells me it's at least stage three. More likely, stage four."

Mia leaned forward. "I don't understand."

"It means the cancer has spread to other organs or parts of the body."

"Cancer," said Mia, recalling the tale of how her grandmother had died.

"There's treatment, but—"

"Pointless, yes?" Auntie Sis said while Sasha hummed a little melody, unaware of the moment's gravity.

"Probably." The doctor removed his glasses and rubbed his eyes. "And expensive."

Auntie Sis rose slowly from her chair, nodded to the doctor, and walked, dreamlike, out of the room. They wouldn't be making any treatment decisions today, Mia realized, taking Sasha by the hand, though it seemed the decision had already been made for them. The diagnosis was a death sentence.

Once they returned home, Mia tucked her mother into bed, pushing the blanket aside and using only the sheet. Even that seemed too much in the day's stifling heat.

"Fetch Billy," Mama said.

Mia recalled the small white card Billy had handed her two years earlier. She kept it in the bottom drawer of her dresser with outgrown clothes and a collection of pictures Sasha had drawn: their cinderblock house with a tidy row of white flowers; rainbows and soaring birds among the clouds; a self-portrait of Sasha's smiling face framed in chin-length braids; a colorful birthday cake with five candles.

Mia once had cheerful memories like this, too. Before Uncle Jean cast his dark shadow over her.

She rifled through the remaining items, finding other treasures—a special silver pen, a straight-A report card from sixth grade, and a palm-sized prayer book from her first communion. She opened the prayer book where the satin ribbon marked a random page and plucked out Billy's card, praying he'd come.

She took the pen and zipped it into her backpack. Uncle Jean had caught her unprepared. She wouldn't let that happen again. In a pinch, the pen could serve as a weapon.

Forty minutes later, Billy rushed into the house.

"I know people," he said desperately, wiping his shirtsleeve across his damp forehead. "There is a program in America for just this type of thing. It's—experimental, but if you agree, the treatment is no cost to you."

"Free cancer treatment?" said Auntie Sis, laying a damp cloth on Mama's forehead. "Do you know how far gone she is? The doctor said weeks. A month at the most."

Billy glanced at Mia, his eyebrows raised, seemingly afraid of upsetting her further. But in her mind, the rape, had become secondary to Mama's imminent death.

Mia went to her mother's bedside and crossed her arms as if it could protect her from the heartache. But the overwhelming heat made her feel lightheaded in the close quarters, and she struggled to breathe the damp air, which was rank with suffering and pain.

"You promise too much, Billy," said Mama. "Nothing and no one can save me now."

"You know that's not true. There is one person." Billy bent low and whispered in Mama's ear. Her head snapped up.

"Ellis?" she said with a gasp.

"Yes."

"That first day you arrived with the box of provisions, you said you didn't know him. You lied to me."

"I—yes. I lied," he said, glancing at Mia. "But he can help. As I said, there are treatments."

Auntie Sis cleared her throat and stepped closer. "In America," she said.

Mama shook her head and slowly placed a hand over her heart. "Never. Besides, it's too late for me. You know it's true."

"It doesn't have to be. And what about Mia? You want her out of here."

Mia listened closely, suddenly understanding what Billy was

really saying. He was thinking beyond treatment. What would happen to Mia after Mama was gone? Who would care for her?

"Not like this. She doesn't even know the man," Mama said with a pained glance toward Mia.

"It's the best option," Billy murmured.

"You can't be serious," Mia said. The notion that she'd be sent away was daunting enough, but to go to her father, the heartless man who'd left Mama alone and pregnant? She'd heard Uncle Jean the day Mama kicked him out.

Was Billy really saying that now that Mama was dying, the man who had abandoned Mia to a pedophile was her salvation? He'd been nothing more to her than a phantom, a fantasy of what her life could have been like had he stepped up and taken responsibility.

"You cannot be serious," Mia repeated, imagining a world where her mother did not exist. Or a world without Jonas, Auntie Sis, or Sasha. "I won't go." Her heart raced as she spun on her heels and marched out of the room, unwilling to process the implications.

A month passed, as the house grew dark and bleak in the shadow of her mother's illness. Volunteers from the mission began visiting regularly. Billy's work with his organization took a backseat to his constant vigil once Mama had convinced him she was against his Hail Mary plan to whisk her off to America for treatment and a reunion with the man Mia held responsible for everything that had gone wrong in her young life. Who's to say this man, Ellis, even wanted her? But any fears Mia had about Billy's intention to send her away after Mama passed melted into the background as they worked to keep Mama comfortable for the little time she had left.

"Mia?" Billy opened the front door and stepped onto the sun-soaked porch, where she sat with Jonas on a white-washed bench. His shirt collar was soaked with sweat. He held a folder with a white sheet of paper peeking out from the side. Mia recognized Mama's signature. "It's time to say goodbye," Billy said.

Mia looked him in the eye. He'd been crying, and his expression was strained. She stood and embraced him with a heartfelt acknowledgment of what he'd come to mean to her small family. This sensitive soul cared for them and never asked for anything in return. Now, after hearing what Billy said earlier, Mia wondered if her father had something to do with that. Then quickly rejected the idea.

Inside, Mama's head lolled to the side, and she struggled to open her eyes. Seeing Mia, she smiled. A beautiful smile. The kind Mia remembered from happier times.

"Come here, Sunshine," Mama murmured.

Mia's eyes stung, brimming with hot tears. Her throat cramped, and a dull ache took hold deep in her chest. She fell to her knees at her mother's bedside and wrapped her arms around the only person in the world who truly loved her.

"Mama."

"You're afraid, baby. But you have nothing to fear. You are a strong, beautiful, intelligent girl." She swallowed hard, and Mia lifted a glass to her lips. The water ran down the side of her mouth and spilled on the bedsheet. The second attempt was more graceful. Normally, they'd share a laugh over things like this, but not today.

"Listen to Billy, eh?" Mama said. "Your father . . ."

Mia nodded, unable to speak.

"I never told you much about him. I had my reasons. But there's nothing for you here anymore; he is all you have."

"I have Auntie Sis, Sasha, and—" Mama shook her head before Mia could mention Jonas and Billy.

"Ellis is your family." She coughed and continued in a whisper. "Tell him that I'm sorry."

Mia grimaced. *Never.* The confusion and sadness and pain she'd always felt when thinking of her father now coalesced into a white-hot rage. He was a stranger to her. He'd abandoned her mother when she was pregnant. He'd condemned her to figure it all out on her own. And he'd sacrificed his child to the abuse and violence of a demon, her Uncle Jean.

"Goodbye, my darling girl. My Sunshine. I love you and always will if you keep me in your heart." She was whispering now with the effort of speaking.

Mia wiped at the steady stream of tears. "Mama! Don't leave me!"

Mama struggled for words but gave up. She'd said what she needed to. Billy stepped in and placed a hand on Mia's shoulder.

Standing at the bedroom door, Auntie Sis began to wail, setting off cries from Sasha, who clung to her skirt.

Mama looked past them, then closed her eyes. Mia thought she heard a whisper, a small gasp that was her last breath. She was gone, and Mia turned to stone, her eyes fixed on Mama's beautiful face, placid and finally at peace.

Mia woke on the sofa the next morning to the sound of loud voices down the street, then a shriek followed by three loud blasts. After their prolonged absence, Mia suspected the gangs had returned.

Billy emerged from the kitchen looking like he hadn't slept all night.

"Sit tight," he said, then left the house, closing the door behind him.

The voices had reached her house. She went to the window and peered out the shutters. There were three of them. Two she'd never seen before dressed in cut-off shorts and matching gray T-shirts. The other, she knew as Flossie, the boy from school who'd slugged it out with Jonas. He looked up and caught Mia's eye with a menacing grin.

Mia heard Billy's soft-spoken plea for peace, no doubt explaining the circumstances in the home. But it did him no good. The gang had no patience for peace, though they demanded payment for supposedly keeping it.

"Unity Makes Strength," Mia said, with her head bowed in grief and fear for a friend's safety.

When Billy opened the door, his glasses were snapped in two, his shirt was torn with two buttons missing, and blood dripped steadily from his nose. Clearly, he'd been coerced into paying their dues. Jonas followed behind Billy.

"They're gone, for now," Billy said. "But we need to find a better situation for you all."

Mia gasped when she saw Jonas's bloody lip. "They hurt you, too!" she said.

"Not really. I'm all right," he said.

"They'll be back, though, Billy said."

"Yes, but you'll be fine. I'll take care of you." Jonas had always seen himself as her protector, but Mia knew a sixteen-year-old boy was powerless against the gangs. He, too, would have to flee or be conscripted.

Mia braced herself for the big changes that were coming.

CHAPTER 11

The church service at St. Cecilia's was beautiful—overflowing with flowers and brightly colored decorations. The women wore yellow, Mama's favorite color. The men wore white. The congregation sang loudly and more robustly than Mia had ever heard them. St. Michel's, where Mama had worked, passed a plate to help cover expenses, and Mia's neighbors laid out a feast fit for Kanaval.

Mia felt numb when Auntie Sis brought her back to the house and, as if Mia were a small child, put her to bed. That bed. The bed she'd shared with her mother as a young girl. The bed where her mother withered and died.

When Mia closed her eyes, she saw visions of her mother, young and vibrant. She thought of words they'd exchanged, words of love and loyalty. She felt her mother close by as if she still lay a breath away, then turned toward that phantom and grieved all over again.

A few days later, Mia heard murmurs on the kitchen radio about a tropical storm and an announcement about another protest outside the state building in downtown Port-au-Prince. She didn't care about the unpredictable weather or which way the wind was blowing in Haitian politics. She just wanted peace.

Sasha giggled in the next room. This was Mia's family now:

Auntie Sis and Sasha. For that small mercy, Mia felt grateful. But the last few months had been a nightmare that weighed heavily on her.

"Hey," said Jonas, standing in the open kitchen door. "How's it going?"

Mia shook her head.

"I have an idea," Jonas said. "Give me ten minutes." He darted out of the house and soon pulled up on a borrowed motorcycle not much bigger than a scooter.

Mia stepped onto the porch. "What's this?"

"Let's go for a ride. I'll have you back in no time," Jonas said.

Mia heard footsteps behind her and felt a friendly tug at the braids Auntie Sis had tightened before the funeral.

"Go," Auntie Sis said. "You need a break." The words melted into Mia like butter on warm toast.

Jonas took Mia to Lake Azuéi for the afternoon to help her clear her head. It wasn't more than forty miles away, but it felt like a hundred for the peace it brought to be out of that house.

They swam, teasing each other about the legendary crocodile lurking in the lake. They collected stones and then threw them back in the water one by one. *Kerplunk, kerplunk.* Mia watched the rings fan out farther and farther, imagining them reaching the opposite bank, where the majestic mountains of the Dominican Republic stood in muted shades of green and purple. It was a beautiful sight. It was a beautiful day.

They lay on a large rock, away from the sand crabs, allowing the warm sun to dry them. The crystal-clear water lapped rhythmically at the shore.

"I love you, Mia," Jonas said.

"You are full of it, Jonas." Mia lifted her face to the sun.

"You tease. I know you do." He nudged her and ran his fingers along her side.

"Stop it. That tickles."

"Don't you love me?"

"Stop it, Jonas."

"Kiss me," Jonas said. Mia looked at his charming smile and giggled. But then he leaned over and pressed his lips to hers. She resisted, and he pressed harder, reaching under her T-shirt to take a breast in his clammy hand. Mia squirmed, then jumped away. Her mind catapulted to the memory of being helplessly trapped beneath Uncle Jean. His hands on her body, his thrusting between her legs.

"No!" She pushed Jonas off and scrambled down from the rocks but had nowhere to go. She glanced at the motorcycle. "Take me home."

Jonas tumbled off the rocks and went to her. "I'm sorry, Mia. That was stupid." He reached out for her, but she leaped back.

"Don't touch me," she said, glaring at him, feeling angry and confused.

Jonas had been like a brother to her. She loved him like a friend and always would, but any thought of more made her whole body revolt.

Clouds crept in as the motorcycle sputtered down the bumpy dirt road, a rising wind at their backs. Mia shivered. Their afternoon lying under the warm sun seemed like a distant memory.

They stopped for fuel on their way into town. A radio perched above the cash register played Michael Jackson's "Beat It." One of those songs that worms its way into your head. Jonas paid for the gas and handed her a bottle of water.

"I'm sorry," he said again. *Beat it.*

Michael Jackson went silent for a special announcement on Radio Caribe`. Tropical storm Jeanne, originating on the coast of Africa, was now predicted to reach hurricane status and was headed right for them. *Beat it.*

Auntie Sis was in tears when they arrived at the house. "Hurry," she said. "We need to get to the shelter." Sasha stood at her side, staring up at the sky with terror. Her first big storm.

Mia ran past her aunt into the house. She picked up her backpack and tossed in clean underwear and a change of clothes in case she couldn't return right away. Then she grabbed what money she could find and two of her mother's prized possessions—the tablecloth and the salt and pepper shakers. Things to remember her mother by if the storm did its worst—which seemed inevitable.

Mia, Auntie Sis, and Sasha were safe enough at the crowded and noisy mission school shelter. Jonas and his mother were there, too, huddling nearby. She couldn't look at him without thinking of the kiss at the beach and his groping hands. *How could he? Such gall!* The storm's roar echoed her fury.

As if Jonas could read her mind, his sad eyes met hers, and he sighed. Then he inched toward her and handed over a fresh bottle of water.

"I'm sorry," he said, looking as dejected as a person could.

Mia turned the bottle over in her hand and fiddled with a small rip on the label, slowly peeling it up and folding it back.

"You're a good friend, Jonas. I don't want to lose that."

"You know how I feel," Jonas said. "How I've always felt."

Jonas was her closest friend. How could he not understand that this was bigger than a violation of friendship? Mia recalled his groping hands, and that instantly reminded her of her uncle's unwanted attention. Was he here? She looked around the room, grateful not to find him or his vile grin.

Jonas took her hand. "You're looking for him, aren't you?"

Mia nodded. With a catastrophic storm raging outside the building, she was more concerned with her future.

"Come live with me," Jonas said. Mia imagined his vision of playing house, but understood the underlying concern for her safety.

What was left for her at the cinderblock? How would Sasha, Auntie Sis, and she fare without Mama and the ever-present shadow of Uncle Jean?

"You'll be safe with us," he said, glancing at his mother, who was deep in conversation with the woman beside her. But Mia knew too well how Jonas felt about her, and she wasn't going to give him any encouragement.

"I'll be fine."

Deseret had once said that Mia possessed Mama's beauty and grit. Mia had never been sure about the former. But she now knew she had the latter. A group of men gathered near the doors, debating how long the storm would last. The sound of water dripping from the ceiling was torture. Then the lights flickered out. Mia was not surprised. Nothing about tropical storms or hurricanes surprised her anymore. Sasha clung to her mother, her whimpers reminding

Mia of when she was small, huddled on her bed with her mother, Uncle Jean, and Auntie Sis, during a storm like this one. It felt like a lifetime ago.

When the storm finally relented and the doors opened, they returned to their home on Rue Janvier. Half the roof had blown away, and the house was flooded with six inches of filth and slop.

Mia heard laughter from the debris-filled street and turned to see Uncle Jean sauntering up to them with a burning cigarette pinched between his fingers and a devilish grin.

"Where do you think you're going?" he asked Mia.

"Home, where I belong," Mia said.

Uncle Jean sneered, shaking his head. "Not anymore, Sweet Thing. This house is mine."

The threat to turn him in as a pedophile was Mia's only play. "I can still tell my story to the police."

"Your word against mine."

"Auntie Sis is my witness."

"Ah, there you're wrong. She's witness to nothing."

It was true. Everything Auntie Sis knew about Uncle Jean's predation and abuse was secondhand.

Mia's head pounded with the weight of what she knew was coming next.

Uncle Jean reached for Sasha, who shrieked and ran for her mother. He locked eyes with Auntie Sis. "You and Sasha are welcome to stay." He turned his back on Mia and draped an arm around Auntie

Sis's shoulders. "We'll be a family again." He murmured something in Auntie's ear. Was it an attempt to reassure her, or a threat to keep her from fleeing?

Auntie Sis looked from him to Mia, desperation bleeding from her eyes. The message was clear. They had nowhere else to go. Sasha needed a roof over her head.

Mia's shoulders dropped in despair. She felt as broken as the fallen palm in the middle of the street. With a lump in her throat and nothing besides what little she'd hastily packed before fleeing for the shelter, Mia trudged down the road through the mud back to the shelter. She was tired and hungry, with nowhere else to go. Maybe she'd been too hasty when she turned Jonas down. Maybe he'd been right.

A hand gripped her arm. She pulled away with a shriek.

"What are you doing out here, Mia?" Billy said, his brows knitted tightly.

Mia gripped the straps of her backpack and stared down at the muddy sandals on her feet.

Billy brought her to his modest apartment above the locksmith. It had one bedroom and a compact kitchen and had lacked power and plumbing since the storm. He kept gallon jugs of fresh water under the kitchen sink, and a one-burner camp stove served him well for cooking. As she got settled, he used it to prepare her a plateful of re-hydrated scrambled eggs. She took it gratefully, fork clenched in her hand.

"Why are you doing this?" asked Mia as she began eating. "You've always been there for us. Now for me. Are you so helpful to everyone?"

Billy laid a slice of buttered bread on her plate and sat beside her. He sighed, thinking quietly to himself before speaking, his own breakfast growing cold.

"I arrived in Haiti about a year before meeting you all. I was working for the US embassy, then accepted a job with an organization that studied the causes of global hunger and poverty, boiled it down region by region, country by country while noting their differences or commonalities. This is something your father still does. But the research is time consuming," Billy continued. "Because the face of poverty is ever changing with the shifting environment, geo-politics, and too many other reasons I don't want to get into right now."

Mia gazed at him, eyes wide and attentive, wondering where this explanation was leading. Then Billy got to the point.

"Research was meant as the first step, Global had always intended to use that information to implement the next phase of the operation."

Mia recalled overhearing Mama and Billy when he came to the house after Hurricane Georges. Billy and Ellis worked for the same organization. "Two branches of the same tree," he'd said. Billy said no when Mama asked if he knew a man called Ellis.

"The organization split in 1989," Billy said. "Starting here in Haiti. We called it Global Healing. Like many new ventures, it floundered at first. My predecessor drew too much attention and was—removed." Billy's sigh suggested an unwilling departure. "That's where I come in. My job is to work within the system to take the next step. Aristide understood my role and set me up with people who could assist me and our program. It was exciting. I saw many possibilities in the face of corruption on an unimaginable scale. Politicians who grew fat while their citizens starved." Billy sat quietly for a moment or two, perhaps gauging how much to share. Mia sensed there was something he wasn't telling her.

"I did my best with limited resources," Billy said. "I couldn't save everyone. It would have killed me to try. But I made headway with a seat at the table and President Aristide's support. You will recall, though, that his power came and went with the political tide. I was frequently at the mercy of some extremely selfish men."

"So why us?" Mia asked. "The special treatment, I mean." They sat in silence as he considered his next words.

"I can't say why, exactly, but you and your family became important to me."

Can't, or won't? Mia wondered. She thought back to the first time he'd visited the house, how kind and attentive he was toward them, returning in time to help deliver Sasha into the world. He'd rescued Mia from Uncle Jean, appearing out of nowhere in the dark side-street. After Mama sent Uncle Jean away, it was Billy she relied on after Mia's rape. And he'd remained close by throughout Mama's illness, visibly grieving after she'd passed.

"Were you in love with my mother?" Her tone wavered on doubt, but it was the only reason she could think of for him to single them out.

"Um, no," Billy said glancing away. "Not exactly."

"Was it because of my father?"

He sighed and squared his shoulders, then looked Mia in

the eye. "I've enjoyed helping you and your family. That is all. I'm not finished, though. Not with you. Not until I get you out of here."

Mia crossed her arms. "I told you before, I'm staying."

"That's out of the question. The riots are intensifying. And Global Healing is thinking about relocating me, so I might not be here to protect you."

"Jonas will protect me."

Billy leaned closer, his elbows on the table. "Jonas is a sixteen-year-old boy, Mia. I urge you to reconsider reuniting with your father. I've been in touch, and—"

"With my father?"

Billy cleared his throat. "He's aware of your circumstances."

"He doesn't even know me."

"He's asked for you to join him in the US," Billy said. "To live in the US. Do you know how fortunate you are?"

Mia folded her arms tightly across her chest. Her body stiffened in resistance. "You lied," she said.

"Excuse me?"

"When Mama asked if you knew Ellis. You lied."

Billy leaned back in his chair, nodding slowly. "I was afraid I'd lose her trust."

"And you expect me to trust you now? You expect me to trust—him?"

"I pray you will," Billy said.

Mia unfolded her arms and pounded the table. How could she rely on the man who'd abandoned her mother and her? How could she ever trust him? More importantly, how could she leave Haiti?

It's all she knew. Her mother was buried here. Her life, such as it was, was here.

"I can't go," Mia gasped. "I won't."

And yet . . . as much as she hated to admit it, she had no way to support herself. How was she going to survive? Grit would not provide food or shelter. She couldn't rely on Billy or Jonas. And staying with Uncle Jean was a non-starter. Slowly, the harsh reality came into focus.

Billy was right.

Billy reached behind him, and from a short stack of papers, grabbed two documents, placing them in front of Mia. A provisional passport and her birth certificate. Mia Louise Ellis-Bacri. Female. Born September 23, 1989. Mother: Luisa Annette Bacri. Father: Theodore Michael Ellis, III.

The official name on the certificate surprised her. All this time, she'd believed Mama had wanted nothing to do with the American who'd run from his responsibilities. Now here was his name attached to hers. Ellis-Bacri.

"How did you get these?" Mia asked.

"With your mother's help," Billy said.

Mia gawped. Mama had been scheming behind her back?

"There's a boat leaving for Florida in two days," Billy said. "You will be on it. Your father will meet you there and take you north to his home in Indiana. It's what your mother wanted."

"I don't believe you."

"She was only looking out for your best interest. That's with your father."

"She hated him," Mia said. But she wondered if that was the

right word. People fall out of love when they have good reason, Mama had said once. But there was a gulf between not loving someone and hating them.

After a long pause, Billy said, "Your father is . . ." He collected himself and began again. "Your father is . . ."

"He's what?"

"He's a good man."

Mia humphed.

"He's your papa," Billy said.

"No," Mia said, offended Billy would use a term so familiar. "Any man who'd abandon his child has no right to be called papa. He's no one to me, and *definitely* not my papa." Mia could see by Billy's pained expression, that she'd gone too far. But she wasn't going to apologize for saying what was in her heart.

"This is a good situation for you, Mia. Be grateful." Billy stood and began collecting the dishes from the table, but Mia pushed her chair back and reached for his plate.

"I'll do it," she said, her heart fluttering as she spoke. Billy looked up. "I'll go."

They drove north for over an hour to reach the only boat leaving that day for the Florida panhandle. It was usually a reliable route into the US from Haiti. But today, Radio Caribe` announced that many Florida ports, thrashed and beaten, were closed to arrivals in the aftermath of Hurricane Jeanne, and there was a risk of being turned away. Hundreds who'd tried to escape Haiti's dire circumstances over the past years had already met that fate.

Billy switched off the radio.

Mia fiddled with the pen she'd found in the bottom drawer. Montblanc, it read along the side. "I'm afraid," she said. "You'll be fine. Everything is arranged, your documents are in order, and your father will be waiting for you on the other side."

"What if he doesn't show? He's abandoned me before." Mia locked her eyes on Billy, daring him to respond.

Billy kept his eyes on the road, as palm trees swayed on either side. "He'll show."

Beyond the trees, Mia could make out long bands of whitecaps on the dark blue sea. Minutes later, Billy turned onto a narrow dirt road and parked in a sprawling gravel lot.

Mia clutched his hand as he guided her through the bustling crowd at the run-down terminal. There was a long line for tickets, and a whiteboard listing canceled charters or rescheduled excursions. A lone clerk at an information kiosk was bombarded by disgruntled passengers. Billy led Mia down the docks to Pier 16. She struggled to keep up.

The boat wasn't much more than a sixty-foot fishing rig. The all-male crew looked like they should be behind bars.

Though Hurricane Jeanne had passed, the rough seas remained. Sailing conditions were poor enough to keep most boats tied fast to their slips. But the captain of Mia's boat believed he could navigate the turbulent waters. She had no choice but to trust him.

An older man approached, his matted white hair contrasting with his dark face. "Good morning," he said in Creole, his body casting a long shadow in the early morning light. "I am Luc Telfort, your captain." His eyes locked on the documents Mia held to her chest, including her Visa application and provisional passport. "I'll hang onto those," he said, reaching for them.

"Uh, no," said Billy. "She's a responsible young woman. She will keep them with her."

"Not if she wants to get on my boat."

Mia tested her newfound grit. "Then I'll wait for another boat."

"You're a minor and my responsibility," the captain said with an exasperated sigh, "from the moment my boat leaves the pier to when I hand you over at the other end."

"And the other passengers?" Billy asked.

"There are five others, none of them underage."

Mia glanced at the orange-and-white-striped windsock flapping in the heavy breeze, then turned her gaze on Billy, sweating through his shirt like when she'd first seen him standing outside her house with a box full of groceries. Was he worried she'd change her mind, that the captain might be untrustworthy, or that the trip was unsafe?

Mia's misgivings were less about the journey—though that concerned her, too—than the man she'd meet at the other end. What did she know about him? He'd been in jail, where he met her uncle. He'd briefly worked in Haiti for the same organization as Billy. He'd seduced her mother, then left her and their future child. What did he look like? What kind of life did he have now? Were there other women he'd left behind? Other children?

"Tell him I'm sorry," her mother had said before she closed her eyes forever. For what? *He* was the one who should be sorry.

"Listen, we have no time for this," the captain said. "I assure you, the young lady will be safe. For the next day and a half, she'll have a berth to herself, meals, and security."

Billy nodded, seemingly reassured, so Mia held the documents out to the captain, who snatched them from her hand.

"Grab your bags; we're shoving off in fifteen." The captain turned to speak with a crew member who nodded at Mia with a seductive smile. She turned to Billy, her chin-length braids swinging wildly in the strong wind.

"Billy, I can't . . ." Mia threw her arms around him. "I can't do this."

"You'll be fine," he murmured. Mama had said to trust Billy. But trusting him on this meant trusting him about her father.

Mia pulled away from him, ignoring the sting of tears welling in her eyes. "Okay, um, I guess this is goodbye?" She hoisted her backpack over her shoulders and turned from Billy to face the boat.

"That's all you got?" said Captain Telfort, eyeing her. "No luggage?"

"This is everything."

He glanced at Billy for confirmation. "Right, then," he said. "Let's go."

Billy waved to her as the boat shoved off the pier, bobbing and rocking. Mia gripped the railing at the stern to steady herself. Fumes from the motor stung her eyes and nose. She waved goodbye to Billy, Haiti, and everything she'd ever known. Then she turned and faced the bow, looking out across the sea—toward the stranger who was her father, toward a foreign country, and toward her new life.

CHAPTER 12

Mia kept to herself in the little berth below deck with a dim light and a door that didn't lock, clutching anything at hand that could keep her upright in the rough waters and praying none of the crew would bother her. She didn't trust their unwelcome smiles or lingering eyes.

She clung to her backpack that first day at sea, hopeful they'd all forget she was there. But that night, she heard a thud outside her door—and a sound reminiscent of Uncle Jean's backroom moans.

"Miss?" a man said, his voice deep and sinister. It wasn't the captain. Mia broke into a cold sweat. Trembling, she fished the silver pen from her bag and held it tightly in her fist.

"I know you're in there," the man said. "Let me see that pretty face." The handle turned, and she lunged at it, pressing all her weight against the door. But it wasn't enough. She could see him ogling her through the crack before he forced the door open.

The pen glinted as she held it up. He stepped back, alarmed at first, then grinned, reaching for it. Mia fell back against her bunk. "Leave me alone," she said.

"In a bit," he said, stepping further into the tiny berth that soon reeked with his body odor. "I just want a look at you, you know?" The boat rocked, and he placed a hand against the wall to steady himself. A narrow shaft of light filtered in from the open door, and she noticed he was not much older than her. His shirtfront was stained with sweat, and his grubby cut-off shorts were frayed at the knees.

"Don't come any closer," she said. Why couldn't her father have come for her in Haiti? He could have waited a few more days for the storm to blow over and fly her out. He could have cared enough to ensure her safety. But he hadn't, and this letch was proof of that.

"Hey!" shouted a voice outside the berth.

"Captain," said her intruder. "I . . . I was only checking in on our guest."

"Out of there!" the captain commanded from the corridor. The intruder was gone in a blink.

The captain turned to Mia. "I'm sorry, miss," he said. "It won't happen again." He looked down at the silver pen in her hand and frowned, then handed her a bowl with fat chunks of mystery meat tossed in with beans.

A wave of nausea rippled up from her belly. "Thank you," she said, taking the hot mess.

The captain held out his hand, palm up. "No weapons on board. That goes for you, too."

"It's just a pen," she said.

"That you intended to use as a weapon," the captain said.

Seconds passed before Mia handed over her only source of security to a man she trusted about as much as the intruder who had just left.

Once the door was closed, Mia returned to her bunk, her nerves frayed, and cautiously tasted the foul-smelling food. Her stomach growled, but she could not eat.

Late the following night, Mia heard shouts from the deck and figured they were approaching their destination. The captain appeared at her door, allowing a shaft of light into her berth.

"We're here," he said, reaching for the backpack on her bunk. Mia pushed his arm away, grabbing the backpack herself and pulling the straps over her shoulders. She rose unsteadily to her feet.

"What time is it?" she asked.

"Midnight, or thereabouts."

The captain took her by the arm and guided her on deck as if she were a child unable to make her way on her own, then jogged ahead to an official-looking person waiting on the dock.

Mia stumbled and fell against the rail, feeling tired, sick, and disoriented. She hardly noticed the other five passengers emerging from below deck and lining up on the dock ahead of her.

She took a moment to get her bearings before following the captain blindly under the lamplight. They waited as the others showed their paperwork. Some were told to stand aside. One man made a fuss. A middle-aged woman dropped to her knees when the official stamped her passport. None of them had a soul to meet them.

The captain led her forward and handed her documents to the official. As the official flipped through Mia's papers, she noticed a man emerge from the darkness. He was tall and looked serious—with thick black eyebrows and a beard.

He stepped close to Mia, his steely blue eyes boring into her. "You," he said, with a slow shake of his head.

She couldn't read his meaning. Was he angry? Disappointed? The official approached him, holding Mia's papers behind his back, and asked a question. Mia couldn't understand him, but she sensed something was wrong.

"I'm her father," said the man sternly in English.

Mia gasped. *Father.* She knew the word. Billy had taught her basic English words like *mother*, *father*, *sister*, and *brother*.

The man wasn't handsome, exactly, but he did have a certain confidence. Was that what her mother considered attractive? She looked more closely, seeking some resemblance to herself, or any sign of familiarity. He was an imposter, as far as she knew.

The man calling himself her father presented his identification and pointed to his name on her birth certificate. The official shook his head, and the man grew more irritated.

Mia shivered, and the captain put an arm across her shoulders.

"Step away from the girl," Mia's father said in Creole.

The captain backed off, and a young woman from the terminal stepped in with a blanket. She was blond and heavy-set, with the name *Carla* stitched into her black polo shirt. Carla escorted Mia into the building, where someone else slapped a yellow plastic band on her wrist and asked her to sit on a cold aluminum chair beside the counter across from two other passengers. Where had the rest gone?

A boombox behind the counter played Madonna's "Material Girl" followed by "Karma Chameleon" and "Electric Avenue." It was 2004, yet Americans seemed fixated on 80s music. A faint recollection of Michael Jackson's "Beat It" drifted through Mia's mind. Then, other memories. The storm. The shelter. Billy's little apartment.

She was a long way from home.

Her stomach grumbled as she eyed a half-empty box of doughnuts. She hadn't had a proper meal in days and was beyond hunger.

Carla set a cup of hot tea on the end of the counter and motioned for Mia to take it. Mia held the cup in both hands, welcoming its warmth in the heavily air-conditioned building.

She stared out the office window at the official and her father. They were both angry—their voices were raised, but she could not understand them. Then they walked away, out of sight. Mia's heart fluttered. Were her documents no good? Was her father going to leave her? Were they going to send her back—or send her to jail?

The woman pushed the doughnuts closer. Mia selected a plain cake doughnut—the least offensive. She nibbled and sipped her tea, fretting over what would become of her if the Americans rejected her. An hour passed, then two, before the woman escorted her to a waiting van holding several of the other passengers.

"No!" shouted her father. "Stop!"

Mia spun around toward his voice. She felt lightheaded, and her stomach roiled. Then she stumbled back and retched. The vomit splattered across the pavement, her shoes, and the official, who jumped away in disgust.

Mia's father pushed past the official and took Mia by the hand. "You're coming with me," he said in Creole.

The van door rumbled open, and two men in black rain jackets popped out. "Sir!" Her father tightened his grip, leading her away. "Sir!" the men yelled again, and one shoved a clipboard forward. "Your signature!"

Mia's father cursed, snatching up the pen and scrawling an

elaborate E on the dotted line. Mia still felt woozy. Her vision blurred, and the world went dark.

Mia woke curled up in the backseat of a compact car with a piercing leg cramp and the taste of vomit in her mouth. She couldn't remember how she'd gotten into the car but had been vaguely aware of the engine's sonorous hum during the all-night drive.

"Where am I?" she asked in Creole.

"Almost there. Go back to sleep."

The sun had barely cleared the horizon when the car turned down a long, narrow road and stopped in front of an enormous white building with broad steps leading to a large red door. Mia rubbed her eyes as a man and woman ran up.

Her father opened her car door, and she stepped out cautiously into the cool air that smelled like the clear open skies over Lake Azuéi. There were no palm trees or bright flowers, but she heard birdsong and the rattle of leaves from a nearby catalpa tree like the one that grew behind Uncle Jean's shop. *Uncle Jean*. Mia shuddered at the memory.

"This is Rosa and Oscar," her father said in Creole. "They'll be looking after you for a while."

"Not you?" Mia asked with a shiver in the passing breeze. Had he really brought her all this way merely to abandon her so soon?

If she hadn't been so overwhelmed by her new surroundings, she might have spoken up, though something about her father suggested it was better to remain silent.

She glanced from one face to the other. Rosa's eyes were kind and soft. Oscar's smile looked sweet and genuine. Rosa put a tender arm around Mia's shoulders and walked her toward the side of the building. Oscar followed. Mia stopped and looked back. "Papa?"

The impulse took her by surprise. She'd never thought of him like that. She'd told Billy as much days earlier.

She saw him wince. This wasn't going well. "Ellis," he said. "You may call me Ellis. Understand?"

She'd waited fifteen years to meet him and couldn't even call him Papa.

"Where are we—Ellis?"

"Meridian, Indiana. This is my home. Rosa and Oscar work for us."

"Us?"

"You'll meet the others later." Ellis stared at her as if he couldn't fathom her existence, then ambled back to the car, a dingy brown Toyota with a missing hubcap.

Rosa smiled warmly, her eyes twinkling, and said something that sounded like gibberish. English, she assumed. Ellis hadn't explained that neither Rosa nor Oscar spoke a word of French or Creole.

Rosa escorted Mia through a small herb garden and beneath a wrought iron trellis tangled in a woody vine with dull yellow leaves. Beyond the garden was a green door that led into a warm kitchen where she was shown to a table and given a bowl of chicken soup with two fat, fluffy dumplings.

Mia took in her surroundings as she ate, noting the terra-cotta floor, the brass light fixture above the table, and the lace curtains over the sink where Rosa stood, humming a cheerful tune. She turned to Mia, holding up the soup ladle.

"More?" she asked.

Once Mia had her fill, Rosa led her down a carpeted hallway and up a broad staircase to a bathroom on the second floor. There, she left Mia alone.

Finally, Mia thought. She'd become desperate for a toilet. She relieved herself, looking from the claw-foot bathtub to the polished stone countertops where Rosa had laid a fluffy blue towel and a change of clothes. It wasn't anything like the home she'd shared with her mother in Haiti. The memory sent a stab of grief through her heart.

Dare she fill the bathtub? It would require gallons of water. That would be decadent by Haitian standards, but here? She heard a tap, and then Rosa spoke softly through the door. A question. Mia opened the door a crack, and Rosa smiled. She entered shyly and approached the bathtub, then plugged the drain.

"Cold water," Rosa said, turning the first valve and inviting Mia to feel the cool stream. Next, she turned the second valve. "Hot water." Mia nodded her understanding. Then Rosa picked up a bottle from the side of the tub. "Shampoo." She went on like this for the conditioner, the floral-scented soap, and finally, the bubble bath, which she squeezed out into the running water. Millions of bubbles burst forth, creating an ever-expanding island across the water. Mia laughed. She'd never seen anything like it in her life.

Rosa smiled, then placed the towel closer to the bath. "Welcome, dear girl," she said. Soap, hot water, dear girl. Mia rolled the new words around in her mind after Rosa left her alone to bathe. She had a lot to learn—but she felt hopeful for the first time since her mother had passed away.

If only Ellis was as kind as Rosa. She hadn't expected much, but he hadn't even said Mia's name. It felt like an insult—like he was continuing to deny her existence.

Mia emerged from the bathroom clean and dressed in a bright orange sweater and tan pants one size too small. Quietly, she retraced her steps to the kitchen.

Rosa tugged at the sweater's cuff and winked, then prattled on in a string of words that went right over Mia's head.

Oscar led Mia out of the kitchen, with Rosa following. They walked past the garage, the equipment shed, and the stable. Rosa ran ahead to unlock the door to a small gray cottage while gesticulating and chattering about what sounded like a list of tasks. Oscar nodded and mumbled his agreement, winking at Mia as if she understood what was happening.

Was she to live in this cottage? Was she to have it all to herself? What about Ellis? Where had he gone, and when was he coming back?

The cottage opened into a dark living room with a brick fireplace on one end and a plush sofa facing a wall-mounted television on the other. Rosa went to the front window and pulled a thick cord that drew open a pair of heavy woven drapes, revealing the small garden bed of bright yellow flowers on the other side.

Rosa continued to speak as she led Mia across the living room and through an open door to the kitchen. As with the bathroom, Rosa patiently identified key items. Oven, cupboard, sink. With each word, Mia's love for Rosa grew. Someone cared enough to try and make her feel at home.

Oscar took pride in opening the side-by-side refrigerator. It took Mia's breath away. So much food!

"Fridge!" Oscar said, beaming. "Food." There was much too much to identify, so they left her to figure things out for herself later.

Next, they climbed the creaky stairs to a room at the end of the hall. There was an L-shaped desk in the corner, with a bookshelf on one side that matched the dresser and bed. They were all old but clean and polished. She admired the blue-and-white braided rug on the floor and yellow gingham curtains in the windows. Rosa pointed to a colorful patchwork quilt on the bed and pointed to herself.

Does she want the blanket? Mia wondered, then pulled the heavy quilt from the bed and handed it to Rosa, who laughed, put it back on the bed, and gave Mia a firm embrace.

"Dear girl," said Rosa, then addressed the quilt with the pantomime of sewing.

"Ah," said Mia, finally understanding. Rosa had made the quilt.

"What's going on?" came a small voice from the doorway.

Mia turned toward a boy looking to be about nine years old with wire-rimmed glasses, short sandy blond hair, and a stained white sweatshirt.

"Oh!" said Rosa with a start. "Um." She turned to Mia, her eyes wide, and said softly, "Mia, this is TJ—your brother."

Though she was still learning English, Mia knew the word *brother*. She blinked, unsure what to do or say. *I have a brother*, she thought jubilantly. *All this time, I had a brother.*

Ellis had moved on from Mama as if that chapter in his life had never happened, but Mia put her anger aside for the moment as she reveled in this newfound knowledge.

Finally, she came up with another useful American word. "Hello."

It took TJ nearly as long to digest what Rosa had said. But once he got it, he said, "Oh, hey," and left the room.

Oscar laid Mia's backpack on the bed and patted it. This was her bed, she gathered. This was her room.

When they reentered the living room, they found TJ on the sofa watching cartoons. He glanced up at Mia, then returned his attention to the TV.

A tall blond woman with a neat ponytail and black turtleneck emerged from the kitchen and looked Mia up and down.

Oscar smirked. "Hello, Francis."

Francis flashed an insincere grin and turned back to Mia. She said something that included the word mother, then pointed at Mia.

"Mother?" Mia said.

"*Step*mother," Rosa said. "Ex."

Now Mia was really lost. These terms meant nothing to her.

Francis frowned as she studied Mia critically. She said something in what Mia thought was a flippant tone, and tugged on the hem of Mia's sweater. *Bouzine*, Mia wanted to call out. A word that might horrify Mama. But Mia knew a bitch when she saw one.

Rosa put a protective arm over Mia's shoulder while TJ's eyes remained glued to the blaring television.

Francis looked around the room and down the little hallway that led past the stairs. Then she smirked and said something snarky that began with *Ellis* and ended with *Princess*. Mia didn't like the hostile tone, and she didn't like Francis.

Francis took hold of TJ's hand and gave it a tug. He whined but crawled off the couch and followed her out the door with a shy wave to the others.

Rosa turned to Mia. "Sleep?" she said, laying her cheek on prayer hands. "Yes?"

Mia nodded. "Yes," she said, though she'd slept for the better part of twelve hours on the way from the Florida port.

Mia awoke to Ellis standing beside her bed. The sun hung low in the sky, casting the room and his face in an eerie glow. How long had he been there? Had he been watching her? Mia recalled Uncle Jean referring to Ellis as a beast of a man. The beast she saw now did nothing to dispel that notion.

Ellis scratched his beard and cleared his throat. "Get up. It's time for dinner."

Mia appreciated his use of Creole but didn't know what to make of his abrupt tone.

"I'm not hungry," she said—though she was famished.

"There's someone I want you to meet." He removed something from his pocket and placed it on the desk. "I'll wait for you outside."

Mia waited for him to leave before looking at what he'd set down: the silver pen from Mama's drawer. It unlocked a chain of memories Mia didn't care to think about, so she climbed out from under the warm quilt and swept it into the top drawer. She straightened her clothes and slipped on the leather sandals she'd arrived in, feeling alert and acutely aware of her new surroundings. Then she circled the room, opening empty dresser drawers and peeking into the wardrobe, empty but for a row of yellow plastic hangers.

Slowly, Mia opened her backpack and removed her few possessions. The tablecloth, the salt and pepper shakers, and the change of clothes she'd packed were wholly inadequate for the brisk fall weather outside her window overlooking the gravel driveway.

"Hey!" Ellis called from the bottom of the stairs.

Mia glanced at her reflection in the mirror over the dresser and grimaced playfully, as Jonas might have. She felt a sudden ache in her chest. What was Jonas doing now? Did he miss her?

Ellis led her to the main house, but they didn't enter through the elaborate red front door. Instead, he took her to the green kitchen door around the corner. Mia followed him down the carpeted hallway she'd walked down earlier, but when they came to the stairs, he walked ahead to the largest sitting room she'd ever seen, and then onward to the dining room. There was a massive tapestry on the wall and a sparkling chandelier hanging from the ceiling.

She'd never imagined a table like the one she found here, set with fine China and crystal glassware. All this for one family? Ellis sat on one end and an old woman on the other, her silver hair pulled back from her face in a neat French twist. She glanced up at Mia, the motion as stiff as her starched white blouse, and nodded as Mia took her seat on one side of the table. Francis and

TJ sat across from her, a vacant chair between them and one on either side.

The old woman cleared her throat and spoke in a superior tone without smiling. Mia listened carefully but didn't recognize any words.

She looked at Ellis as he responded to the woman. Then, in Creole, he introduced the old woman as his mother.

Mia glanced at the woman, whose diamond stud earrings twinkled like tiny stars. "She looks like a movie star," she said.

Ellis shook his head. "This is your grandmother."

"*Grann?*" said Mia.

Francis hmphed and spoke curtly in English through a forced smile.

The old woman shook her head and said, "I understand you speak French, *oui?* You will refer to me as *grand-mère, s'il vous plaît.*" She spoke with a perfect accent. Mia blinked. It would be French, then. "Tell me about your trip," the old woman continued in French. "The weather was nice?"

Mia looked at Ellis. She needed help not with the language but with the idiocy of the old woman's question.

"The water was rough, grand-mère, but I was delivered safe and sound," Mia said in thickly accented French.

"Delightful. I was on a cruise last spring that surely tested my constitution. Eight weeks on the Atlantic from Amsterdam to Morocco. Just one rough patch, thankfully. I don't think I could have borne more."

"Oh, Christ," Francis said in English, smirking at Mia across the table. "French?" Mia sat in the awkward silence that followed wondering if it was French Francis didn't care for, or her.

Ellis grumbled something under his breath with an annoyed glance toward Francis, who rolled her eyes. Grand-mère straightened her shoulders and glared across the table in a proud display of dominance. Mia looked from face to face. When she got to TJ, he seemed oblivious, and much more interested in what lay beneath his fingernails.

Finally, Rosa entered the room with a tray full of something that smelled delicious and laid it on the table. Mia leaned forward to see.

"Sit back, *jeune femme*. Don't be rude," said Grand-mère as Rosa served five small bowls of the orange-colored soup. Mia wanted to smell the soup before tasting it but didn't dare under the old woman's watchful eyes. Instead, she waited, spoon in hand, as the others started in. Then she sampled it, relieved and grateful to Rosa for serving something familiar—pumpkin soup with loads of cream. The next course arrived, and Mia trusted that Rosa had taken equal care—chicken, potatoes, and what looked like tiny cabbages. The latter tasted disgusting but for the crispy bacon mixed in. She ate them anyway, washing them down with plenty of cold water.

"Cold water," she murmured, smiling to herself for remembering the new words. She looked to Rosa for approval, but Rosa had already left the room.

Ellis had heard, though. "What's that?" he said in Creole.

Mia looked away, afraid that if her pronunciation were poor, he'd have one more reason to think badly of her.

Rosa arrived with dessert. The five thin layers of chocolate with whipped cream filling and coated with crushed mint candies were heavenly. Mia might have licked her plate if she'd been home in Haiti.

"It's TJ's birthday next week," announced Francis, using the agreed-upon French. "I expect you'll be busy, though, hmm, Ellis?" Ellis quietly picked up his fork and held it lightly in his fingers as if weighing his response. Francis continued with a flip of her hand in Mia's direction. "Too busy with your new charity here?"

Yes. Of course. It all made sense now. That was why he preferred being called Ellis over Papa. The reason he'd taken her in. Daughter or not, she was nothing more to him than a charity. Her heart might have broken at that moment had she not already steeled it against him.

Ellis glanced at Mia, but his expression gave nothing away. "I'll be there," he said to Francis.

"You won't be off on some mission?" Francis said. "Some godforsaken village on the other side of the world?"

Ellis cleared his throat. "I said I'd be there."

"Stop this, you two," Grand-mère said, pushing her chair back from the table.

The adults moved to another room, holding tiny glasses of liqueur. Grand-mère took Mia by the shoulders and told her to remain with her brother until they returned.

What strange people, thought Mia, but went to join TJ in a small room down the hall. He'd already plugged himself onto a cream-colored loveseat and flipped on the television that sat on a heavy chest of drawers with clawed feet and shiny brass handles. A picture of a pastoral village hung above it in a gilded frame.

Mia looked from the picture to TJ. "Do you speak French?" she asked, hoping to relate to him on some level. TJ turned to her with a blank stare.

"TV," he said finally, in English. "Remote."

He handed her a controller, then picked up a pen and paper

from the side table and drew a stick family. "TJ, me, brother," he said, tapping the pencil on the smallest of the stick figures. "Ellis is Father. Francis is Mother." He drew a large X over the pair.

After each revelation, TJ looked deep into her eyes to ensure she'd heard and understood. Then TJ pointed to the largest figure—not Ellis, but Grand-mère. "GG."

"GG," Mia repeated, guessing GG was his own personal name for his grandmother the way Mimi was Sasha's name for Mia.

TJ clapped his hands and giggled in delight, then pointed excitedly to the TV. "SpongeBob."

She nodded and turned her attention to the television. TV. SpongeBob. This was TJ's world—and now, Mia was part of it.

CHAPTER 13

Mia lingered in bed the next morning, tucked snugly beneath the warm quilt, and welcomed the sunlight showering over her from the bedroom window. She recounted the events of the past few days: from Billy's tiny apartment to the foul intruder on the boat to Ellis's harsh scowl at the dock. And finally, to her new surroundings. She glanced around the room and noticed her empty backpack hanging on a hook beside the door. As if it belonged there more than she did.

Would she ever feel at home under this roof?

With a heavy sigh, Mia peeled back the blanket and pulled on the ill-fitting clothes from the previous day. Then she ventured downstairs, where she found Ellis brooding over a cup of coffee at the kitchen table.

"Where is TJ?" she asked in Creole.

"With his mother," Ellis said without looking up. "He lives with her but stays here on weekends when I'm in town."

"Are you often gone?" she said, lifting a mug off a hook beside the sink.

"It's my job."

As Mia helped herself to the remaining coffee in the glass pot, she recalled Billy's explanation of Ellis's job. Traveling the world to understand the causes of poverty and hunger. She also remembered what Mama had said to Auntie Sis years ago; that Ellis "loved his job more than he loved me—or her." Was that true of Francis and TJ? If so, no wonder Ellis and Francis were divorced.

How anyone could be married to either of them was a mystery. What had Mama seen in this man?

She took a sip and set down her cup while she picked through the fridge for something to eat. But eggs were too much trouble, and nothing else looked appetizing.

"Fruit," Ellis said, rising from his chair and reaching for a shallow bowl of oranges, bananas, and a pair of large, green apples sitting on the counter. Mia chose a banana. She ate as Rosa appeared at the kitchen door with a woven tote bag slung over her shoulder and car keys dangling from her fingers.

"Get your shoes," Ellis said in Creole. "Rosa is taking you shopping." He handed Rosa a slip of paper and a credit card, then nodded at Mia, barely making eye contact as he left the room.

Shopping, she soon learned, meant a trip to the mall—a fantastic place, all indoors, where everything could be found amid bright lights and polished floors. Mia had never seen that many white people in one place, their purchases swinging in crisp paper bags. Rosa laughed at Mia's wonderment as they passed a well-stocked cellphone kiosk, a shop window with finely dressed teddy bears in various poses, a stationery store with towers of greeting cards, and a store with nothing but soaps and lotions. A white girl about Mia's age was standing out front handing out samples from a pink basket. She handed Mia one, which she hesitated to accept. Rosa nudged her with her elbow, though, and the girl, grinning, gave her two.

Rosa led Mia into a massive store called T.J. Maxx that made the rest of the mall irrelevant. It had everything one could possibly want.

Mia bounced from clothes rack to clothes rack, looking but not daring to touch as Rosa selected a colorful array of shirts, sweaters, and slacks meant for someone older, periodically holding them up to Mia to gauge the fit. Finally, she sent Mia into the fitting room. The three-way mirror was a marvel. The bright overhead light was spellbinding. Mia felt giddy as she put everything on, like an actress in a play, dressing in floral prints and knee-length skirts. No—no—no. They were all wrong. She took them all back to Rosa, who then allowed her to wander. Jeans, T-shirts, black socks, and tennis shoes. It wasn't exciting, but the style was authentically hers. With Rosa's encouragement, she walked away with a pair of pullover sweaters and a jean jacket, though she'd wanted the leather one.

Beggars can't be choosers.

They returned to the mall's bright lights and gleaming floors. Mia stole glances at the other shoppers, who looked away as she approached. She was an oddity here, like a black stone on a white pebble beach.

Finally, Rosa led her to a shop with a little red schoolhouse picture outside. A poster in the window showed pictures of pencils, notebooks, and other school supplies.

"Huh?" said Mia. Then she realized what Ellis had in store for her.

School.

She wasn't ready. She was only starting to get her feet under her. Being thrown into a classroom full of strangers was a lot to ask of someone who'd just left her home, her country, and her language.

Mia needed more time. Apparently, Ellis wasn't willing to give her that, Mia thought.

When they returned home that afternoon, Rosa left Mia alone to put her new clothes away. Filling the empty dresser and wardrobe with the unfamiliar things felt odd. Odder still to dress in them, like an imposter. But Mia imagined that, in time, she'd get used to her new clothes as she'd get used to everything else in her new life.

She went to the top of the stairs and listened for signs of life—signs of Ellis. But the house was quiet, so she walked outside and looked up the narrow gravel road leading into a wood. Then she looked the other way and saw Oscar entering the stables whistling a cheerful tune. Curious, Mia followed. She grinned when she heard the whistling at the other end of the barn. The sharp scent of fresh hay instantly struck her as her eyes adjusted to the dim light.

There were three stalls but only one horse, a curious speckled gray filly who leaned her long neck over the stall door. Mia jumped back, her heart racing. She'd never seen a horse up close. It was immense.

The whistling stopped. "Ah," said Oscar, understanding her hesitance. "Like this." He stepped closer and murmured sweetly to the horse. "This is Liesel," he said to Mia. He laid a hand gently on the horse's cheek and ran it down her neck. The horse batted her eyes and snorted softly.

Then Oscar reached for Mia's hand and placed it on Liesel's velvety soft nose. The hairs tickled. Mia felt slightly calmer with Oscar nearby. She smiled nervously, patting the horse's long neck.

"Come," Oscar said, motioning for Mia to follow. He opened the door at the rear of the barn to a fenced paddock. Beyond that was a wide pasture where two other horses nibbled at tufts of dried grass. One was black with white boots, and the other was chestnut brown with a black mane. Both lifted their heads to have a look at the newcomers. The brown horse ambled toward the fence. It snorted and bobbed its head as if trying to get Mia's attention.

"This is Freddy," Oscar said, climbing onto the first rung of the fence and reaching across.

Mia laughed when Freddy nudged her hand with his nose and puffed warm air from his nostrils.

"Hello, Freddy," Mia said, grateful to Oscar for the introduction. For the first time since arriving the previous day, she felt like she might find happiness in Meridian, Indiana.

The following day, Ellis took Mia for her first day of school. A banner with an image of a mountain lion waved over the front door. Gray decals of the same image clung to each of the four glass doors leading into the old brick building. Mia followed Ellis to an office window, and once he'd signed them in, a tall man in baggy black pants called them back into his private, windowless office and shook Ellis's hand like they knew one another. Then he spoke to Mia, his words tumbling out of his thin-lipped mouth so fast she couldn't have caught one if she'd tried.

"This is Mr. Gottlieb," Ellis said in French. "He's the principal." Then a woman with large, red-framed glasses entered the room and swiped her long black bangs to the side. Ellis said, "This is Mademoiselle Spencer, the French teacher."

Ellis sat down first, Mia beside him, and the others sat down on the other side of the desk.

"*Bonjour*, Mia," Mademoiselle Spencer said with a warm smile. She continued in French, explaining that she'd act as Mia's intermediary throughout the school day. Mia remained silent as the teacher described what the day would look like. Though old enough to be a sophomore, Mia would begin as a freshman to give her more time to adapt.

Ellis grumbled but didn't object until Mademoiselle revealed Mia's schedule, which included four classes: gym, algebra, biology, and French.

"French? That's ridiculous," said Ellis. "She already speaks French."

"The others do not," Mademoiselle Spencer replied with a polite smile, then turned her attention to Mia. "And learning works both ways. You help them. They help you. Do you understand?"

Mia nodded.

"Is that the best you can do?" Ellis said. Mr. Gottlieb looked around uneasily. Apparently, he did not speak French.

"I've seen it work firsthand when I was in college, Mr. Ellis. With this method and my personal tutoring, I'm confident Mia will be up to speed before the end of the term."

"Hmm," Ellis said. He sounded unconvinced but had little choice but to accept the proposed method. He turned to Mia. "Oscar will pick you up and bring you home."

Mia nodded again but had to look away from him. Home? The word stung unexpectedly. He was referring to his tidy house on acres of land with a mansion, a stable, and servants, but that wasn't her real home. Home was where Mama was buried. Home was Haiti.

Mademoiselle took Mia's hand and led her to her first class, biology. It seemed like a pointless exercise. The class was taught in English. She wasn't going to learn anything. *Not with that attitude,* Mia thought, remembering her teacher back in Haiti when Jonas whined about the assignment.

On the way, Mademoiselle explained to Mia that Meridian was a small community that preferred things a certain way.

"What do you mean?" Mia asked.

"You'll see."

The class was already in progress—not exactly the ideal moment for Mia to enter. The other kids stared at her, eyes bulging, necks craning at the only person of color in the room. In fact, from what Mia gathered, she was the only person of color in the town. This must have been what Mademoiselle meant by "a certain way."

Mademoiselle took the seat behind her and roughly interpreted what was going on. The cardiovascular system wasn't anything Mia had any experience with, but it seemed that no one else here did either, judging by the blank looks on their faces. At least the attention was off her and on the diagram at the front of the room.

Algebra was a little better. Again, there were whispers and stares, but several kids had been in her biology class, and the initial shock had worn off. Also, the subject was familiar. Numbers. She could do that. She was unprepared for gym class, though, playing volleyball in her jeans and not having anything to change into after the mandatory shower. She stood out among the white skin and pink nipples, self-conscious of the stretchmarks from when her body had rocketed into puberty.

Then, Mademoiselle had to leave to teach her first class and enlisted another student to take Mia to lunch. The student wasn't thrilled. Neither was Mia, who looked up into the deep blue eyes and cynical smirk of a girl with tight jeans and an oversized sweater that barely covered the port wine birthmark at her neck.

"This is Natalie," said Mademoiselle. "She'll be in your French class. Perhaps you two could learn a few things from one another."

I doubt it, thought Mia. Natalie made an art form of avoiding eye contact. All through the lunch line, then after finding a seat in the busy cafeteria, she chatted up other students while introducing Mia to no one. The isolation Mia had felt that morning was nothing compared to this. She was rejected; a nobody. She felt invisible.

Finally, she reunited with Mademoiselle after lunch and a study hall break and breathed a sigh of relief. Mia waited as the other students took their seats, wondering which desk would be left empty. She groaned quietly when the only vacant seat was beside Natalie.

"*Bonjour mesdames et messieurs,*" called Mademoiselle from the front of the room.

Mia felt exhausted. She wasn't in the mood to do the vocabulary reading they'd been asked to do. *Maison, oiseau, homme, ciel.* House, bird, man, sky. She sighed, remembering sitting beside Jonas in French class while he moaned about how useless it was. Jonas. She felt a tug at her heart for the boy she'd loved like a brother since she was a small child. "I'll take care of you," he'd said.

"Mia? Is everything okay?" asked Mademoiselle in English, forgetting that Mia wouldn't understand.

But Mia knew *okay* and answered, "Yes. Okay." The other students laughed. Had she said something wrong? Something funny? Or was she the joke? Whatever their reason, she wanted to spit at them. Instead, she reconciled herself to learning English faster than they could learn French.

"Let's just see them try to learn Creole," she said to Mademoiselle after class as the other students rushed to leave the room.

Her teacher nodded. "Give it time, Mia. They'll come around."

Mademoiselle was right. High school became easier as the weeks ticked by. After some encouragement from Mademoiselle, Natalie became a friend. The transition was slow, initially, but Mia felt sorry for the girl when she struggled to recite a simple passage from their text.

"Slow down," Mia whispered in French. Natalie blushed, took a deep breath, and tried again. Afterward, they helped one another in class, studying after school and on weekends. French to English, English to French. Mademoiselle's teaching method took hold, and a friendship was forged.

Mia was so excited by the prospect of having a new friend that she tore out a sheet of notebook paper and wrote of her latest success to Jonas, who wrote back several weeks later with a vivid description of his geometry teacher, who was 'totally hot' and really into him. Mia had always loved Jonas's confidence. He'd signed his letter, Your brother, Jonas.

Now, Mia had an actual brother.

That November, during one of TJ's visits, he took her through the garden behind the big house where a grove of aspen trees with leaves as golden as the sun shielded them from view.

"This is my fort," TJ said, pointing to a gray shipping pallet surrounded by a collection of stones from the size of his fist to a small melon. "Don't tell anyone, especially Ellis."

Mia nodded. TJ's fort lacked walls and a roof, but she understood. This was TJ's special place. With a delighted grin, he reached under one of the pallet slats and pulled out a black plastic bag filled with superhero comic books and a deck of colorful trading cards. He sorted through the cards and handed her one.

"Cat?" Mia said.

TJ laughed. "No, silly. Pikachu! You don't know Pokémon?" He fanned the deck, pointing to the fantastical characters on the cards. "Charmander, Bulbasaur, Jigglypuff . . ." He went on, his face aglow. Then he sorted through the deck and pulled out twelve duplicates. "For you," he said, beaming as he presented them to her.

TJ was sharing his treasure with her, and Mia's heart swelled with affection.

GG was more of a challenge. During one of her special dinners, she'd let slip that she didn't believe Ellis to be Mia's father, referring to Mama as *la putain*, the whore.

Mia pushed back from the table with a huff, looking from GG to Ellis. She debated whether to fight it out with her grandmother or wait for Ellis to defend her mother. Ellis cleared his throat.

"Stay where you are," he said. Mia glared at him. "Mother, you will apologize." He set down his fork and waited for the old woman to speak.

"*Je suis désolé*," GG said, meeting Mia's gaze and lifting her water glass, as if that made her apology sincere.

Mia didn't buy it.

The old woman set down her glass. Ellis picked up his fork, and Mia was left to mourn her mother's memory alone.

CHAPTER 14

Ellis was frequently gone for weeks on end, which restricted TJ's visits. And although Rosa and Oscar worked for the household during the day, they returned to their home in town in the evening. That meant Mia spent many hours alone in the cottage, but though Ellis arranged for her to stay in the big house during his absences, she always refused.

"I prefer my own company, thank you," she said and was grateful when Ellis didn't argue. It occurred to her that he'd been alone in the cottage before she'd arrived, and perhaps that suited him as well.

The cottage was quiet, except for the few times Rosa would stop in to clean up. Mia could have handled that but didn't object to the pleasure of Rosa's company. They would often do housework together. Mia came to know the cottage so well that she finally started to feel at home everywhere but in Ellis's room.

TJ had warned her early on to stay out of there. "Off limits," he'd said, furrowing his brows like their formidable father.

But one winter day, when Mia was alone in the quiet house, she stood in Ellis's open doorway and scanned the room—looking for anything to help her understand this mysterious man.

A queen-size bed was at one end of the room, topped with

what Mia assumed was one of Rosa's quilts. A nicked-up rolltop desk on the opposite wall stood open, revealing many small drawers and cubbies. Its surface was cluttered with a jumble of papers, some sorted into a pair of wire baskets, but most hastily pushed to the side. Books, stacked four and five high, lined the top, their spines hidden from view. Two windows facing the front of the house flanked the desk. The shades were drawn, casting the room in sepia tones. A tall dresser stood in the corner with its drawers in various states of closure. Above it hung a yellowed world map.

Global Vision had directed Ellis to Haiti. Where was he now? The answer was likely somewhere on that desk, but Mia was unable to cross that threshold. This was a man who'd left her mother to raise a child alone.

The sound of a car outside interrupted Mia's train of thought. Ellis was home.

Quickly, she shut the door and bolted up the stairs two by two, her heart hammering. From her bedroom window, she watched Ellis pull a faded blue duffle bag and heavy backpack from his dull brown Corolla. His beard had grown, and he wore an unfamiliar green-and-blue plaid jacket. Then she noticed something else.

A dog.

A German Shepard mix with large upright ears and a white tip at the end of its tail bounded from the backseat and sped up the snowy drive toward the woods. Then it doubled back, darting frantically this way and that as if trying to find its way out of a maze.

Ellis looked up at Mia's window as if sensing her staring at him, and their eyes met.

"You!" he bellowed. "Get down here!"

She flew down the stairs and burst out of the front door, eager to meet the dog. One moment, she was standing—and the next, she was on the ground with two paws on her belly and the dog excitedly licking her face.

Oscar and Rosa soon appeared to see what all the commotion was about.

"The mutt was wandering outside the gates," Ellis said to Mia in Creole, though her English had gotten stronger since she started school. "No tags. I'll need you to look after him until we find his owners. Can you manage that?"

Oscar ducked into the shed and emerged with a leather collar a moment later. A silver tag dangling from the D-ring read, *Ezra*.

Something left behind by a former pet, Mia assumed. Good enough. Ezra.

Eight weeks later, Ezra was still living with them. In fact, since Ellis was spending so much time away from home, the dog had become her closest companion. He slept in her bed, sat by her side while she studied, and delightedly played with her in the snow, as if this was his first time seeing it, too.

In early spring, Mia would wander into the stable to spend a little time with the horses, Ezra at her side. She'd speak with them in Creole, and they'd snuffle and huff as if they understood. As if they knew how lonely and broken she felt, with no true sense of belonging. Her friendship with Natalie hadn't gone beyond shared study sessions. Mia wanted more—a true friendship.

Ellis hadn't been home in weeks, Oscar and Rosa were gone for the weekend, and TJ was at his mom's. Emboldened, Mia threw a blanket across Freddy's back and strapped on his cumbersome saddle by herself for the first time, going through the protocol just as Oscar had taught her. Mounting was tricky, but Freddy was ready to go once she was in the saddle, cooing sweetness into his ears.

They explored the estate, ducking into the woods behind the big house. Ezra bounded over tufts of tall grass, sniffing at trees and plants along the way. Freddy's pace along the neglected dirt road was slow and steady. Mia absorbed his calm and scanned the leafless trees and brush, listening to the chirps and peeps of small animals.

Then, something in the wood caught her attention. A building. A—house? She clicked her tongue and steered Freddy toward it. Then she dismounted, walking closer through the brush.

The wooden shack looked like it had been abandoned for decades. The windows were missing. Peeking in, she saw a space the size of the sitting room in her Haitian cinderblock home. But there were no furnishings, just a rough wood floor. She gripped the door handle and pushed. It was either locked or stuck.

A loud rustling in the woods stopped her cold and set her imagination running wild. A bear? Some other beast? Mia was struck with another jolt of memory. A man? Recalling the rape on the floor of Uncle Jean's shop, she mounted Freddy and kicked him into a canter until they reached an open field and found a gate at the other side.

It was a sunny day. Nearby, tufts of dry golden-brown grass framed a stand of cattails, puffed and billowing with seeds like a molting bird. The cattails gave up their fluff to the wind, which collected like snow along the banks of a lake that mirrored the clear blue sky.

Ezra ran ahead as Mia and Freddy circled the lake. The water looked clear and clean, untouched by civilization. Mia imagined Native Americans stopping for a drink of fresh water or setting up camp close by. She pictured schools of fish beneath the glimmering surface. Or maybe a crocodile, like the rumored one in Lake Azuéi.

She inhaled the smells of damp earth and rotting plant debris. Blackbirds picked at the cattails, calling boastfully to one another. Finally, at the far end of the lake, Mia dismounted again and approached an outcropping of flat rocks jutting into the lake. She stepped just close enough to see her reflection.

Staring back at her was the real Mia. Here at this lake, in this spot, she felt whole, liberated, and content. Under Ellis's roof, whether he was home or not, there'd been an undercurrent of anxiety, she realized, and a deep loneliness. She was still grieving the loss of her mother, her country, and the familiar sights and sounds of Haiti. What was it about this lake that lifted that from her shoulders? Solitude? Peace? Whatever it was, she was grateful.

"Whoop!" she shouted, laughing at her audacity. When was the last time she'd raised her voice? Her mother's funeral? Did it always have to come to that? Times of high emotion when there was no better way to express oneself than to cry out loud? Freddy stomped. She went to him and ran her hand along his warm neck to soothe him.

"This is our spot, Freddy," she said confidently. "You, Ezra, and me."

When Ellis was home and holed up in his office for hours, Mia tiptoed about, easing open the refrigerator or avoiding the squeaky board at the top of the stairs. She did not want to draw Ellis out to gawk at her, like he often did, as if she were an extraterrestrial. *What are you doing here?* his eyes would say. *Where did you come from?*

She'd often slip across to Rosa's warm kitchen or sneak away to the lake for the peace it brought her. She'd spend hours on the flat rocks, warmed by the sun, with her dreams and cherished memories. Ezra would duck into the brush, chasing real or imagined prey. Freddy would stand with his ears alert. And Mia would focus on the glassy water where fish jumped, or bubbles rose to the top, forming ever-expanding concentric rings.

She would watch, mesmerized, as each ring swallowed the next until the final ring faded away. This was what her life had become since Uncle Jean had first led her into the back room of his little shop. She'd been swallowed up by one assault after another, one storm after another, powerless. But the same rings that swallowed her up had also joined to embolden her. Someday, she'd hold the cards. Someday, she'd be free to make her own choices, to live where she wished, and to do as she wanted. *Be patient*, she told herself. *Your time will come.*

Mia grew frustrated with her outgrown braids late that winter and decided to cut them off rather than try to find anyone in Meridian who could fix them. She stood in front of her bedroom mirror and snipped.

The old braids dropped to the floor one by one. Each represented something from her Haitian life. Uncle Jean's ugly grin. Rue Janvier buried in mud and the smell of rot and death after a hurricane. Auntie Sis's wails when she'd miscarried. These thoughts were overcome by images of Mama's tender, golden brown eyes. The bed they shared when Mia was young. Jonas sitting beside her in school. The joy of Kanaval and Sasha's sweet coos as a baby. Mia was near tears when the last braid fell.

"Hello?" called a voice from downstairs. It was Rosa. Mia took a deep breath and left the room, meeting her at the foot of the stairs.

Rosa was holding an envelope. She stared at Mia for a second or two.

"Oh, dear girl, what have you done?" Rosa said, placing a tender hand on Mia's head. She led Mia to the kitchen, pulled out a chair and sat her down. Then she left the room to fetch a black electric razor. The attached guard reminded Mia of a bear's claw.

"Hold still," Rosa said.

Mia closed her eyes as fine snippets of hair showered down on her cheeks and chin and tickled her nose. When she opened them again, she saw Rosa's smiling face.

"Much better," Rosa said.

Mia dashed upstairs to have a look in her mirror. Her reflection was a shock at first, and she felt a moment's regret.

"Out with the old," Rosa said, entering the room behind her with a broom and dustpan.

"Right," Mia said, unconvincingly.

Rosa pulled the envelope from her apron pocket and laid it on Mia's desk. It was addressed to Mia Ellis-Bacri.

The sender was Billy Krieger. Mia's heart soared. "Billy!"

She slid a finger beneath the seal, careful not to tear the return address, then unfolded the letter. It was printed neatly in French on Global Healing stationary.

Mia dropped onto her desk chair, a broad grin stretched across her face, and began to read.

February 3, 2005

Dear Mia,

I hope this note finds you well and apologize for not reaching out sooner. Believe me, I intended to, but the days seem to slip by as quickly and easily as butter on hot pavement. You're often in my thoughts, as is your father. Come to think of it, I owe him a letter, too. Maybe an email.

Everything is fine on my end. I'm being relocated to the Australian Outback to live among the native population there. My new address is below.

Before I leave town, I wanted to give you an update on your family, still ensconced in your childhood home on Rue Janvier. Your Auntie Sis works long hours at the shop with Sasha at her side when not in school. I've been assured that there isn't a moment when the young girl is not supervised. Your uncle still runs the shop, but I seldom see him there.

Jonas sends his love, but not all of it. He has a

girlfriend, Poppy. I have not met her, but Jonas says she reminds him of you. If you have a moment, he'd love to hear from you, as would I.

I'm eager to know how you're getting along in Meridian and your new life in the US.

Yours sincerely,
Billy

Mia read the letter twice through. Any regrets for cutting off her braids turned toward thoughts of Billy, Jonas, Auntie Sis, and Sasha. She tore out a few sheets of paper from a nearby spiral notebook and wrote first to Auntie Sis, then to Jonas, and finally to Billy to thank him for thinking of her.

She'd cut her hair, but she couldn't cut away the people she loved.

CHAPTER 15

Mia's friendship with Natalie blossomed, and Mia's English improved every day. They'd often walk to Natalie's after school or go to school events together.

Natalie's family were standoffish at first. Her brother, an upper classman, would often leave the house when Mia visited. Her mother would hide behind a book or a magazine. Mia overheard Natalie's father whisper, 'What's *she* doing here?' one afternoon when he found the pair doing homework together at his kitchen table. Mia suspected, but couldn't be certain it was because of her skin, it might have been the language difference. Either way, she was as alien to them as she was to just about everyone else in Meridian.

Once, she noticed a woman on a street corner point her out to her companion. It could have been nothing, or it could have been what Mademoiselle meant by the community preferring things "a certain way."

"Don't worry about her," Natalie said. "She doesn't know you."

She never will, thought Mia. But it bothered her just the same.

As the months passed, though, there were fewer curious glances and ignorant remarks. But Mia's darker skin still set her apart. If it wasn't for Natalie, Mia would have had no one.

It was a warm afternoon in May when Mia first brought Natalie to the lake. They sat on the rocks sunning themselves as Freddy nibbled the tender grass nearby. Ezra circled them until he finally settled under the giant cottonwood.

Mia balled up her cardigan and tucked it under her head. She stared up at the passing clouds thinking how perfect everything felt. The sun, the birdsong, Natalie lying beside her. She glanced over at her friend, whose blond hair looked like sweet honey in the sunlight, her lips as soft and pink as a ripe peach. Mia wondered what it would feel like to kiss those lips.

"Natalie?" Mia said.

"Mm-hmm?" Natalie turned her head, shielding her eyes from the sun.

"Thank you."

"What for?"

"For being my friend." Mia reached across to pat Natalie's arm, thinking of the risk Natalie had taken. "You're brave."

Natalie rolled her eyes and laughed. "Shut up. I'm not half as brave as you." Mia had shared many details of her life in Haiti. Her little house, the street gangs, the storms, and political unrest. She spoke of Kanaval, the foods she missed most, and her lifelong friend, Jonas. She shared her grief about Mama's death, too. The only thing she left out was Uncle Jean.

"No, really," Mia said. They lay back on their towels, listening to the water lap at the rocks and the wind rattle the cottonwood leaves. "You're my great friend."

"I think you mean *best* friend," Natalie said, grinning.

"Best. Yes." Mia reached across her towel and took hold of Natalie's hand. "You are the best."

Mia and Natalie returned to the lake regularly that summer, dodging TJ when they could, taking him along when they couldn't. He was great company, always joyful, always kind, but Mia preferred to have Natalie to herself.

They'd swim all day, laughing and splashing in their own little world. Natalie spent so much time at Mia's that her mother joked that she would start forwarding her mail.

Mia's birthday landed on a glorious sunny day in late September, though no one seemed to remember but her. The slight was quickly forgotten when Natalie called that morning. The girls rode out to the lake, Mia on Freddy's back, Natalie on Liesel's.

The rocks felt warm under their bare feet. Once they'd laid out their towels and made themselves comfortable, Natalie handed Mia a small white box.

"What is it?" Mia asked.

"Just—nothing," Natalie said. "Open it."

Mia held the box in the palm of her hand and lifted the lid, revealing a necklace coiled on a square of soft cotton. She pinched it between her fingers and held it up. A small red polished stone shaped like a heart hung from a delicate silver chain.

"It's jasper," said Natalie. She was suddenly bashful, looking from the stone to a distant point across the lake. "My aunt says it symbolizes friendship."

Mia flushed with affection as she wove the chain through her fingers. *Friendship.* "It's the nicest thing anyone has ever given me."

"Really? It's not . . . weird? You know . . ."

"Not weird." Mia stood, and Natalie helped her fasten it around her neck.

"Happy birthday," Natalie said, blushing.

"Thank you." Mia put a hand to her chest, feeling the necklace in her palm. Her heart raced as she turned to face Natalie and, without thinking, kissed her. Natalie stood motionless, a small gasp escaping her lips. Mia stepped back with a wave of regret, fearing she'd lost her best friend in an impulse.

But Natalie took Mia's hands and drew her closer. Their lips met again. This time, it was Mia who was surprised.

"Where did that come from?" asked Ellis at dinner that night. GG glanced at the stone dangling from its chain as Rosa set a platter of appetizers on the table.

"It was a birthday present from my friend," Mia said, lightly touching the red heart.

Ellis blinked, and Mia saw a tug at his mouth. A wince? No. Couldn't be.

Rosa grasped Mia's shoulders from behind. "All the best, dear girl. I've made a special treat—"

"Oh, yes. Your birthday," GG said, interrupting Rosa. "How old are you now?"

"Sweet sixteen," teased TJ from across the table. "Never been kissed."

Mia smiled shyly, touching the stone. Ellis glanced at the necklace and cleared his throat as if to speak but said nothing. Then his eyes met hers, and he froze, staring at her, lost in thought.

What did he see? Or who? Mama?

Later that fall, while Natalie was out of town to see her grandparents, Mia rode out to the lake, leaving tracks in the morning frost. The sun hid behind a thick bank of clouds, but Mia loved the vibrant fall colors and the earthy smell of fallen leaves. She'd been seeking solitude.

She sat cross-legged on the rocks, then fastened the top button of her dark wool coat and pulled her stocking cap down to cover her ears. Geese honked overhead, flying in two uneven Vs. A copper-colored wood duck glided lazily by and picked at a clump of wet leaves along the shore. Mia sighed contentedly.

On her return home, she spotted Ellis standing outside his car in front of the cottage. She stopped mid-stride, wondering if he'd seen her and weighing whether she could slip away unnoticed.

"You," he said, opening his car door. "Get in."

She flinched. "Mia," she said, under her breath. "My name is Mia."

She eased into the passenger seat. Ellis slipped in behind the wheel and locked eyes on her. Mia's heart began to race. It had been over a year since he'd first greeted her as *You*, but this was the first time she'd found her voice to confront him on it. Had he heard?

"Mia," he said, starting the car. It was barely audible but

unmistakable. It felt like a million butterflies coming together all at once, fluttering from belly to chest and back again. He'd said her name. Did it mean as much to him as it did to her? Mia glanced at him, looking for a sign, but his eyes were fixed straight ahead as he shifted into gear.

He drove along the overgrown dirt road that led into the woods behind the cottage. Then he parked in front of the dilapidated shack she'd discovered the previous winter.

TJ had told her that the old cabin had been part of the homestead when the Ellis family first settled in America. That was back when the tired, hungry, and downtrodden were welcomed with open arms.

Well, not *all* the tired, hungry, and downtrodden, Mia had learned in her US history class. Only the white-skinned ones.

After bringing the car to a stop, he got out and opened the trunk, then knocked on her car window. He was holding a black box. He opened it, revealing a silver pistol nestled inside. It glinted in the dappled sunlight. Mia stepped out of the car and closed her door, not once taking her eyes from the pistol. It was the first time she'd seen one in real life. Ellis carefully removed the gun and turned it over in his hand.

"This is the barrel," he said, pointing along its length. "This is the grip." He showed her how to hold it, how to load it, and then how to fire it. Ready, aim, *shoot*. The bullet punctured a paper target pinned to a tree fifty feet away.

That day, he taught her to shoot. A skill that both thrilled and repulsed her. She recalled hearing gunfire the day her mother died. The gangs used the threat of gun violence to both strike fear into and elicit payment from the very citizens they said they were protecting.

There were gangs in the US, too. She'd heard of the turf wars in Chicago, Los Angeles, New York, and every other big city in this enormous country. In America, it seemed to her that guns were a necessary part of life. The tool of choice for revenge, assault, and self-defense. Kill or be killed.

As they drove back to the cottage, Mia glanced at Ellis, wondering why he'd gone to so much trouble? She'd barely gotten the question out of her mouth before he told her.

"My father taught me to shoot when I was a young boy. His father taught him. I—" he swallowed hard as if the thought were painful. But Mia got the message; it was a family rite of passage. Was he warming to her? Had he accepted her at last?

"Thank you," she said, uncertain how to address the years of pent-up resentment that had built a wall between them.

CHAPTER 16

The summer of 2008 was bittersweet for Mia. On the upside, she'd graduated from high school, and her acceptance to Northwestern University meant she'd be miles from Meridian and Ellis's watchful eyes. On the downside, it was Mia and Natalie's last summer together before starting college. They'd be splitting up for the first time since their friendship blossomed in Freshman year since Natalie was accepted to Columbia University.

One blistering August afternoon at the lake, Mia and Natalie lay on their towels under the cottonwood tree amid suffocating humidity and merciless mosquitoes. Ezra sniffed around, then curled up on a soft tuft of grass nearby.

Mia swatted at a mosquito on Natalie's bare back. "Let's go for a swim," she said lazily. "I need some relief."

Natalie sat up and reached for her watch. "Crap. It's late," she said, putting her loose-fitting sundress back on. "I was supposed to be home an hour ago."

She looked down at Mia, still stretched out on her towel. Natalie was leaving for New York the following day, but Mia had three more weeks to pack before leaving for Chicago. There, she'd share a dorm room with a perfect stranger.

"What's the rush?" Mia said, rolling onto her back. She dreaded the separation. Every day that summer had brought them closer to this moment.

Natalie knelt beside Mia and kissed her sweetly. "My mom's waiting. I can't let her do all the packing, or I'll be stuck with all the clothes I hate. And we both know that sweater set my grandma gave me last Christmas will be the first thing in the box." She laughed.

Mia didn't want to imagine what high school would have been like without Natalie. Not only had their friendship assuaged Mia's loneliness, but it also buffered her from the blatant scrutiny of the others at the school. There were always students, parents, and even a few teachers who couldn't look her in the eye or say a kind word. As the years went by, however, Natalie's support helped Mia feel like her differences mattered less and less. She excelled in school and on the volleyball team. She ignored the bigotry. But ignoring them was easy because she had Natalie.

"Will you think about me?" Natalie asked.

Mia touched the stone heart that had never left her neck since Natalie had given it to her on her sixteenth birthday. "Every minute," she said. "And you?"

Natalie looked at her watch again. "Every second."

All summer, Mia considered telling Natalie that she loved her. But she always rejected the thought. This moment was no different. Love is binding. Love is a promise. Love is something you can't take back.

People fall out of love when they have good reason, Mama had said once, suggesting love's fragility. But love was the only word that fit.

"See you at Christmas," Mia said, already wistful for the

long days sunning together on the rocks, their afternoons drinking *café au lait* and eating French pastries in town, and their tender explorations.

"I'm counting the seconds," Natalie said, rising to her feet.

Mia felt her heart break as she watched Natalie walk her bike through the brush where the dirt road led toward Argyle Street.

This was it. This was goodbye.

Finally, it was Mia's turn to leave. All that morning, she had moved about as if she'd been sleepwalking. Ellis had holed up in his bedroom with the door shut. TJ, there for a long weekend, was riveted to his new cell phone, playing Angry Birds, but Mia felt his eyes on her whenever she passed him on the sofa. At fourteen, he'd gotten very skilled at ignoring her, but she didn't take it personally. She'd also ignored him in favor of Natalie.

Oscar loaded his car with Mia's few personal belongings. Most of them fit into a single suitcase she'd borrowed from Rosa, who stepped in with a hug.

"I'm going to miss you both so much!" Mia said through the painful lump in her throat.

Oscar, who would be driving her to school, held the car door open and waited patiently for Rosa to pull away from Mia while Ezra nudged her hand with his warm, wet nose.

From the corner of her eye, Mia saw Ellis standing at the front door to the cottage, his brow as furrowed as she'd ever seen it, his hands stuffed deep in his pockets. She turned toward him and met his eyes, waiting to see what he'd do or say. He took one step forward and opened his mouth to speak—but then he turned away.

Mia wondered what was on his mind. Good riddance? She was out of his hair at last. But as the car pulled away, she noticed the shade open in his bedroom window as he watched the departure. For a split second, she believed she saw his hand rising as if to wave goodbye.

"Stop the car," said Mia, looking back toward the cottage.

"Chica?"

"*Stop!*"

The car gave a jolt as Oscar slammed on the brakes. "Is there a—"

Mia thrust open the car door and ran back to where Rosa was still standing, now mystified. Mia's heart pounded as she charged into the cottage. It stopped cold when she saw Ellis in his open doorway, arms at his sides. He appeared dark and ominous in the light from his bedroom window. They stood no more than eight feet apart in that hall, but the distance felt like a chasm.

"*Say* something," Mia said. Ellis took a step forward. She stepped back, realizing her fists were balled up as if ready for a fight. Calm down, she told herself, but she was too far gone for that. Too angry. Too hurt. "Four years," she said. "Four years, I've lived in this house, and you are just as much a mystery to me today as when I first heard your name."

"But I—"

"As a child, I wondered who you were. What you'd be like. Would you be kind and patient, like my neighbor, old Mr. Desante? Or a monster, like my Uncle Jean?" The latter name sent a shiver up her spine. "Did you know about him? Did you know what he did?"

Ellis looked down at his feet and then slowly raised his eyes to meet hers.

But she wasn't done. "I knew nothing about you but bits and pieces picked up along the way. I tried putting them together in every way imaginable, but never imagined you would be like . . . like this."

"Like what?" Ellis asked. He took another step forward. Mia backed up.

"So—cruel."

He stepped forward again, but this time, Mia stood her ground.

"Cruel?" he said. "I gave you a family. A solid roof over your head instead of a flyaway tin roof on a cinderblock shack. I gave you food, security, and education. You are on your way to one of the most prestigious universities this country has to offer. *That's* cruel?"

"Try love. Try some genuine emotion. Try getting to know me."

Ellis stepped closer, and she could finally see his face. He looked crushed. "I know you," he said.

"You know nothing!" she said, trembling with emotion. "And now it's too late."

"It isn't," Ellis said. But Mia had said her piece and turned to go. She was nearly out the door when she heard, "Mia?"

She stopped. This was the second time she'd heard him use her name, but it was too little too late.

Mia stomped out to the car, where Oscar waited for her with the engine running.

"Let's get out of here," she said.

Fury surged through Mia's blood as Oscar drove them out of town. He hadn't gotten more than five miles before anxiety took hold, and the butterflies in Mia's stomach rose up as if to choke her. Serves me right, she thought. Her first instinct was to blame herself. She didn't *have* to confront him. She'd gone years without doing so. But Ellis had it coming.

Mia reflected on the hardships she and her mother had endured. They could have been lifted so easily by Ellis, if he had made a different choice. And he had the nerve to rub it in her face, telling her what he'd done for her. Food, safety, a solid roof. "He left us and didn't look back," Mia had heard Mama say to Auntie Sis.

Of course, she'd also said, "Tell him I'm sorry."

But Mama had nothing to apologize for, just like Mia had no reason to blame herself for her own discomfort. Her stomach roiled. She breathed heavily through her nose, afraid to open her mouth in case—

Oscar looked across at her, just as she began to gag, then jerked the car onto the shoulder of the two-lane highway. He jumped out and came around to open her door. Mia practically fell out of her seat as she retched into the gravel. Oscar took her by the elbow and led her further from the car. She vomited again into the weeds.

Oscar spoke, but she couldn't hear him over the traffic zipping by. He held out a bottle of water. She couldn't drink but used it to wash the acrid taste from her mouth.

Finally, she got her footing and made it back to the car.

"Should we turn back?" Oscar said.

"No!" Not a chance. She had a new life waiting for her in Chicago.

"These big changes can be stressful, but . . ." He went on, and Mia didn't stop him. He wouldn't understand why she was so distressed. She wasn't about to tell him, either. He might ask why she hadn't said something sooner. She didn't know. He might ask her to apologize. She couldn't possibly. He might tell her she'd regret her outburst. She already did, and for reasons she couldn't understand.

Oscar pulled in front of Mia's dorm, which had been randomly assigned to her. It was co-ed, with men on the even floors and women on the odd. But as Oscar helped her lug her things up to her room, Mia saw plenty of guys checking things out on her floor, though they didn't live there.

She closed the door behind her and looked around the room as Oscar set down her heavy suitcase. Light flooded in from floor-to-ceiling windows on two walls. The room was split equally down the middle, and the roommates shared a tiny bathroom.

A pair of identical desks were positioned at the feet of a pair of identical beds. A bundle of clean sheets and a flat pillow lay stacked in the center of each. Oscar reached for the sheets.

"I've got this," Mia said, though she suspected Oscar wasn't ready to say goodbye. In some respects, neither was she.

"You'll do fine, Chica," he said, patting her hand. Mia threw her arms around him the way a daughter hugged her father.

"I love you, Oscar," Mia blurted in a rare show of emotion.

He held her a little tighter, then released her with a tender smile. "You'll do fine," he said again, then left her to the next phase of her life.

Mia took a deep, revitalizing breath as she looked around at the blank walls, the unmade bed, and the clean desk. A blank slate. Grinning with a new determination, she set to work.

Mia had just finished putting her clothes away when a tap on the door announced the arrival of Chrissy Cosgrove from Bloomington, Illinois.

Chrissy stepped into the room with an apologetic nod that Mia only understood when Chrissy's parents and two rambunctious younger brothers barged in behind her.

"Sorry, sorry, sorry," Chrissy whispered, sweeping her long, sleek ponytail off her shoulder while scanning the room with big brown eyes. Mia noted a small gold cross hanging from a chain around the girl's neck and assumed it was as treasured as the jasper heart that Mia wore.

Introductions were made. The boys looked on, slack-jawed and with blank stares, as if they'd never seen a person of color before.

"It's a pleasure to meet you," Mia said, freshly aware of how her unique accent identified her as foreign. Mrs. Cosgrove hugged Mia briefly, then released her as if they'd never touched.

In Haiti, the Cosgroves would have been the ones out of place. Chrissy and her mother began unpacking boxes of clothes, bedding, lamps, and throw rugs, all in multiple shades of pink and purple.

The boys darted around the room as their father did his best to corral them. Mia decided to make herself scarce, dodging Thing One and Thing Two on her way out the door.

She worked her way down the crowded hall to the stairwell, sidestepping students along the way and the occasional hand truck with stacks of color-coordinated boxes. Eventually, she found her way to the grassy commons outside, looking for someplace to quiet her mind.

She walked along broad sidewalks, under gothic-style arches, and past a stately church until she reached Campus Drive, where a narrow footpath emerged from a distant grove of trees. It branched off to the left and right, extending along a small body of water that was too small for a lake but too big for a pond. A chain of fountains erupted from its center.

Mia followed the path to her right, which curved around the little lake and opened to an extraordinary view of Lake Michigan. Nearby, a concrete bench warmed by the sun awaited her. She took a seat and kicked off her shoes. It was mid-September. The weather was pleasant, though a cool, easy breeze brushed Mia's face.

A student sped past on a sleek road bike. Mia wondered why they were in such a hurry. Registration wasn't until the following day. Classes wouldn't start until next week. A pair of joggers came the other way, chatting and laughing. One was dark like her. The other was Asian. Mia was lightyears from Meridian's 'certain way'.

What a pivot from where she'd begun her day, she thought, attempting to wipe Ellis's image from her mind.

She wasn't done with him, that family, or Meridian. There was the matter of tuition. Ellis had her there. She owed him something for the leg up.

There he was in her mind again. *Get out!* She jumped from her bench and ambled back to the dorm. By the time she got there, Chrissy's family had gone. But they'd left their imprint on Chrissy's side of the room—from the matching bedspread, dust ruffle, and toss pillows, to the pink gauze lampshade and daisy-shaped bookends on the desk.

Mia couldn't help comparing her own side of the shared room. The colorful quilt on her bed, hand-stitched by Rosa, looked like a flea-market cast-off compared to Chrissy's setup. But she longed to climb under it and feel Rosa's warmth and love. She looked at the embroidered tablecloth draped over her tiny desk at the end of the bed with the out-of-place salt and pepper shakers. The talismans of her Haitian roots meant nothing to anyone but her. She was proud of those roots—proud to be Haitian. Something she'd forgotten in the four years under Ellis's roof.

CHAPTER 17

Once classes began, Mia and Chrissy often spent late nights studying and listening to music in their room, closing the door to block out the constant commotion in the halls or guys sniffing around for a hook-up—a term Mia had only just learned.

"Let 'em sweat, eh?" Chrissy said one rainy night after locking the door. "Boys just take what they want and won't look back."

Mia shifted uncomfortably in her desk chair and stared down at her finger as she traced the tendrils stitched into her cherished tablecloth. "That's what I've heard." The undercurrent of anxiety was always there, like a dull headache that's gone ignored.

"Have you ever . . . you know, been with a guy?" Chrissy asked, dropping onto her bed with a bounce.

Mia's thoughts went dark as she recalled Uncle Jean's contorted face and the rage in his eyes as he thrust himself into her. The devil himself. She promptly pushed the image aside. "No, not like that."

"Not even a kiss?" Chrissy said, fiddling with the cross at her chest.

The memory of Jonas's youthful spit-laden attempt was quickly replaced by the memory of Natalie's sweet mouth. But Mia shook her head, unwilling to share details that might provoke Chrissy's judgment. "How about you?" she asked.

"Never," Chrissy said.

Mia wasn't surprised. Chrissy was pretty buttoned up—much more so than Mia, who took a year adapting to the mandatory showers in high school, wanting to hide the body her Auntie Sis might call Ti-Quitta, the vodou loa of sexuality. Mia hated that reference. It undermined all the other characteristics she valued in a woman—strength, patience, fortitude, compassion, and intelligence. Loa Erzulie, goddess of love and beauty, possessed those qualities. Mia closed her eyes and pictured Natalie.

As if by magic, Mia's phone pinged, and a text appeared from Natalie.

All cleared for winter break. See you then.

Missing you. 

They'd only been apart since August, but it felt like an eternity.

Mia thought about their reunion. Then she thought about seeing Ellis, and her stomach flipped. But if Ellis was home, TJ would be there. Cartoons, junk food, and video games would fill the void left by their father's silence.

Mia recalled the carefully selected Pokémon cards TJ had given her. She'd kept them on her desk at home beside the special pen she'd found in Mama's dresser. She made a mental note to bring them back to school after the break.

Then there was Ellis. "I gave you a family," he'd said. Mia was beginning to wonder if he'd been right. She had employed many strategies over the years to push the negative thoughts from her mind. They were handy when triggered with memories of Uncle Jean and other horrors from that time in her life. But now she needed them to push Ellis from her head because she couldn't face the idea that she may have been wrong about him all these years.

Mia returned home for winter break, and Ezra did everything short of a backflip when he saw her, plowing into her arms with the power of a bullet train. He didn't let her out of his sight for days, reassuring himself that she was there to stay. She was glad to have his unconditional love, but it broke her heart to know she'd have to leave him again when the break was over.

Mia was thrilled to see TJ. She'd only been gone a few months, but it seemed TJ had grown half a foot. He'd put on weight, too, and his face was dotted with acne. He beamed with joy at seeing her, and it warmed her heart.

Mia and her brother did their best to avoid their father in the following days, slipping out of the cottage to sit in Rosa's kitchen or riding the horses into the woods and around the lake.

"I missed you," said TJ one afternoon as they walked the horses into the stable after a ride. Mia unstrapped Freddy's saddle, thinking how nice it felt to hear those words.

"I missed you too," she said. It felt even better to say them.

TJ hoisted Liesel's saddle and blanket over a low beam dividing the stalls, then handed Mia a curry comb to remove mud splatter from Freddy's legs. The barn was quiet but for the shuffle of hooves and Freddy's contented grunts.

"It's not the same without you," TJ said. "Ellis just mopes in his room all the time."

Mia smirked. "He mopes even when I'm here," she said.

"Not like this. I think he's even letting Ezra sleep in his room."

"No!" Mia said with a hearty laugh. That was unimaginable. Mia set the comb down and took up a brush.

"Not on his bed, I don't think, but there's a blanket on his floor," said TJ with a grin.

Mia laughed again. "You went in his room?"

"Are you nuts? Never—but I saw it from the hall," TJ said, straightening his glasses. "And I think Ellis misses you."

Mia laughed. "You're high."

TJ giggled. "Why, yes, I am," he said proudly. "But I also think I'm right."

"You're teasing," she said, thinking of that innocent boy she'd met when she first arrived at the cottage. "High?"

His grin widened. "As a kite."

The following day, Ellis took both Mia and TJ shooting in the woods behind the estate.

It had been two years since Ellis first brought Mia to the old shack for target practice. They had returned occasionally, though it was always awkward, with Ellis instructing in an emotionless, businesslike manner. The addition of TJ meant he, too, had been introduced to, what Mia assumed, was this family rite of passage.

Mia gazed into the gray forest, quiet but for the sound of TJ's boots as he stomped to the shack through the thin layer of old snow.

"You," Ellis called, standing at the open trunk of his car. Mia turned away from the shack and joined Ellis. Laying in the trunk were three rifles atop their padded cases. Beside them was a box of shells that Ellis tucked into the deep pockets of his lambskin coat. He handed Mia one of the rifles and TJ another, then slung the third over his arm before slamming the trunk closed. The sound alarmed a cottontail, who bolted from the brush into a tangle of briars behind the shack.

Ellis walked out into the woods, where he posted tactical targets in red, black, and blue, each color pertaining to a particular distance.

Mia and TJ waited in the shack, their hands and toes growing colder as they watched their father through an open window.

"How far is he going to go?" Mia asked.

"Two hundred yards, max," TJ said, then sniggered. "Two hundred yards, Max. Get it?" He pulled a half-smoked joint from the fleece vest beneath his down coat. "Think there's time?"

"No! Holy crap, TJ. We're handling lethal weapons. Put that away."

"Too late." Grinning, TJ drew her attention to the blackened end of the joint. "What?" he added with an impudent huff.

Mia cursed again, and TJ put the joint away just as Ellis neared the shack. They both stood back when he came through the door, stomping the snow off his boots.

"Let's get started," Ellis said.

TJ already knew his way around a shotgun, and Mia got the hang of it quickly.

The rifle was surprisingly heavy and awkward until Ellis showed her how to balance the weight between her hands, arms, and shoulder. The mechanics were straightforward enough. TJ teased that she had the training wheel model, but Mia was grateful. Loading was simple, the scope was powerful, and the trigger tight but easy to pull.

They squatted in the shack with Ellis at the window beside her, their guns trained on the closest target. TJ giggled at nothing Mia could discern on the other side of the shack.

Pang!

Ellis turned sharply toward TJ, whose rifle had kicked back and left him stretched out on the floorboards, his hunter-orange hat cockeyed on his head and his wire-rimmed glasses crushed under his arm. Mia looked out TJ's window and saw a rabbit blown to bits at the foot of an oak tree, shards of bark scattered in the blood-spattered snow.

"God damn it!" Ellis said in an uncommon show of emotion. "We are not shooting rabbits!"

TJ stifled a laugh. "Duck season?" he said. Ellis looked at him in dismay.

Mia dropped down beside TJ to see if he was all right. "What the hell is *wrong* with you?" she whispered, taking his hand and helping him up to a seated position. TJ suppressed a giggle.

"Stop!" Ellis said. He stormed away, then turned on TJ. "There are eighty-million gun owners in the US—more than anywhere else in the world. Most are responsible. But then there's the few . . ."

His eyes shot from TJ to the gun lying on the floor before continuing.

". . . the few who go too far. Those are the men and women I fear. Those are the men and women who give gun ownership a bad name. They've gone beyond hunting and recreation to kill indiscriminately. Sometimes allowing their anger or . . ."

Hands trembling, voice cracking, Ellis returned his gaze to TJ.

". . . or their poor judgment to override their better instincts. For most, it's lack of training; for others, ignorance; and for some—I don't know what got into you today, TJ, but I don't ever want to see this behavior again." Heat radiated off Ellis as he struggled to regain his composure. "If I do, you will not be welcome under my roof."

Mia peeled her eyes away from Ellis's tirade and focused on TJ, who remained on the floor, his lower lip quivering and his hands fisted together staring up at Ellis.

This was the first time Mia had witnessed Ellis's temper; he usually kept his emotions well hidden. It seemed by TJ's demeanor that it was also a first for him.

Ellis collected the three rifles and stood motionless, staring out the window toward the three posted targets. "Back to the car," he grumbled, then stormed out of the cabin.

Mia took TJ's hand as he cried silently, his eyes focused on the floor. She resisted telling him off. He'd heard enough. As a rule, she didn't like to agree with Ellis, but in this case, he was right.

Once home, Mia retreated into a hot shower. When she returned to her room, TJ sat beside Ezra on her bed, pouting and cradling his broken glasses in his lap.

Mia took TJ's glasses and taped up the broken hinge.

"The king is displeased," he said, putting the mended frames back on.

"Are you hungry?" she asked. He nodded.

She tiptoed downstairs and into the kitchen with Ezra at her heels. Rosa was gone for the day but had left a pot pie on the stove for them to heat up. When Ellis appeared at the door, Mia had just clicked on the oven to preheat.

"Come with me."

Mia followed him as far as the threshold to his room.

Ellis shook his head and harrumphed. "I can't very well show you this unless you come in now, can I?"

She took two cautious steps into the room, Ezra at her side.

The room looked tidy. Ellis's desk appeared in order, with thick, manila-colored files tucked into narrow cubbies on either side and an odd assortment of reference books stacked neatly along the top. An atlas on one end, and on the other, a three-volume set entitled *Tribal Politics in a Volatile World*. A black-and-white-and-gray-checkered quilt lay folded at the foot of his bed. Mia glanced here and there, taking in the room's changes since she'd spied on it years earlier.

Why had he invited her here? Was he going to address the accusations she'd laid on him before she'd left for college? She prayed not.

"Look here," Ellis said, pointing to a darkly stained two-drawer file cabinet he used as a bedside table.

It had a deep scratch across the front, reminding Mia of old

Mr. Desante from her neighborhood back in Haiti. A gold plate with Ellis's initials was tacked above the keyhole on the top drawer. T.M.E. The same initials as his father and grandfather. Theodore Michael Ellis. Battered as the file cabinet was, Mia wouldn't have been surprised if it had belonged to them. The same for the roll top desk. TJ, or Teddy Jr., would be next in line.

"I'm going away for a while," Ellis said, looking into Mia's eyes. Her heart skipped a beat. It unnerved her whenever he looked directly at her. It was as if he was searching for something or wishing she were anyone else.

Again, he motioned to the cabinet. "If something happens, everything you need to know is there." Mia wondered what he could possibly mean by something, suspecting that he meant in the event of his death, but remained quiet. Ellis narrowed his brows, looking as terrifying as he ever had. "This is important to me," he said. "Do you understand what I'm telling you?"

Mia nodded uncertainly. "It's locked?" she asked, glancing toward the tarnished keyhole.

"I have a key, but your grandmother has a copy if you need to get in."

"Do I get a copy?"

Ellis scratched his beard. "No."

"Where are you going?" she asked. She'd never asked before, but the moment begged the question.

"Afghanistan, but I have an excellent team. Do you understand what I'm saying? I'm just telling you in case . . ."

Afghanistan was one of those places people, especially Americans, didn't come back from.

"Do you understand?" he said again.

"Yes. I understand."

There was a moment of silence. "All right, then," he said, waving Mia out of the room.

She left, and he didn't speak of the file cabinet again.

Ellis was gone in the morning. TJ sat in front of the television with Cartoon Network's *Adventure Time* on the screen and a bowl of Fruit Loops on his lap. He was in full vacation mode.

Mia was headed out to see what Rosa was up to when a text popped up from Natalie. Mia's heart soared.

> Just got into town. Do you have time for a quick visit?

> All the time in the world.

> Big news. Be there in ten.

Mia flung off her coat and hung it by the door, her heart pounding with anticipation. *Natalie.*

The next ten minutes seemed like an eternity to wait. But one *Adventure Time* bled into the next. A half hour went by. Finally, there was a soft tap at the door.

With Ellis gone and TJ zoned out on the sofa, the two slipped upstairs to Mia's room and shut the door.

It had been four months since they'd seen one another, touched one another, kissed one another, and the moment was as awkward as if they never had. Mia sat on the side of the bed, leaving plenty of room for Natalie, but Natalie sat at the desk, distracted by the colorful tabs on one of Mia's textbooks.

This wasn't how Mia had seen their reunion. She was overcome with nerves and second-guessing the Northwestern sweatshirt she'd wrapped in red and green paper, thinking how fun it would be to have a little college rivalry when she bought it. A lighthearted matchup between Northwestern and Columbia.

"I'm seeing someone," Natalie said abruptly. "A guy." She looked away as a slight grin tugged at her mouth.

Mia wondered if she was joking. But when her gaze returned to Mia, the truth was clear.

Mia put a hand to her chest where the jasper pendant lay under her thumb, her own broken heart beneath it. Though the heartache was impossible to ignore, she refused to show it. Not to Natalie. And not to anyone else, either—because no one knew of their relationship. The secret, once a treasure held between them, was now a cruel fate.

Mia sat up straight, squaring her shoulders in a show of strength. "Good for you. What's he like?"

She didn't really want to know. But Natalie went on at length. His family was from Connecticut. She described how they'd met, their first kiss, and the great sex. Mia choked on the tears she held back as heartache blended with the sting of betrayal.

Didn't she deserve an apology? Shouldn't she ask for one? But Mia remained silent, just as she had before they'd parted. There'd been no declarations of love, no promises, nothing that bound them. Mia felt foolish for any assumption she'd had.

They switched to more mundane topics. Classes, dorm life, and the weather. Mia felt relieved when Natalie picked up her keys to go.

She would have walked Natalie out to her car, but her legs threatened to buckle the moment she tried to rise from the bed.

"We're good?" Natalie said.

"Yeah," Mia said, her heart aching. "We're good."

She listened to Natalie's rapid footsteps on the stairs. When the front door thumped closed, Mia went to the window to watch Natalie as she practically skipped to her car.

Visions of long summer days at the lake and afternoons at the café blurred as Mia wiped her eyes. The ache in her chest rivaled how she'd felt when Mama died.

A *guy*.

Why not? Mia considered her own sexuality. Was she a freak, or had she been influenced by the years of abuse by Uncle Jean? She wondered if Ellis's abandonment and disinterest played a role. It wasn't the first time she'd considered and rejected these possibilities.

No, her attraction to women had nothing to do with Uncle Jean or her abandonment. Mia believed deep in her soul that women were God's most beautiful creatures. Clever, compassionate, and sensuous creatures.

She unwrapped the Northwestern sweatshirt and put it on. Then she went to join TJ on the couch.

He glanced at her. "She dump you?" he asked. It shouldn't have surprised her that TJ knew. He was an intuitive kid. How could he not have noticed?

"Yeah,"

TJ snatched two video game controllers and handed her one.

"Mario Kart?" he said. "I'll let you be Yoshi."

Mia grasped the controller gratefully.

CHAPTER 18

By February, Mia was back at school. On Valentine's Day, she did everything in her power to distract herself from memories of Natalie. Then, a week later, she noticed a poster pinned up in the common room of her dorm.

GUN CONTROL Rally and March.
Save Our Youth.
Save Yourself.

This had no doubt been spurred on by the recent shooting at Northern Illinois University, where twenty-seven-year-old Steven Kazmierczak killed six students with a shotgun and injured twenty-one.

After Ellis's tirade about irresponsible gun owners that winter, Mia couldn't look the other way.

Kazmierczak showed the world there was more to gun violence than hatred, ignorance, and poor judgment. He proved to the world that the mentally ill should come nowhere near a lethal weapon.

On the day of the rally, Chrissy and Mia trudged through slush and mud into the crowd under overcast skies.

Counter-protesters gathered on a side street, waving American flags. Their cries for Second Amendment rights were drowned out by the rally cries for gun control.

"Enough is enough!"

The rally accentuated the passionate differences of opinion. It probably wouldn't change anything, but the energy she drew from the event was intoxicating.

A year later, as Mia and Chrissy were finishing their lackluster dinners in the cafeteria, someone turned up the volume on the big-screen TV mounted on one end of the room.

Haiti. Earthquake. Magnitude 7.0. The date—January 12, 2010—flashed red amid the horrific footage.

What had been the presidential palace was now a pile of rubble. The streets were unrecognizable, and the people were devastated, terrified of the powerful aftershocks.

Chrissy placed a comforting hand on Mia's shoulder.

Mia recalled the people she'd left behind in Haiti. Jonas, Auntie Sis, and Sasha. All imprinted on her mind. She hadn't heard from Jonas in over a year, but Auntie Sis had recently written with a school photo of ten-year-old Sasha. Mia struggled to imagine what their lives looked like now. The cinderblock on Rue Janvier had withstood countless storms and several minor earthquakes, but how did it hold up to a 7.0 earthquake? Certainly, no better than the presidential palace. She thought of Sasha living in the street as an ill-equipped government labored to keep the peace. The gangs running rampant.

Mia held her hand to her chest, glancing around at the other students in the cafeteria. Some had already returned to their meals and picked up conversations where they'd left off. Their lives remained unaffected while Mia's was shattered.

Mia couldn't sleep because of the terrible images that flashed across her mind that night.

A month later, she received an email from Billy. He'd been out of Haiti for years, but was back now because of the earthquake, returned to a living hell. He wrote that Sasha was among the 200,000 dead.

Mia gasped, recalling the day Sasha was born, with Billy arriving just as Auntie Sis went into labor. Auntie Sis, though sick with grief, was safe, Billy wrote. He'd arranged for her to stay with a contact of his in Alangui on the mountain.

Mia's heart nearly stopped when she read the next line. Jonas, too, had died, after a blow to the head.

Mia remembered the morning after Hurricane Gordon, when, as two five-year-old children, they'd seen a dog with its head bashed in. She'd written to him only a week ago. Now Jonas was gone forever. The news shattered Mia's heart. She read on, hands trembling, hoping Uncle Jean would be among the dead. But Billy said Uncle Jean's disappearance was a mystery.

A mysterious disappearance. Not a death. A shiver ran up Mia's spine.

That night, Mia woke to Chrissy's voice, her hand on Mia's shoulder. "Mia—Mia. Wake up. You're having a bad dream."

Mia opened her eyes wide and gasped. Uncle Jean had come to her in a nightmare, his tobacco-stained fingers pinching her face as he removed her panties in the backroom of the shop.

"Not a dream," she said.

In 2011, Mia and Chrissy packed a tent, sleeping bags, and a bundle of placards and joined a small group from their dorm attending the Occupy Chicago demonstration, an Occupy Wall Street offshoot in Hyde Park. The demonstration had been all over the news and its mission to throw light on corporate greed held great appeal for them. The cause, Mia thought, was worth skipping classes for a couple of days.

Mia threw herself into the rally cries. As the demonstration grew to more than 3,000 activists, she boldly stood her ground against bullying counter protesters and police brutality.

She couldn't understand why their "We Are The 99 Percent" cries didn't resonate with 99 percent of the country.

On their second night, as the sun was setting behind the Chicago skyline, Mia stood back from the crowd and took in the scene. "What is it with people and their blind support of corporate America?" she said to herself.

"We only know the half of it," said a woman standing behind her.

Mia turned toward the voice and came face to face with a slim, fair-skinned woman with wine-red lips and piercing black eyes that said, *I know you*. She was older than Mia. A grad student, maybe. Her wavy dark hair fell loose around her shoulders. It looked so soft that Mia had to resist the temptation to reach out and touch it. Mia's breath caught in her throat. She lowered her sign, taking a moment to find her center. This distractingly beautiful woman made that difficult.

"But isn't that the responsibility of the public?" asked Mia. "To overcome ignorance?"

"I'm not challenging you. I agree with you—but corporations are not the only ones at fault. Check the politicians' pockets. Are they really on our side, or just gorging on power, stuffing their coffers while they can?"

Mia nodded in agreement. She knew well the tight hold major corporations had on politics. It was one of the reasons she chose her major. If corporate America could spend millions convincing people to spend their money on things they didn't need, she, working for a non-profit, could convince people to spend their money to help others.

Behind them, the protesters chanted, "We are the ninety-nine percent!"

Their eyes locked. Mia's heart raced. Her mouth went dry. Any October chill she'd felt moments earlier was replaced by sweaty palms and a burning heat that would have her looking like a tomato if she'd had lighter skin.

"I'm Mia."

The woman flashed a flirtatious grin under the park lights. "I'm Kali."

Mia stared into Kali's dark eyes and felt a rush of adrenaline as every cell in her body tingled with excitement. There was something here. Something powerful.

It had been years since Natalie—years since she'd kissed or been kissed. But there'd been no one who'd piqued her interest. Until now.

Kali reached for Mia's hand. They joined palms, and Mia

was convinced she could feel a pulse. One pulse. Two hands. Mia wondered if Kali felt the same connection. Then her phone rang from a zipped pocket in her fleece jacket. She didn't want to break the spell, but Kali nodded for her to see who it was.

"It might be important," Kali said. "You never know."

"Life-changing, maybe?" Mia said with a grin, thinking nothing could be more important than this moment. But she slid the phone from her pocket.

TJ's number beamed brightly in the dim light. Mia answered.

"I'm in trouble," he said.

Mia glanced at Kali apologetically, and then stepped away.

"Wait, what? Where are you?"

"I'm fucked," he said. "They've arrested me—goddamned Meridian police. Whatever you do, don't tell Ellis. Got it?"

He'd been caught selling four grams of cocaine at a high school dance. It wasn't even his own high school. He went to school in Indianapolis.

"I have to tell Ellis," Mia said. "You're a minor."

"No," he hollered into the phone. "He'll kill me." TJ gasped for breath.

"Can you call your mom?" Mia asked.

"Fuck, Mia, just come get me out of here," TJ said, his voice cracking with emotion.

She was hours away from Meridian. She didn't have a car, and she didn't have any money. "I can't."

"Try," TJ pleaded. Then the line went dead.

Mia stared at her phone, wondering what to do next. This whole business was way over her head.

She'd only called her father three times since she lived under his roof. Each time, to her relief, the call had gone to voicemail.

This time, it didn't.

"What is it!"

Mia paused, surprised to hear his gruff voice. "Ellis?"

"I said, what is it!"

She spoke hurriedly. "It's TJ. He needs your help." She tried to explain what TJ had said and where he was.

Ellis heard her out. Then he said, "He needs bail?" His breathing sounded heavy, labored, almost as if he were drunk. Mia paused; unsure what TJ needed. "Where are you?"

Mia looked around at the thinning crowd. Their chants quieted; their placards set aside for the next day's push. Kali stood five feet away, and Mia felt grateful that her obviously emotional conversation with TJ hadn't scared this woman out of her life. "I'm at school," she said.

"Go on, then," Ellis said impassively. "I'll take care of TJ."

"Everything all right?" Kali said, stepping up beside her.

Mia looked up. "No."

Kali slipped her hand into Mia's. Mia turned to face her, thinking of TJ and how she might have handled that situation better. But there was nothing she could do for TJ, and her helplessness tore her up inside. "Whatever you do, don't tell Ellis." But she did, and she feared TJ would never forgive her for that.

They'd only just met, but the empathy in Kali's eyes tempted Mia to open her heart, tell her everything. Not just what happened with TJ, but the history with Ellis that made her decision so difficult.

"It'll be fine," Mia said, staring at their joined hands, though she didn't believe it, and, she suspected, neither did Kali who mercifully let it go.

After returning to her dorm the following day, Mia braced herself for TJ's call. He'd either curse and scream or whine and cry. But the call didn't come. The next morning, he still hadn't called. Three days passed with this silent treatment, then four. Finally, on the fifth day, her heart heavy with the weight of responsibility, she called him to explain, ashamed she hadn't done so earlier. The call went right to voicemail.

"TJ, I'm sorry. You—I mean, *I* couldn't deal with that."

Her accent had softened since she'd arrived at fifteen, but when Mia left this voice message, the old voice was all she could hear. The poor Haitian girl TJ had taken under his wing. Accepting her into his life, no questions asked.

A week after TJ's arrest, Mia met Kali at the coffee cart outside the humanities building. They'd been texting, calling, and meeting up for coffee since that night at the demonstration. Their attraction to one another was mutual, but there wasn't anything official about their relationship yet—it was mostly flirting and getting to know one another.

Kali handed Mia a coffee. "What's wrong?" she asked.

Mia considered every relationship in her life. One way or another, she'd lost them. Mama, Auntie Sis, Sasha, Jonas, Natalie, and now TJ, her brother. She should have tried harder. She should have come to his rescue. He would have done the same for her.

"Nothing. I'm fine," Mia said, removing the lid from her cup.

"You don't look fine. Talk to me. What's the matter?" Mia noticed that Kali had already assumed the psychologist's role, two terms into her doctorate. But Mia wasn't ready to talk about her brother. She was afraid of where it would lead. She might start with TJ, but then what? What if the dam burst and she let it all out—her grief, her pain, her uncle, her screwed-up relationship with Ellis . . . if it could even be called a relationship? For now, she wanted to keep things simple. She was afraid to scare Kali away, lest she lose her, too.

"Mia?" said Kali, still waiting for an answer.

Mia stopped, turned toward Kali, and kissed her full on the lips. That first kiss effectively ended the consultation.

In the weeks and months that followed, Kali drew much of Mia's life story from her. She spoke about life on Rue Janvier and the cast of characters like old Mr. Desante, Jonas, Auntie Sis, and, of course, Mama. There wasn't a day that went by that she didn't miss them all, but especially Mama whose voice Mia could still remember. *My Sunshine.*

Mia hid the ugly story of Uncle Jean, feeling it was too soon and too much to lay on Kali's shoulders. She wondered if the right time would ever come.

That spring, Mia left the campus career fair with three solid prospects, but one position stood out from the others. Assistant Marketing Analyst with a prominent Chicago firm. It was the job of a lifetime and would guarantee the experience she'd need for her ultimate goal of working for a non-profit. When Laila Porter called to offer her the job, Mia felt like she'd won the jackpot.

"Oh, dear girl. I knew you'd do well," Rosa said when Mia called, unable to contain her excitement. "I'll spread the good news."

Mia wondered how GG and Ellis would take the news. Would they be proud, too? Difficult as it was to admit, she hoped they would.

A week before graduation, Mia unpacked her purple gown from the plastic bag and draped it across the bed beside the black cap. She reached back into the bag for the tassel, thinking about the invitations she'd mailed weeks ago. There'd been no reply from Meridian. Not from Rosa or Oscar, and nothing from TJ or GG. Her own father couldn't be bothered to RSVP. All he'd had to do was return the postcard.

Kali wouldn't be at the ceremony, either—but at least she had a good reason. Her parents had drowned when a ferry went down while they were on vacation in Indonesia. And she returned to her hometown to care for her recently widowed brother's infant son— one tragedy after another. Mia could relate, thinking of her final weeks in Haiti.

"I'll catch up with you in Chicago when the dust settles," Kali had said.

Mia sighed. Chicago. She still couldn't believe her good fortune. To have landed a job in one of the greatest cities in the world seemed like a miracle. Having them set her up in a furnished high-rise apartment with a Lake Michigan view only sweetened the deal.

Rosa said she'd spread the good news. But, as with the invitations, she hadn't heard a peep from Ellis. The slight made Mia's heart ache.

Chrissy opened the door, leaving it open to the noise in the hall, and bounced across the room. "Oh, nice!" she said. "The gowns have arrived." Graduation also meant saying goodbye to her roommate of four years.

Mia glanced at the gown spread out on her bed and shrugged. What was the point? It wasn't as if she'd get the real diploma at the ceremony. That would come in the mail. To her new address in Chicago. Her new life.

She thought of the countless folding chairs she'd seen set up in Ryan Stadium. One of them was meant for her, and there would be no one to stand behind her in the bleachers to congratulate her. The invitations she'd sent had seat reservations. Mia knew exactly which empty seats she'd be focused on.

"I'm not going," Mia said.

Chrissy did a double-take. "Wait. What? You're joking, right?"

Mia collected the graduation paraphernalia and dumped it all in the trash. Chrissy's eyes narrowed, and she dropped her backpack with a *thunk*. "You're not joking."

Self-pity crept up on Mia, and she pushed it back—the same way she'd dealt with unwelcome emotions her whole life.

Tomorrow, she'd start her new life. Ellis be damned.

PART THREE
The Notebooks

CHAPTER 19

Mia fled the hospital as fast as two wheels could take her while recalling the spectacle she'd just witnessed—the fear in Ellis's eyes, the staff intent on saving him, and then her parting words. *I always hated you.*

She hoped Ellis hadn't heard.

She passed the high school, the Wildcat banner flying proudly above the doors. Maybe the drugs were so potent that he couldn't understand. She passed the cafe where she and Natalie sat for hours drinking *café au laits* while getting to know one another. Two blocks past the bank tower, as the freeway on-ramp came into view, she pulled over. Traffic flowed smoothly across the overpass.

She removed her helmet with trembling hands and held it to her chest as she considered her next move.

Stay and see this through with Ellis, TJ, and GG, or return to Drake, Kali, and the security of the world she'd created beyond Meridian? She had to choose.

Where was the grit she'd supposedly inherited from her mother? She could have used it now. All she could feel was grief and pity for a man she'd never been close to.

Where were you when I needed you? When our tiny Haitian

cinderblock home was flooded, when the gangs roamed the street outside, when Mama got sick, or when . . . Mia had a vision of her Uncle Jean but quickly pushed it away. She wanted to remain inside the protective shell she'd created for herself to keep the traumas of her past at bay. But that shell was crumbling.

"Goddamn you, Ellis!"

Mia strapped her helmet on and put the bike in gear. She eased ahead, ever closer to the on-ramp . . . and then sped past toward the estate.

TJ's car was parked outside the cottage, but Mia needed some space. She left her motorcycle behind the shed and trudged through the overgrown pasture, pushing past shoulder-high thistles and briers until she saw the lake. Merely the sight of it lifted her spirits.

She walked around it, spread her coat out on the flat rock that jutted out into the water and lay back, looking up into the clear blue sky.

The lake stretched before her, shimmering in the sunlight, surrounded by burnt golds and rusty reds. The silence was broken by marsh wrens perched on cattails along the shore as water lapped at the massive flat rock in a slow, easy rhythm that calmed her soul and opened her heart to the past. She recalled Ezra snoozing in the warm sun, Freddy nibbling at the soft grass, and Natalie diving in for one last swim.

They were all gone now. All that remained was Ellis's cottage and the dysfunction that came with it. Was it better than Haiti?

There was no substitute for Mama, but Mia had to admit that she owed a debt to Ellis. Her heart sank.

I always hated you.

She cringed, wondering what awaited her back at the hospital.

Slowly, she rose from the sun-warmed rock and put on her coat, then walked back to the cottage. It was time to stop sulking and get to work. Where was that health directive Dr. Patel had asked for?

Mia found TJ in the kitchen, rummaging in the cupboards like a mouse on the trail of something good. Then he held out a bag of marshmallows, triumphant.

"How old are those?" Mia asked.

"Don't know and don't care," TJ said. Mia groaned and left TJ to his prize, then went upstairs to call Kali.

She hung her coat by the door, kicked off her shoes, and dropped onto her bed. The headboard creaked against her weight as she leaned back, her phone pressed to her ear.

"Mia! Oh, thank God! How are you? How's your dad?"

Mia told Kali what Dr. Patel had said. "He's stable."

"And you?"

Mia thought about this. *I'm tired. I'm miserable. I stood by as a team of professionals intubated Ellis.*

"I did something stupid," she finally said.

"What is it? What happened?"

Mia locked her gaze on a strip of flaking paint over the wardrobe. "I let him have it, is what happened."

Kali sighed. "Tell me everything. Start from the beginning." This was Kali, the therapist; Kali, the friend; and Kali, the lover—all rolled into one. Mia wanted to cry with relief.

She started with what it had been like to see Ellis for the first time in over seven years. How he looked and behaved. His cockeyed smile that may have been a sneer, or the other way around. How her second visit brought back memories of his neglect, abandonment, and disinterest.

"I was so angry. Frustrated, too, because he couldn't answer for himself. It sounded like all he could say was *All there.*"

"What's that mean?"

"I don't know. He was so distraught because I couldn't understand him. Then everything went haywire." Mia described the scene of the stroke and, finally, the hateful words. "Those might be the last words he hears from me."

"Did you mean them?"

Mia took a deep breath. "I . . . don't know. No. Maybe." A long silence followed. "The doctor wants me to find his health directive. Said I was listed as next of kin."

"Then you find it," Kali said.

Mia scanned Ellis's room, sidestepped the pile of sheets by the door, and turned her attention to the cluttered roll-top desk.

First, she pushed the files into two neat stacks, paying little attention to the identifying tabs. A few loose scraps of paper remained. She laid them on top, then picked up an overturned picture frame and set it right. A 3 x 5 photograph of a black child peering through the open slats of a broken window shutter. It had an artsy look to it; black and white, perfectly centered.

She blinked. *That's me*, she thought, suddenly transfixed. She remembered the man who'd taken it—his white skin, his thick black beard, his bushy eyebrows.

He'd snatched her up in the street, a hurricane bearing down on them. Mama tore her from his arms. A few days later, he turned up in front of her house.

That was my father. *That was Ellis.*

Mia rocked back on her heels, lightheaded, as the memory slowly came into focus. He'd been there at her house, speaking with Uncle Jean. "I have a right to see her!" he'd said.

Had he been talking about Mia or her mother?

She could almost feel Uncle Jean's grip on her face as he said, "That man is the devil." Mia envisioned Ellis in his hospital bed, unable to communicate more than the odd facial contortion and random gesture, reaching for the bedside table.

"There," he'd said. "All—there."

He'd once brought her into this room. She strained to remember the details. He'd motioned to the file cabinet beside his bed, saying, "Everything you need to know is there." Mia turned and locked her eyes on the old cabinet. She knelt in front of it and tugged at the tarnished brass pull, but it didn't give. The keyhole stared back at her with its beady eye.

Where was the key?

She cautiously approached the desk, feeling Ellis's eyes on her as if he were looking over her shoulder. But he'd *wanted* her to have the key. So why did she feel such guilt?

Many of the cubbies were already open. Had Ellis been

looking for the key? Had *he* thought this was the end? She shook off the possibility and got to work. Beginning with the top row of miniature drawers, barely big enough to fit a box of matches, Mia worked her way across, but found no key. There were five other drawers in the credenza, one in the middle and two on either side. She slid open the middle drawer and found a black velvet box among loose paper clips and replacement staples. Curiosity piqued, she withdrew the box, thinking the key might be inside. What she found surprised her.

A ring. It was brushed gold with a tiny stone, the color of her mother's eyes, set within four prongs. The band stuck upright in a narrow slot that looked worn. Like the ring had been removed and replaced often. Mia ran a finger across the stone, wondering if the ring would fit.

She stopped herself. The key. She must find the key.

She closed the box, set it aside for later, and then checked the two drawers on her left. The top one stuck, and she pried it open, only to discover it was stuffed with checkbooks dating back to the early 90s. The bottom drawer held receipts and odd scraps of paper with illegible notes. She turned over an old newspaper clipping. It read, *The crime of which I stand accused is the crime of preaching food for all men and women. Fr. Jean-Bertrand Aristide.* Mia folded it neatly and tucked it into the drawer before closing it.

The two drawers on the right were equally disappointing. So, the key was not in a drawer. Mia rifled through a pair of upright pigeonholes stacked with file folders and dusty envelopes. The longer she searched, the more driven she became. She emptied the coffee-cup-turned-pen-holder, hoping to find the key at the bottom. Nothing.

When she'd finished searching, the desk looked like a tornado had swept through. But still, there was no key. She needed to get into that cabinet.

Mia marched across the room with determination, drew her foot back, and kicked it.

"Ouch!"

But she'd heard a rattle. Something was inside.

Then she remembered what Ellis had said back when he'd told her about the cabinet. *I have a key, but your grandmother has a copy if you need to get in.*

It was dark outside as Mia tracked through the thin layer of fresh snow to the big house. GG sat on the sunporch, in a comfortable wicker chair, with a half-full tumbler of single-malt Scotch—her norm when she felt the need.

"*Grand-mère*, do you remember Ellis ever giving you a key?" Mia said, sitting in the chair across from GG. "It would have been years ago. Ten, maybe eleven."

GG stared into her glass, exhaling through her nose. Then, slowly, she turned her face toward her warped reflection in the darkened window. "It's snowing tonight. Did you notice on your way over?"

Mia leaned closer. "The *key, grand-mère*."

"What on earth are you talking about?" GG's drink nearly sloshed onto her lap as she relaxed in her chair. "Did you notice the snow? The news said we'd get an inch tonight."

Was she demented? Mia wondered about the old woman she'd never had any love for. But she was more worried that she'd never get into the cabinet.

"The hospital called," GG said, her gaze focused across the room at a Limoges statuette of a mother cradling her baby. "Our Teddy has taken a turn for the worse."

Mia snapped to attention. "Since when? I saw him a few hours ago and—"

"Yes, a few hours ago."

Dr. Patel had Mia's number. If anything had changed, she'd hear about it. "I need that key, *Grand-mère.*"

GG took another drink and then set her glass on the side table. "For heaven's sake, girl," she said. "There is no key."

Mia stormed out of the house and into the freshly fallen snow. No key! She clenched her fists until they ached, ready to hit anything. Life was so unfair! It wasn't just the fact that she couldn't get into the cabinet. That was just the most recent affront. She'd been to hell and back several times with devastating storms, abuse, and loss.

"Ahhhh!" she shrieked, thinking of her mother, Auntie Sis and Sasha, Jonas, and Billy. The people she'd treasured most in Haiti. And then there was Uncle Jean. Her jaw began to quiver, and her hands began to shake.

She'd been bottling it in for decades. Now, she was ready to explode.

Driven by rage, Mia marched to the barn. The heavy door

groaned open. The vacant stables broke her heart. Gone were the days when she'd saddle up Freddy and head out to the lake. Gone, too, was Freddy. Her heart grieved as she rummaged for something to help her break into the cabinet. An ice pick. A screwdriver. A . . .

She found it. A sledgehammer. That would do the trick.

Mia stormed back to the cottage, slamming the door behind her. TJ remained planted on the sofa with his headset firmly in place, his fingers manipulating the controller as his assailant charged into battle, wielding an ax in one hand and a club in the other. Mia noticed his water pipe on the coffee table and the empty marshmallow bag beside it.

He was oblivious as she marched down the hall to Ellis's room with the sledgehammer gripped in both hands. *All there.* She charged at the old oak cabinet the hammer held high over her head. *Thunk.* She swung again. The cabinet split along the side. On the third swing, the file cabinet broke wide open, shattered, and the contents spilled at her feet.

It wasn't the last will and testament or health care directive she'd hoped to find.

It was much, much more than that.

An odd sensation overcame Mia as the room fell silent. It was as if she wasn't truly there, but merely an observer standing amid the thousands of splinters and shards.

The daze didn't last. In her next breath, she took stock of the scene with astonishment. A jumble of spiral notebooks, bound journals, and those mottled composition books she remembered from her school days. All interspersed with scrapbooks and a pair of old shoeboxes.

Mia picked through a collection of manila folders labeled "Project This" or "Project That." Folders for Afghanistan, Rwanda, Bangladesh, and others. Then she locked her eyes on a red leather notebook—scuffed, ragged, and held together with disintegrating twine.

She set the remaining folders aside. Then she leaned back against the bed, cautiously opened the notebook to the first page, and began to read.

CHAPTER 20
The Red Notebook

May 18, 1988

I arrived in Haiti three weeks ago on a two-prop plane from Manaus, Brazil, and waited in the scorching heat for my passport to be stamped. There were six sets of eyes trained on me, two of which belonged to the man who'd pulled me out of line and, without explanation, shoved me into a van bound for the municipal jail in Port-au-Prince. What was the charge? What was my crime? I hadn't a clue what triggered such a dramatic turn of events. My appearance, perhaps.

I'd been in the Amazon for the previous six months, researching the Manakieaway village and their struggle with poverty and hunger as I've done elsewhere for Global Vision.

All hell broke loose when an industrial corporation blew in and threatened the little community. Max, my boss, pulled me out without any warning. But instead of sending me home to Indiana, he gave me another assignment. I don't think a Haitian jail was what he'd had in mind.

I would have much preferred the gentler climate of the Midwest while being pushed through the booking process. A noisy ceiling fan clicked as it spun, offering no relief as I read the documents dated April 12, 1988. *That,* I understood. Nothing else. Haitian Creole, the dominant language spoken here, shares many qualities with French (with which I am more familiar, thanks to my high school French teacher). But it is not French.

Over the past three weeks, as Global worked day and night for my release, I became more familiar with my cellmates.

One of them, Jean Bacri, a lively man in his mid-twenties, volunteered as my interpreter. The other two—a drug dealer and a petty thief—seemed harmless enough. Jean was serving six weeks for brawling. "Self-defense," he'd claimed, after a group of men attacked him in a bar for flirting with "the wrong kind of girl." He did not elaborate.

When he asked what I'd done, I could only say I'd been in the wrong place at the wrong time. "It's always the case," my cellmates replied, laughing. I didn't realize how right I was until they filled me in on the existing political climate.

Global hadn't had much time to prep me for Haiti. All I knew was that the current president, Leslie Manigat, was recently nominated in a highly contested election set up by the military. A nationwide boycott ensued, resulting in only a four percent turnout; Manigat won.

I also knew that the Reagan administration and America's allies had boosted much-needed trade and financial help to Haiti for years, believing Manigat's predecessor, Jean-Claud Duvalier, would turn around the atrocities of his father's reign, but the plan failed.

Duvalier, commonly referred to as Baby Doc, was a monster, using the Tonton Macoutes, his father's volunteer militia, to kill, torture, and arbitrarily imprison citizens who disagreed with his regime.

Massive protests followed, shedding light on continued human rights offenses, so Reagan cut US support, forcing Duvalier into exile. Yet nothing had changed. Reagan's financial embargo remained while these human rights abuses continued.

My cellmates informed me that Manigat's election, a feeble demonstration of democracy, failed to convince President Reagan to lift the embargo.

President Manigat, like Duvalier, doesn't care for outsiders, though the country is full of them—an international palette of do-gooders. They are necessary but unwelcome. I count myself among them, but it's not official, not until the government signs off. Otherwise, I'm just another American, which is, in part, why I ended up in prison.

Global Vision's 'negotiations' for my release placed a heavy financial burden on the already cash-strapped organization. I don't understand how they did it, but I was free to go this afternoon, three weeks after my arrest. I was released the same afternoon as my cellmate, Jean, though I had nowhere to stay. Between my untimely exit from Brazil, and the funds needed for my release, Global was unable to make their usual arrangements, generally a host and a stipend. I was on my own. Thankfully, my new friend, Jean, kindly offered me a place to stay in the meantime, with Global's promise to compensate him, of course. It was either that or catch the next flight back to the States, which was not my first choice. I had research to conduct and a report to complete here in Haiti, and after failing to complete my Amazon assignment, I was eager to get started.

❧

It was a miserable bus ride to the outer banks of Port-au-Prince—blazing hot and stifling humidity. I hadn't bathed in weeks and was desperate for a shower and a clean change of clothes, so when Jean finally led me down Rue Janvier, a dirt road dotted with shacks, I prayed there would be indoor plumbing. He stopped in front of a little whitewashed cinderblock house with blue shutters and a plain white bench on the front porch.

The moment we walked in, a young woman appeared as if from a dream. She was barefoot, dressed brightly in an orange sundress, her waist-long braids tied back by a golden headscarf. The soft brown skin of her bare shoulders glowed in the sunlight streaming through the open kitchen door. She was breathtaking.

Jean introduced her as Luisa, his little sister. At a loss for words, I just stood there, dumbfounded.

She did not appear altogether pleased by Jean's arrival. She spoke in a low and measured voice, in what felt like a scolding—though with that knife in her hand, I think she meant business. Then she looked at me, waving the knife as if assessing my character.

I didn't need a mirror to know I probably looked like the loa Kalfu the men had spoken of in prison. (A loa, I've learned, is part of the voodoo culture. Vodou, they call it here. The African slaves took their gods and goddesses and merged them with their Christian counterparts. Kalfu is the Vodou loa for the devil.)

Jean stepped closer to his sister and took her by the shoulders. His next few words were inaudible, though their aggressive tone was disturbing. Luisa squirmed out of his grasp, humbled. Then Jean turned to me and told me to take off my boots. I did so, then flushed with embarrassment when I noticed my crusty socks, unwashed like everything else I owned. I needed a bath, a shave, and a comb.

Jean laughed. "Not before me, my friend," he said. So, I took my boots outside and waited on the bench.

Luisa stepped out and gazed at me with soulful eyes. They were golden-brown like gems and rimmed in thick dark lashes. She apologized and said Jean had explained my visit and that I could stay as long as I needed, though they could only offer me a cot she'd set up in Jean's room. Her French wasn't much better than mine, but I understood every word.

Then she bent to collect the filthy socks I'd just peeled off. Intending to wash them, I suppose. Mortified, I clutched her wrist to stop her and felt an electrifying jolt from my hand to my heart.

This isn't a metaphor. I think Luisa felt it, too, because she pulled away, her eyes locked on mine before she turned and walked back into the house, leaving me alone to think about what had just happened.

✣

After a shave and much-needed bath, I settled in. I yearned to lie down but was called to dinner. More hungry than tired, I joined them at the table, sitting across from Luisa as she served the simple meal of fish stew and brown bread. It was all I could do not to stare at her beautiful face.

I've always been shy with women. Awkward and quiet and

never sure where to look or what to say. Perhaps Luisa suffered from a similar affliction because she didn't say a word all night.

Jean didn't help matters any, continually referring to me as a "beast." "Just look at the old dog," he said. I'm not even thirty, though I'm sure living rough over the past few years makes me look older than that.

When I turned in, I heard Luisa's bedroom door groan shut; then the tumbler clicked as it locked behind her.

May 19, 1988

Luisa had already left for work when I woke up this morning. She's an aide, Jean told me, at St. Michel's Mission School.

I had work of my own but needed to speak with Max before I could get started. Unfortunately, Jean and Luisa don't have a phone. They mostly used the phone at JC's, a nearby general store where Jean worked.

We walked from his house to the hectic main road. It was crowded with pushy sidewalk vendors who approached us to buy their fruit, shaved ice, or fresh fish. Shouts, horns, the rumble of traffic, and sirens enveloped us as Jean pointed out certain landmarks, like a bar he frequented, a popular food cart parked on an empty lot across from the bus stop, and another bar he frequented on the next corner. He invited me for a drink, but I declined, eager to connect with Max.

When we finally arrived at JC's, Jean thrust the door open and introduced me to a heavyset old man named Jacques, who scowled at Jean from behind the counter. Jean declared that we'd both been released from jail and introduced me as his American friend. *Friend?* I thought. Jacques, also skeptical, offered his fleshy hand and looked up at me with a guarded smile.

Jean pointed me to the phone behind the counter as Jacques turned to him with some heated words in Creole. It seemed Jacques was not eager to have him back either, making me doubt if staying with him was a good idea.

While they bickered, I ducked behind the counter to call Max, despite the one-hour time difference.

The connection was poor. After some back and forth about my accommodations and the food, and his moaning about how expensive my Haitian assignment had become, Max asked me to reach out to someone named Jojo Martin, who worked in the social welfare department. It's not unusual for me to have a government contact, but . . . *this* government?

"This is our only shot," Max said. "Think of him as a guide, or—a chaperone."

I hung up and dialed the number for Monsieur Martin. He answered in Creole, and I stumbled into French, though I soon learned that he spoke perfect English. We agreed to meet for lunch at the Royal Palm, a bar he liked in the center of Port-au-Prince.

Jean pointed me to the bus stop, where I did my best to ignore the discomfort of the sweltering heat and oppressive humidity. I'd sweated through my linen shirt by the time the bus let me out at *Place L'Ouverture.* I passed the enormous bronze statue of the Black Maroon, an escaped slave, kneeling with a broken chain attached to his left ankle—a powerful representation of black freedom.

The interior of the Royal Palm was quite nice, despite its hole-in-the-wall appearance from the outside. As my eyes adjusted to its dim lighting, I noticed well-groomed men sitting at linen-draped tables in pairs or groups of three—lobbyists, I suspected, given the neighborhood, or government officials.

A slight black man in a fine suit waved at me from the ornate bar that looked as old as the city itself. He grinned as I approached.

"You must be Ellis," he said in English. "Could I get you something to drink? Coffee?" He held up his cocktail glass. "Rhum?"

Rhum, I learned during my stint in jail, is a Haitian favorite—made from pure sugar cane juice and more potent than traditional rum.

I ordered a beer in French, and the bartender looked me up and down with a frown.

"Did I say something wrong?" I asked Jojo after the man left to get my beer.

"It's the French," he said, though our speaking English probably didn't do me any favors either.

Jojo suggested I learn some Creole as my beer hit the bar, then asked me where I was staying. When I said Rue Janvier, he nodded as if he knew the neighborhood. In his line of work, I gathered he was familiar with the poorer areas of town. I gave him my pitch about studying poverty, noting that no two countries were equal when it came to the root of the matter.

I asked for Jojo's help; data, contacts, any information he could get.

"I'll do what I can," he said. "But if you're asking me to spy or take any risks, you're looking at the wrong man. I'm nobody. I live in a one-bedroom flat on the north side of town. I have a wife—two years now, thank you—and a kid on the way.

Spy? That would be a first for Global. All I needed, I told him, was a cultural leg up, somewhere to start, perspective.

"Perspective?" Jojo fished around for the lime wedge in his cocktail with a long finger and told me I was wasting my time in Haiti. There was no local industry. The farms were dying. The drop-out rate was nearly half. Haiti couldn't even educate its own—the non-profits or the churches did it. The problem, he said, was a lack of education, local food, and no industry. Add to that the inconsistencies in leadership, and you have yourself a country on the edge.

Job done, I thought. I may as well pack my bags.

Jojo glanced over his shoulder at the other patrons. They didn't look like they were hurting. Men who worked within the system, I assumed.

"My research focuses on the big picture of hunger and poverty," I said. "A global picture."

I told him I didn't bring solutions on the matter and didn't intend to interfere with those guys' ability to afford a hundred-dollar meal. "I want to see the conditions on the ground and how poverty is being addressed," I said.

"I'll save you some time," Jojo said, laughing. "It isn't." He said that the applications are too complicated for the beneficiaries to fill out. His department does home visits but is understaffed and by the time they get to the family in need, it can be too late. The requirements have changed, or the benefits reduced. "It's like everything else. What's law today can be wiped off the books tomorrow. Just ask the last administration—or the next."

∽

After dinner, as Luisa cleared the table, I asked Jean where I might take Creole lessons. "Don't look at me," he said, laughing. But later, as I was getting ready for bed, standing half-naked beside the cot, Luisa walked in on me and said she'd teach me Creole, but only if I taught her English.

I looked into her beautiful eyes and determined that I had the better end of that deal.

June 17, 1988

It's the middle of June already and it seems to get hotter every day. But I've made myself comfortable on the shady porch this evening, my treasured Montblanc pen in hand to catch up on the past few weeks which have flown by since Luisa started my lessons.

We began with a trip to the Pantheon, a national museum and mausoleum dedicated to Haiti's forefathers; a band of escaped and freed slaves who fought to liberate Haiti from the French long before any other nation had abolished slavery.

On the way to the bus stop, we met an old man with one arm who Luisa introduced as Mr. Desante. They visited briefly. He seemed fond of her in a grandfatherly way. As we continued to the bus stop, she explained how he lost his arm in a protest. The volunteer militia beat him so severely that his arm was dislocated, crushed, and nearly ripped from his body. A medic finished the job.

"My father was shot and killed trying to stop the assault," she said. "I was just a child." Luisa quickened her pace, as if putting distance between her and Mr. Desante would put the grief behind her as well.

The Pantheon was a marvel, built entirely underground, beneath a lovely botanical garden. Inside its heavy doors was history and art on every wall and pedestal. Not just focused on the revolution, but figures like Christopher Columbus, who colonized the island of Hispanola on behalf of Spain and enslaved and wiped out the native Taino people before trafficking Africans. The Pantheon, though, was testament to Haitian fortitude as they fought for independence.

My college studies in sociology had only glazed over these facts. I know now how much more there is to learn about Haiti and its people.

I realized that by bringing me to the Pantheon, Luisa had chosen to begin at the beginning. I looked at her admiringly, and she met my eyes with a grin. She'd realized, without my having to ask, that before learning a people's language, I needed to learn more about the people.

Later, Luisa and I visited other notable landmarks, such as the hard-won mountaintop fortress, Laferriere Citadel, and Port-au-Prince's Cathedral of Our Lady of the Assumption with its high steeples and elaborate Romanesque arches, where we watched a guest priest, Father Jean-Bertrand Aristide, preach to a packed house.

He spoke in Creole. I understood nothing. But the way the parishioners received his message suggested that he knew how to reach them, and that he was loved.

She brought me to the mission school where she worked, and proudly guided me through the classrooms, stopping at a bulletin board in the hall with a display of student photos. She pointed to a little round-faced girl with ponytails tied back in red ribbons. "I'm not supposed to have favorites, but—just look at that face," she said with a delightful grin.

Luisa also took me to the cemetery where her parents were laid to rest. I gazed down a winding dirt path that wound through a maze of concrete tombs. Epitaphs, both Christian and Vodou, adorned the limited space in between, where ornate crosses and brightly painted cherubs came face to face with macabre statuettes like scythe wielding skeletons, and headless babies painted red and black. An overcast sky contributed to the grim landscape.

Luisa pointed toward the crumbling stone wall at the far end of the path. "That is Mother's grave." She turned slightly to the right. "And over there is Father."

I recalled my father's funeral service. With so many attendees, there wasn't room in the church. They only loved him for his money. Hypocrites, all of them. Only three attended the burial. Mother, Granny, and me. Following Luisa down the trail, I remembered how I'd stood by his freshly dug grave, staring down at my polished black shoes, my heart burning with hatred for the man who'd made my young life a misery.

Luisa stopped at a plain slab of concrete that covered the plot. She pulled a strip of cloth from her skirt pocket and swept the dust from the engraved text: Emeline Patrice Bacri, 8 Jan 1944 - 7 Jan 1977. She'd died the day before her thirty-second birthday.

"How old were you when your mother died?" I asked.

Luisa looked away and sighed. "Fifteen." She sat on the side of the slab, legs crossed, and motioned for me to join her. "She had cancer, I think. Nobody knows for sure. It happened so quickly."

Luisa glanced at her father's tomb nearby.

"A brave man," I said, recalling how he'd saved Mr. Desante's life.

"I suppose—to many. I was too young to really know him. But Jean did, and he'd never tell you Papa was brave. He'd tell you that Papa was a bully. Jean hated him."

"I was ten when my father died," I said, swallowing hard. I told her how Father used to take me to a ramshackle cabin behind our house to shoot small animals and then make me skin them. If I refused, there'd be hell to pay. The memory made me ill.

Luisa took my hand in hers, her eyes downcast. "You would never be such a father," she said.

I glanced at our joined hands. "Never."

In the month since I crossed the threshold of the little house on Rue Janvier, I'd memorized the tilt of Luisa's chin, the gentle curve of her neck, and the shape of her lips.

As I walked with her in that cemetery, I wondered if she still remembered the jolt we'd felt that afternoon on her porch. The instant that bound me to her.

June 20, 1988

I'm somewhat distracted tonight as I make this quick entry. I can hear Luisa preparing for bed on the other side of the wall. I think of her clothes falling to the floor, her bare skin sliding between the sheets. Is she thinking about the conversation at dinner? Is she playing it back in her head as I've been all evening? My God, she's beautiful. The fact I'm still here in her house seems like a dream, especially after the news I received this afternoon.

My stipend finally arrived with enough to settle up with Jean for room and board, extra for his trouble, and the address of an available apartment just a few blocks from JC's. No more sleeping on a cot in the corner of someone else's room—in someone else's house.

I should have been glad.

When I returned to Rue Janvier to break the news, I was met by the mouthwatering aroma of roasting meat, something far more decadent than I thought possible on Jean and Luisa's budget. Either it was a holiday, or Luisa was trying to impress me.

"Are you hungry?" she asked, her eyes bright, her smile welcoming as she emerged from the kitchen just as spellbinding as the day I'd first met her—though this time, her hands held a folded tablecloth, not a kitchen knife.

She laid the cloth out on the table and smoothed out the creases. I admired the embroidered vines, delicate blue flowers, and the inscription on either end. *L'Union fait la Force,* and *Inite se Fòs.* The first was in French, and the second, in Creole. Both meant the same thing. Unity Makes Strength.

She placed the little blue salt and pepper shakers on either side of a jelly jar that had been filled with chamomile, the tiny white daisies that grew like weeds beside the house.

Midway through the meal, I retrieved my wallet and returned to the table with a wad of Haitian Gourdes. Jean dropped his buttered biscuit and nearly choked when I handed him what I owed.

"This much?" he said.

I thanked them both for their hospitality and explained that Global had arranged another place for me and that I'd be moving out.

I glanced across the table at Luisa for her reaction. There was none. She was stone-faced, staring at the pile of yellow rice on her plate. My heart sank. We'd gone from strangers to friends in one month, and I'd silently hoped for more. But that was an unfair proposition, considering I'd be gone from Haiti in a few more months.

"What's the rush?" Jean said, thumbing through the cash. "Stay. What do you say, Luisa?" I held my breath, waiting for her answer.

She set her fork down, her eyes locked on mine. I thought my heart would stop.

"Stay," she said, a gentle grin tugging at her mouth. How I didn't kiss her on the spot mystifies me.

Then Jean turned up his radio for the suddenly breaking news. General Henri Namphy had stepped in as Haiti's new leader. He'd proclaimed that Haiti had only one voter—the army.

When I said I'd never understand Haitian politics, Jean sighed and switched off the radio. "It's like this," he said. "What if a powerful American general decided he wanted to be president? And what if the army agreed?" I shook my head at the notion. "Okay, then say your Ronald Reagan chose to be president for life?"

"That's impossible. The people wouldn't stand for it," I said.

"Is it impossible? He could just make the decree."

"We have fair elections," I said. "Democracy."

"Democracy. Ha! No such thing. Men want power, Ellis."

"We have a solid constitution. Term limits. Oversight. And an objective supreme court," I said.

Jean raised an eyebrow and chuckled. "How long do you think *that* will last?"

His little jab disturbed me. Was American democracy so fragile? What would its demise mean to the rest of the world?

September 12, 1988

Jojo met me at the Royal Palm yesterday with a warm hug and a cold beer to discuss the bombing on the St. Jean Bosch Church that killed over fifty worshipers and left eighty injured. Tragic, horrific, and completely out of the blue.

Jojo said otherwise. He'd seen something like this coming and said the attackers were after the parish priest, Jean-Bertrand Aristide, whom I'd seen preach at the cathedral. This was the fourth attempt on his life. Rumor had it that Mayor Romain, the bombing's mastermind, had acted on orders given by General Prosper Avril.

Jean had told me about Avril back in May. He'd been Jean-Claude Duvalier's advisor before the Reagan administration forced him out. The suspension of all aid to Haiti followed.

Jojo said that Aristide would be in greater danger should Avril ever come to power.

༄

As if the day's political upheaval wasn't enough, Hurricane Gilbert was gaining speed over the Atlantic. Jean and Luisa prepared for the worst. A transistor radio played in the background as we put what we could up off the ground. Luisa filled cooking pots with fresh water and stuffed rags under the doorsill. Then we all sat together on her bed, our backs flattened against the wall opposite the window with Luisa's bare arm against mine. Though we'd been sweating throughout our preparations, she still smelled like a garden, earthy and sweet.

The storm hit with a ferocity I'd never experienced before, violently battering the little house as if intent on its destruction. The window shutters came loose and slapped against the frame, then ripped away. Later, a terrifying clatter and wail screamed at us from outside the room. Jean's curses were overwhelmed by the deafening storm as Luisa gripped my hand, wriggling her body closer. I put an arm around her shoulders and held her to me as if holding onto a piece of myself.

I woke this morning with my arm still firmly around Luisa as we lay nested together like spoons in a drawer. The storm had finally released its grip.

I could hear Jean cursing on the other side of the wall, "Christ to hell and back."

"Good morning, Luisa," I whispered, feeling the steady rise and fall of her chest with each breath until she finally woke. She tensed, then just as quickly relaxed and rolled over to face me.

"Good morning . . . *You*," she said, with a bashful smile.

The moment felt intimate, like we were new lovers the morning after. Awkwardness and familiarity rolled into one.

You. That one word felt like a bond. I know you. I love you. I would do anything for you.

"You," I murmured as I cupped my hand to her cheek, feeling the impulse to kiss her. I would have, except for Jean.

"Christ to hell and back," he shouted again. Luisa slid out of bed and straightened her shirt, which had inched up to reveal the curve of her waist and hips. I wanted to pull her back to me, return her to our nest, ignoring the mayhem that awaited us outside.

Jean appeared in the doorway, his hands and feet covered in mud as he glanced from me to Luisa and back again. He'd been curled up inches from us on the bed throughout the night. He wasn't blind.

"The roof," he said curtly, his eyes burning into me in what I could only interpret as a warning. I looked at Luisa, who'd seen the same thing and made a quick exit.

I put Jean's glare behind me and followed Luisa out of the room. Then I saw what Jean had referred to. Multiple sheets of the tin roof had peeled away from over the kitchen and part of the sitting room. I shielded my eyes from the blinding sun, overcome, and ankle deep in a pool of muck. The scene was horrific, but was multiplied when we stepped outside, where neighbors trudged through the mud, collecting what they could salvage. I've never seen anything so tragic.

Jean pulled me aside when Luisa left us to join the others.

"Leave her be," he said. "Or I'll send you packing."

Message received.

September 18, 1988

Hard to believe it's only been a week since the storm. It feels like a lifetime. The neighborhood is mourning the loss of one of its own, the surviving widow, barely three months pregnant. Jacques took ill immediately afterward, leaving Jean in charge of the shop. So, as well as lending a hand to rebuilding Mr. Desante's shack, I volunteered to patch up Jean and Luisa's roof. Not a particular skill of mine, though I did my best and was grateful to Luisa for her help—including the motherly first aid she applied to the scrapes and blisters I'd earned while wrestling the corrugated tin into place.

Each time she touched me, I recalled the feeling of waking up with her in my arms and had to remind myself not to get involved.

Leave her be.

Several days later, I was at the hardware store to pick up a few things for the roof. While in line, I glimpsed Luisa passing by on the street outside. She was accompanied by a young man with a charismatic smile.

My skin prickled at the sight, and I reacted like a fool, jumping out of line and out the door.

I quickly caught up to the pair and introduced myself, blathering on about nothing, intellectually challenged by blind jealousy.

Finally, the man excused himself and left me alone with Luisa.

She seethed through clenched teeth. "You can't just do that," she said, punching me in the chest. "He's a nice guy." She walked on ahead, her long braids swinging in time to her step. The physical impact of the punch was nothing compared to the emotional blow.

"Luisa," I said, chasing after her. "Wait." She rounded on me, and I was momentarily trapped in her steely glare. Then, fists clenched, she stormed off.

"You," I called after her, as sweetly as I could, remembering the term of endearment she'd used during our intimate moment on the morning after the hurricane. Instantly, she slowed her pace.

We'd gone a block without a word once I'd finally caught up to her when a rumble of armored trucks filled the street. Military guards started shouting warnings accompanied by shots in the air. The bullets showered down, and bystanders scattered as I grabbed Luisa and ran for safety. JC's was around the next corner. We burst through the door and I slammed it behind us.

Jean looked up in alarm as Luisa grabbed the TV remote from his hand and turned up the volume to hear the announcer on Télé Nationale.

The three of us stood in silence as we learned of another coup d'etat. This time, it was General Prosper Avril who'd assumed power, as Jojo had warned.

"Christ to hell and back!" Jean blurted.

We waited, but it took a while for the ruckus in the streets to die down. Finally, as the sun was sinking on the horizon, we walked home in relative peace, consumed by the day's events. As we passed the corner bar, Luisa stopped and turned to me.

"Do you like me?" she asked, sweeping her braids off her shoulders. I paused, wondering if she was referring to my shameful behavior outside the hardware store.

Three men stumbled out from the bar and into the dark street. One shouted a slur against one of the others, who responded with a string of profanity.

"Let's get out of here," I said, her question still echoing in my head. *Do you like me?* It was more than that. I'd completely fallen for her, and it wasn't fair. Not to her. Not to me.

Once home, Luisa locked her sultry eyes on me. I recalled the morning after Hurricane Gilbert, holding her close, whispering her name. Jean must have seen us. It's why he'd told me to leave her be. He was right. This road only led to heartbreak. I was flying down it at breakneck speed.

She took my hand and led me into her bedroom, where she stood in the moonlight spilling through the shutters. I watched spellbound as she slipped her dress from her shoulders. She walked toward me, her hips shifting gracefully, dancing to a rhythm I could not hear. I drew her closer, entranced by the golden glow of her eyes and the voluptuous curves of her body, needing to feel her warm sweet flesh against mine. Her lips tasted like ripe plums.

My logical mind whispered, stop. Stop now. But I couldn't, and neither could she. We fell onto her bed, feverish with passion. There was no going back.

The sound of footfall outside the house cut our euphoria short.

Jean?

My heart thumped wildly. I leaped from Luisa's bed and pulled on my pants, closing her door behind me, eyes trained on the door for Jean. Then I heard a knock. Palms sweating, I opened the door . . . and sighed with relief.

It wasn't Jean, but Jojo Martin. Instead of a fine suit, he wore a navy-blue T-shirt and a pair of tan slacks.

He'd come to tell me he'd lost his job. Shortly after taking power, Avril had quickly surrounded himself with sycophants to make a clean sweep inside and out. They'd turned the whole department on its head and were bolstering his claim of "country first." No outsiders welcome.

That position went back to Jean-Claude Duvalier, who'd ruthlessly singled out political rivals, journalists, trade unionists, and anyone suspected of opposing him. Illegal detention was also rampant. Detainees were kept incommunicado for long periods of time and frequently subjected to torture and ill treatment.

Duvalier had encouraged his volunteer soldiers to carry out much of his dirty work. They'd patrol the streets carrying rifles and swords, threatening anyone in their path.

Jojo reminded me that General Prosper Avril, now President Avril, had worked for Duvalier. "Cut from the same cloth," he said.

Ironically, Avril gave a grand speech this afternoon boasting of his ambitious human rights agenda. He was sending a message to Ronald Reagan to get what he wanted most—an end to the embargo. Though his speech sounded righteous, it was self-serving—Avril was securing his seat in power.

"Politics," I said. "Reagan will never fall for it."

Avril was bent on ousting foreign aid organizations and NGOs like Global Vision, targeting us in whatever wicked method imaginable. He planned to use us for leverage until Reagan gave in.

Reagan stated that the embargo could only be lifted if Avril showed a legitimate attempt at democracy. Avril's approach was anything but.

"These men are ruthless," Jojo said, "and if you don't get out, they'll throw you in prison, where you'll either be beaten to death, or starve. Go."

Luisa stepped out of the house wearing nothing but my T-shirt, her bare legs, exposed. "It's okay," I said, wondering if she'd overheard any of our conversation. "I'll be in shortly." She looked from me to Jojo, who nodded in greeting. Then she closed the door behind her.

"Ah, I see," Jojo said. "That complicates matters."

"It does. And I'm far from finished with my report." I was in unfamiliar territory, romantically, and reluctant to leave Haiti the same way I'd fled the Amazon.

Jojo proposed I take shelter in his family's summer cabin in the mountains. It was that or go back to the States.

Once Jojo left, I sat alone, listening to the crickets nearby and the far-off peel of sirens, thinking of the personal danger I faced and the impossible choice I'd have to make.

Stay, and I endanger Luisa. Go, and I lose her.

I returned to her bed and lost myself in her embrace. "*Tout bagay ap byen bèl*," she murmured in her soft voice. Though it remained to be seen if everything would be fine as she'd said.

Abandoning all thoughts of Avril, Jojo's predicament, or my own, I drew Luisa closer, intoxicated by her scent, her voice, and her body as we moved as one, deaf and blind to the world outside her walls.

Sleep eventually overcame us, though I couldn't rest for long. I needed to figure out my next move regarding Global Vision, Avril, and my report.

To hell with the report. But giving up on it would mean giving up on the Haitian people, Luisa among them. It would also do neither of us any favors if Jean found us together.

Leave her be.

I gazed at Luisa's peaceful face, aglow in the moonlight, and reluctantly pulled myself from her bed, grateful that Jean had made a late night of it elsewhere.

"Everything will be fine," Luisa had murmured. But no one knows what will become of today's events. I will just have to cross that bridge when I get to it.

September 19, 1988

I woke this morning to a jab in the ribs. "Get your ass up," said Jean. "We need to talk."

I panicked, wondering if Luisa had said something about the previous night. But Jean went off on a rant about the Macoute soldiers making the rounds. "Hungry for Americans," he said, grabbing my pack and dropping it beside me as I put on my pants. He told me to get out before he and Luisa got swept up in my mess, then marched out of the room.

Luisa stepped in, still wearing my T-shirt, and snatched the red notebook from under a folder marked Project Haiti—my unfinished report in its most raw form. Jojo's offer, I decided, was too good to pass up. I had everything I needed for urban Haiti, but the mountains would give me precious insight into the country's rural communities.

"Give me the book," I said, throwing on my rumpled linen shirt. She looked at me with a face so forlorn it broke my heart. "I don't *want* to go," I said. "I *have* to."

She'd overheard my conversation with Jojo, which made it easier to explain where I'd be. Though I didn't know for how long. I opened the pack wide, and she dropped the notebook in.

We could both hear Jean in the kitchen. Luisa tugged at the collar of my unbuttoned shirt as her lips brushed mine.

"I'll come with you," she said. But we both knew it wasn't safe. We kissed, our lips lingering as we longed for more time.

I walked to JC's and called Jojo, who drove me out of town where I could catch the bus to Alangui. From there, I'd have to walk.

He assured me I'd made the right decision and handed me the keys to the cabin, a hand-drawn map, and a note he'd written to the caretakers—a neighboring family that looked after the cabin and its surrounding coffee farm.

The bus ride into the mountains was a grueling five hours, along primitive dirt roads riddled with potholes. The driver stopped whenever a local flagged him down for a lift. I don't know what was worse: the stifling heat or the dust billowing in through the open windows. But either was preferable to turning back.

At last, the bus reached Alangui, a sleepy village overlooking a lush green valley. We passed an auto garage with an old pickup truck and two compact cars parked out front and came to a stop outside a market with a hand-painted sign hanging lopsidedly on two mismatched chains.

I walked past a group of young men huddled together outside the market. Mounted to the wall behind them was a payphone. The moment I tripped the bell at the door, the clerk, a stout woman, locked her eyes on me in a steely glare. Everything about me screamed "foreigner."

The shop reminded me of JC's, stocked with necessities like kerosene, pantry items, and somewhat fresh produce. I did my shopping, and then headed back out. The boys out front had moved on by then, so I swallowed hard and called Max. He answered promptly.

"Hey, Max," I said, wiping sweat from my face with my shirt sleeve.

"Ellis. Where the hell have you been? The news down there is terrifying. Every organization in Haiti is calling their people home, including us."

I explained that I was going to ride it out in Jojo Martin's cabin in the mountains. The last thing I wanted was another aborted mission like the one in the Amazon. I asked for three months, promising to return to the States afterward, with or without the finished report.

In true Max fashion, he was not happy, expressing himself with colorful language. But he backed down when I told him how remote the cabin was and that Jojo would be by to check on me from time to time.

☙

From the market, I followed a path east along a narrow ridge. Beyond that was a verdant grove of coffee trees. Not much further was a stone farmhouse where I'd find the family hired to care for Jojo's property. The cabin, halfway down the ridge, wasn't much more than a shanty slapped together with warped boards and a tin roof, partially shaded from the late-afternoon sun by a giant catalpa tree.

I found the inside dark and dusty but well-stocked with cooking gear. The cabin lacked electricity, but it had its own well and, to my great pleasure, running water—a rarity in this remote community.

The upstairs loft had barely enough room to turn around, but a spectacular view of the sloping hills dotted with shrubby trees, six feet tall and higher.

I tossed my pack on the bed and sorted through my few

belongings. After setting my journal on the small writing desk, I popped out to explore the property before sunset.

It was oppressively warm outside, but the air smelled sweet, like honeysuckle. I ventured past the outdoor shower into the grove. I'd never seen a coffee tree before. The fruit resembled a berry more than a bean. The dark and rigid leaves made me think of my mother's glassed-in porch and the gardenia that bloomed in the late spring. Which is not to say that I was homesick—it was hard to be sentimental about the loveless shell I'd grown up in.

I hiked out to the gravel road, past a rusted plow that looked like something from a museum. A forgotten tool without purpose.

According to Jojo, the farm is large—four-and-a-half acres in all. Most farms are less than three. They are spread across the mountainside, in a patchwork of manioc, yams, and coffee. The latter had been Haiti's number one export until the embargo. The thought of all the unnecessary suffering caused by that policy made me ill.

Though the Haitian government is twisted and its leaders greedy, US policy has played a huge role. I've seen enough poverty in my travels to know what does not work. An embargo is a stick; aid is a carrot. The carrot will always win, even in the presence of a corrupt government—a point I mean to highlight in my report.

Inspired by that thought, I turned back to the cabin and noticed a man waiting for me beneath the catalpa tree. His hand was braced against the trunk as if to hold himself up.

"*Sa ki mwen di*," he said, head tilted as if to challenge me.

"Jojo Martin is my friend," I said, with a tentative step forward. "He invited me."

My unpracticed Creole seemed to make the man more

skeptical, so I switched to French, hoping to express myself more clearly.

His eyes narrowed to a squint. "A man who speaks French is a man who cannot be trusted," he said in French.

I raised an eyebrow. "So, am I not to trust you?" He burst out laughing.

I removed Jojo's note from my back pocket, worried that it wouldn't satisfy him. He glanced at it and tossed it aside.

"My name is Dee," he said, before graciously inviting me to dinner with his wife and two sons. I happily accepted.

∽

Dee's house was a half mile up the hill. Millie, his wife, emerged from the stone house to greet me. Their two teenage boys held back, wary yet curious. As was their dog, a black terrier mix that made me think of my dear childhood spaniel, Ezra, a gift from Granny Ellis after Father died.

At dinner, I felt uneasy when I noticed the family taking far less while they heaped food onto my plate. Millie fussed and scolded the boys when they left the table early. But their exit allowed for a frank conversation about the realities of life on the mountain.

Teachers came and went, meaning regular school closures, or disenchanted, truant students. An eager young doctor might come through once and then never return—as if this outpost was just a stamp for their resume. Fresh water, too, was a major issue. The family stored most of it in cisterns above Dee's farm. But there was no filtration, and it needed to be boiled before drinking. The only other option was the public water spigot outside the market, a mile away. Locals went there several days a week, lugging five-gallon buckets.

"And the roads," Dee said. I recalled the potholes and fallen debris from my bus ride. But that wasn't the worst of it—during a storm, complete washouts or landslides would block portions of the road.

"I guess I got lucky," I said. "The road crew must have cleared the bulk of it before I arrived."

Dee laughed. "We are the road crew—my family and the others here on the mountain. We clear the roads with nothing but shovels and buckets. The government has forgotten us."

"Not entirely," said Millie. "They remember when it's time to collect the taxes."

In short, the situation up here is tragic and will only get worse the longer the embargo lasts, and the coffee trade languishes.

It's late now, and I've returned to my temporary home in Jojo's cabin. As I think about the difficult Haitian situation, I find I need to cleanse my mind. I just reread the passages I've written about Luisa. The words—so heartfelt and immediate—brought everything rushing back: her scent, the feel of her skin, the taste of her lips, and the intensity in her eyes. My heart races to think how overwhelmed I'd been when I first saw her and how she still affects me.

November 9, 1988

I was at the market today and noticed a well-dressed man watching me from outside. When our eyes met, he tipped his dark brown fedora, as if in greeting. Once outside, I looked around for him, but he'd vanished. Had Avril's arm reached this little village? Was I being followed?

I didn't mention the man when I called Max to give him an update and learned that he'd booked a flight home for me early next year, on January 29. Under no circumstances was I to miss it.

As I hiked back to the cabin, the firm deadline nested in my chest like a stone. And then there was that strange man in the fedora.

When I returned to the cabin, someone was waiting for me on the front porch. As I came closer, I realized, to my relief, that it was Jojo. A delightful surprise to see his friendly face.

I put on a pot of coffee and asked about life in the city, though I suspected he hadn't come all that way for a casual conversation.

Jojo leaned back against the counter. "Still hell, I'm afraid."

Avril had followed up on his promise to round up the foreign aid workers and anyone working for an NGO. He sees them all as threats.

NGO's, like Global, are on the front lines, we see how corruption hits the most vulnerable, and share our findings with our respective countries. We're the watchdogs that force Avril, or anyone like him, to disguise their depravity.

"There's no end in sight," Jojo said. "But you're safe up here."

"Being up here isn't a permanent solution, Jojo," I said, pouring the coffee into our mugs.

"It's a solution for the time being. You'd be an idiot to return to Port-au-Prince now. A sitting duck."

We walked outside and sat across from one another on two

stumps near the catalpa tree. Jojo toasted to life on the mountain. A refreshing breeze swept in, rattling the long seed pods dangling from the tree.

"It truly is special up here," I said, lazily picking up a fallen pod, "but what I've learned about the conditions is heartbreaking. What can be done?"

"From what you've told me, Ellis, it's not your job to fix things. You provide information that others can act on or not."

I nodded, frustrated by Global's inability to implement the second part of their plan. Even then, however, that would be out of my hands.

"How are Sheila and the baby?" I asked, shifting the conversation.

Jojo whipped out his wallet and flashed photos of the one-month-old Maci. Her big brown eyes stared right into the camera lens with a smile that was pure joy. "She's the light of my life," he said.

"Maybe someday I'll be so lucky."

Jojo grinned. "I bumped into your friend Luisa a few days ago. You may soon get company, I think."

My heart quickened like a teenage boy with a desperate crush. Then I recalled the odd man I'd seen outside the market.

As I think of him again now, I pray she doesn't come. Then again, I pray she does.

January 6, 1989

Jojo wasn't wrong. Two weeks ago, as I was helping Dee and his boys dig a new culvert for their well, I looked up to see Luisa staring at me.

"Good morning—*You*," she said. I stumbled back into the deep mud.

Trying to regain my composure, I struggled to my knees. Luisa reached out to help me. Impulsively, I pulled her into the mud with me. Her squeal drew attention from Dee's boys. Their jaws dropped when they saw Luisa with her arms wrapped tightly around my neck, smothering me with mud-splashed kisses. I felt embarrassed at first, shy in front of the boys for the public affection. Then I let it go.

We walked to the cabin and bathed in the open-air shower before heading upstairs, where we lingered in one another's arms till the loft glowed orange with the setting sun.

I held her tight, imagining what it would mean to call Haiti my home. A romantic fantasy and impossible in the current political climate. I wondered if she would consider coming to the States with me instead.

Yet the way I travel . . . gone for weeks, often months at a time . . . it wouldn't be fair to her, would it?

I abandoned my work for the rest of the week as we hiked and explored the area. When Christmas Eve rolled around, we packed a picnic and watched the sunset from the ledge above Dee and Millie's house. Luisa lay back on the soft earth, the golden light kissing her face.

She'd told Jean she was on a church retreat for St. Michel's Christmas break. We were determined to make the most of our time together. But it flew by too quickly, and today, we had to say goodbye.

It was a beautiful, sunny day, though my soul was filled with dark clouds as I walked with Luisa to the village to catch her bus home. I carried her pack. Luisa carried the conversation.

The bus arrived ten minutes early, and I cursed, recalling Loa Kalfu and his evil ways. We waited until the last moment to say our goodbyes. I was due in Port-au-Prince on January 27. Max had booked a room where I would wait for my flight back to the US two days later. Luisa agreed to meet me there. And then what? The uncertainty is still tearing me up.

She gazed into my eyes, as if reading my thoughts, and placed her hand on my arm. I felt a jolt, as with the first time she'd touched me. I took it as a sign.

In whatever form it takes, Luisa is my destiny.

When the bus pulled away, I noticed the odd man with the fedora sitting in a silver Corolla across the street. Avril's man? I still don't know, but his recurring presence can't be a coincidence. Whether or not he is a threat, his presence reminds me I am on borrowed time.

January 28, 1989

I woke this morning beside the most beautiful woman in the world. She is my world, and I'm going to prove it to her. However, before I set off on my private mission, I'll take a moment to jot down some important details that led me to this momentous decision.

I returned to Port-au-Prince yesterday in a van loaded with dried and bagged coffee beans bound for the commercial roasters. Luisa, as promised, met me outside the hotel, and we climbed the stairs to my small, second-story room. I set my bag down by the door, aware of her eyes on me. She took my hand and sighed, then led me to the open window and gazed despairingly down at the bustling street.

But with only two days remaining, I felt her pain when we made love. Her all-consuming urgency made me wonder if it was merely our limited time that concerned her or something more.

"Ellis," she said after. She'd used my name—not the charming endearment, *You*. The change stung a little, and I snapped to attention. "I think I'm pregnant," she said.

My emotions whirled between fear and joy, like a spinning coin. I wondered if I'd heard her right. I looked into her searching eyes. "I'm only a week late," she added, "but I've never been late before."

I recalled the weeks we'd spent on the mountain without regard for the consequences.

A child.

"You're going to keep it?" I asked.

Luisa shrugged. "I don't know."

We lay in bed, both of us staring up at the ceiling, listening to the din from outside through the open window. I reached for her hand.

"Come home with me," I said, rolling over to face her. "To the United States."

She grinned, then shook her head. "I have a life here, Ellis. A job I love. A home I own."

I told her she could make a life in the States, too—with me. She could get a job, and we'd make a home—together.

"We'll be a family," I said, wracking my mind for the key that would convince her of my devotion. Three words I never thought I'd say. "I love you."

She stroked my beard and kissed me lightly. We made love

again—slowly, as if time was on our side. "Please," I whispered in her ear. "Marry me."

$$\backsim$$

There wasn't much sleep for Luisa or me last night. She gave me a parting kiss before leaving for work. She said she'd return to the hotel later with her answer.

That wasn't a *yes*. It wasn't a *no*, either, but she held my hands to her heart as if all was right with the world. Encouraged, I'm off now to do what I need to do. I'll be ready when she returns.

CHAPTER 21

Mia turned the page, eager to learn what happened next.

It was blank. In fact, the remainder of the red notebook was empty.

She jumped at the sound of the door handle turning. TJ ambled in. He stopped cold when he saw the splintered remains of the file cabinet and the half dozen notebooks stacked beside the mess: blue, black, green, and two yellow spirals.

"What the hell?" he said. "Have you completely lost it?" His eyes skipped from the pile of notebooks to the boxes and scrapbooks Mia had set aside. "What is all this?"

Mia wasn't ready to share. Not this. Not yet. She was still digesting the weight of it. She rubbed her tired eyes, then stood and stretched, the red notebook still clutched in her hand.

"I don't know," she answered.

It was the truth. She wasn't sure of what she'd found. The journals were just the beginning. She still had the scrapbooks and shoe boxes to go through. "I was looking for Ellis's health directive—couldn't find the key." She stooped over the remaining notebooks, wondering which one picked up where the red notebook left off.

TJ pointed to the sledgehammer resting against Ellis's bed. "A pretty drastic solution, don't you think?"

"Maybe," she said. She prayed he'd leave her alone. The notebooks and everything within them called to her.

TJ knelt and began picking through the mess, turning over a scrapbook and opening it to the first page.

"Hey," he said. "Is this you?"

Mia knelt beside him and gazed down at the book. The photos were of her at her first Kanaval, in full costume. It was after the parade. In the first photo, she, Auntie Sis, and Jonas stood in line for water. Auntie Sis seemed distracted, as if searching for someone in the crowd. Jonas's head was turned away.

Mia's heart surged with grief. She recalled Jonas's face: his joyful smile and kind eyes. "I'll take care of you," he'd said that day at Lake Azuéi. He'd only been fifteen then. Yet he'd revealed the good-hearted man he would have undoubtedly become had he lived through the 2010 earthquake.

It was Billy who'd told her of Jonas's death. Billy must have taken those photos of her at Kanaval.

"Who's that?" TJ asked, referring to the next photo. "She's beautiful."

"Mama," Mia said softly. In the photo, Mia was speaking with Mama. Both were dressed in colorful halter tops and flowing skirts.

TJ looked from the photo to Mia. "I should have known. You look just like her."

In the photo, Mama studied Mia's face, her head tilted as if listening—as if hanging on her daughter's every word. If Mia had been able then to foresee the dramatic events that followed, would she have done things differently? Would she have said something about Uncle Jean sooner? Would she have held her mother closer? Would she have noticed the signs of Mama's illness when there was still time to save her? Mia sighed, feeling her heart would burst with love for the mother she'd lost.

Then she noticed Uncle Jean in the photo. Standing back in the crowded street, watching them. An icy chill ran through her body. She snapped the book shut, her pulse racing, her skin prickling. She willed herself, as she always did, to push the memory of Uncle Jean into the furthest corners of her mind. Seeing his name in Ellis's journal had already set her nerves on edge.

"What's up with you?" TJ said. "You're shaking."

Mia pushed the scrapbook aside. "I'm fine."

"Sure?"

"Really," she said. "I'm fine." He was better off not knowing, and she wouldn't know where to begin.

TJ wandered over to Ellis's stripped bed and stretched out on it.

"What side of the bed do you think he sleeps on?" he asked. "And why does he keep his room so dark?" Then, after a long pause, he added, "Did he ever even love my mom?"

Mia laid down beside her brother and listened to the lazy cadence of his voice as he rambled on. She wondered about her own parents' feelings for one another, thinking again about the pages she'd just finished in the red notebook.

After TJ had drifted asleep, she rolled over and rested her eyes on the shattered cabinet. "It's all there," she murmured as she dozed off.

When she woke, the room was dark. TJ was gone, but he'd covered her up with a wool blanket that smelled like it had been put away damp and never aired out.

She considered climbing the stairs to her room when she noticed the time on her phone: 3:40 a.m. She still had so much material to go through, but time was not on her side. She'd need to read more selectively. Not every book. Not every entry. Yawning, she switched on the light and picked through the remaining notebooks until she found a corresponding date on the front page of a black leather journal embossed with Ellis's initials. *Fancy*, she thought.

She climbed back onto the bed and settled in.

CHAPTER 22
The Black Notebook

March 21, 1989

Max greeted me at the Indianapolis airport this afternoon, two connections and sixteen hours after leaving Haiti. He'd grown a mustache since I'd seen him last—a bushy thing that hung over his upper lip.

His ashen face and deep-set worry lines conveyed the stress he'd been under since I'd landed in Haiti.

"I should never have allowed you to stay," he grumbled, reaching for my pack and slinging it over one shoulder. He called me stubborn, difficult, insubordinate, and the bane of his existence. Then he wrapped his arms around me in a suffocating embrace.

It was a quiet two-hour drive back to Meridian, the radio barely audible as I drifted in and out of sleep.

"Is there anything I can do for you?" Max asked when we reached the house at last.

"Take me back," I said, knowing how crazy it sounded.

Max shook his head. "Get some sleep. I'll see you in a few days, after I've read your report. It's finished, yes?"

I looked up at the house and groaned. Then I grabbed my pack and dug out the report. It *was* finished, though it lacked my usual polish.

Max drove off, and I ducked beneath the arbor dripping with fragrant violet clusters outside the kitchen door. Rosa met me at the door with tears in her eyes. I'd been missed. She'd read reports of the explosive events in Haiti, and when my trip went longer than expected, she dreaded I'd been caught up in it. Her fears were confirmed when Max called Mother with the news. Never underestimate a housekeeper's aptitude for eavesdropping.

I found Mother tucked comfortably into the sunporch, drinking her coffee and reading a home decorating magazine. I waited for her to see me, to acknowledge me in some way.

When she finally looked up, she said, "Well? How did that turn out for you?"

☙

From the day I first told Mother about Global Vision, excited for the opportunity to make a difference in the world by working for this newly minted NGO, she'd made it clear she was against it. It was beneath me, she'd said. Unworthy of an Ellis.

Didn't she watch the news? Was she blind to the suffering of others? It seemed unfathomable that she wouldn't pull her head out of the sand long enough to recognize that she was in a position to help—that she could be a voice for the underprivileged, and a purse for the organizations that do the most good.

We are as different from one another as Father was from his

own mother. Granny was a tender soul who volunteered at Saint Sebastian's food bank three days a week and at the animal shelter every weekend. Father repeatedly mocked her for doing so.

⁓

I left the sunporch in disgust, then retreated up to my bedroom.

The past few months have been a living nightmare. I feel both absent and present in a world so ludicrous that I cannot fathom how I've muddled through. All I can do now is try my best to document what happened. Perhaps I can make sense of it, if there is any, by putting it in writing here.

The morning after I proposed, I set off for a jewelry store I'd seen near JC's, my heart thundering with excitement. I imagined tears and kisses and a long night of lovemaking.

The streets buzzed with activity. I passed vendors calling out from their food carts or visiting with locals outside their stores. Young boys giggled and teased each other as pretty girls walked by. There was laughter everywhere, as if the world knew how I felt.

The jeweler smiled from behind a long glass case as I entered. I pointed to my ring finger, and his smile grew. The first case held necklaces and brooches; the next held bracelets and earrings. The jeweler led me to the last case. Rings.

My eyes fell on a simple one with a tiny golden stone. "That one."

The ring I'd chosen was ideal for Luisa and perfectly matched the color of her eyes. I counted out my cash as he placed it in a satin-lined box which I held in my cupped hands before tucking it into my pack.

I hurried from the shop and slowed as I passed JC's, wondering how Jean would react to the news. You see, I was confident Luisa would say *yes*. The sign in the shop window said JC's was closed, though the lights were still on.

Strange, I thought. But I kept walking, turning the corner. Then I noticed smoke from the firepit behind the shop. I approached the back door to check on things.

"Quiet, Sweet Thing," I heard from the other side. I opened the door. A small girl looked up at me, pleading for help with her eyes. She was no more than six or seven. Jean turned to see me.

I was flirting with the wrong kind of girl, he'd said when I asked why he was in prison.

Seeing her chance, the child fled. I charged at Jean, knocking him flat.

"How could you?" I said, my heart bleeding for the young girl. "What is *wrong* with you?"

"It's not what you think," he said. "The girl was just lost, is all."

I didn't believe him. I think he knew, because his eyes narrowed on me, vengeful and dark.

"I'll have you behind bars," I said. But my threat was as toothless as Mr. Desante, since the police would surely arrest *me*, an enemy of the state.

Jean raised a fist. I snatched it and twisted his arm behind him, resisting the urge to snap it in two.

"You make me sick," I said, releasing him.

"It wasn't what you think," he shouted, then quickly rounded on me with a punch in the ribs.

I pushed him against a shelf stocked with T-shirts and shop

supplies that tumbled to the floor. He spit in my face before I stormed out through the open back door. I was more determined than ever to get Luisa out of Haiti. Did she have any idea what kind of man her brother was?

The cheerful streets I'd walked an hour earlier felt grim and sinister as I turned the next corner. The pain from the blow to my ribs inflamed my anger. I heard footsteps behind me. Believing it was Jean, I stopped and balled up my fists, ready for a fight. But a hand gripped my arm and pulled me back.

"Identification, sir," a man said in a deep and gravelly voice. His English was perfectly enunciated, as if he already knew who I was. I turned to see two men wearing the uniform of Avril's volunteer army—the Tonton Macoutes. My heart flooded with dread.

This was it. In my haste, I'd let my guard down. *Idiot!*

I reached for my pack. In seconds, both hands were bound behind me.

My body stiffened. I shouted for them to stop, to wait, to let me explain. They wouldn't have it.

A silver Corolla rolled past. The driver wore a fedora like the man from the market in Alangui. But then I spotted Jean across the street, standing beside a newspaper stand. After a long draw from his cigarette, he nodded to the men. My blood went cold.

"That man!" I shrieked. "That man is who you should arrest. He's a pedophile!"

The soldiers laughed. My plea fell on deaf ears.

❧

A week into my incarceration, I was finally allowed to call Max. But there wasn't enough time to explain my circumstances, much less ask him to get a message to Luisa. I can only imagine what she thinks of me, or what kind of lies Jean filled her head with.

The men in prison joke about Loa Kalfu. But now I've met the devil, and he is no joking matter.

My new cellmates worked for the many non-profits who'd dedicated valuable resources to Haiti. Each man's organization was as bent on their release as mine. As were their home countries.

In a brief call with Max, I learned that Alvin Adams, the new ambassador to Haiti under George Bush's fledgling administration, informed his State Department that all future financial assistance to Haiti could resume. It was unclear whether a conniving President Avril had convinced Adams that he was different, and that Haiti was a changed country, or whether Avril's scheme to use foreigners for leverage paid off. Either way, Congress went along with it. The embargo lifted, and we political prisoners were extradited to our respective countries, with one condition—we were banned from ever returning to Haiti.

I pleaded to see Luisa right until the helicopter lifted off and swept me away.

∾

"Marry me."

My words haunted me as I unpacked the bag that the prison guards had handled, but which by some act of charity still held the red notebook and little ring I'd bought for Luisa. If not for those two things, I might come to believe I'd imagined the events of the past year.

Now, the words *I think I'm pregnant* overshadowed visions of Luisa waiting at the hotel or what Jean might have told her.

Once I'd gotten settled in my room, I reached for the cordless phone beside the bed and dialed Jojo. There was a lot to unpack since I'd seen him last on the mountain. We spoke for the better part of an hour. I told him about Luisa's visit, her possible pregnancy, my proposal, the altercation with Jean, and finally, the arrest. He'd read about the detainees' release in the paper and expressed relief that I'd arrived home safely.

He was still unemployed and quickly running out of savings, a source of great anxiety for him and his wife. If something didn't come up soon, they'd have to move from the apartment to the mountain cabin. He didn't want that for his daughter.

An idea occurred to me. My thorough report on Haiti laid the groundwork for Global's next step, taking action to combat the diverse causes of poverty I'd outlined so thoroughly. I told Jojo I'd speak with Max and get back to him. In return, he'd get word to Luisa about my untimely arrest.

"I'm banned from returning," I told him. "She must come to me."

"Leave it with me, my friend," he said.

March 30, 1989

Anticipating Luisa's arrival, I moved out of my mother's house today.

"And where will you go?" Mother said when I told her. "This so-called job of yours doesn't bring in enough salary to support a flea, much less a man like you."

A man like me. I always hated it when she referred to me that way—implying I was better than other people. Thank goodness for Granny Ellis, Rosa, and Oscar. They kept me grounded over the years, as Mother threw one upper-class entitlement after another in my path. I was raised acutely aware of my advantages. They were a source of personal conflict for me, given how many others lived on the brink of survival—the poor, homeless, sick, or abandoned.

However, I'd had one privilege for which I was most grateful—my education. My only regret was that Purdue hadn't been further away.

Difficult as it is to admit, Mother was right about one thing. I can't afford to move out. But, determined to make good on my brave declaration, I collected my belongings and lugged them across to the old gray cottage on the estate.

Rosa and Oscar had left the partially furnished cottage vacant years ago when they opted to live in town. I intend to make it a home for Luisa and our future family.

I brought a few comforts with me from the main house. Most notably, the antique roll-top desk and matching file cabinet from my father's office. Both fit snugly into my new bedroom, and the desk, once purged of Father's papers, will be ideal for my own work. I used it earlier to write to Luisa. The third letter since my return. I included what money I can spare and hope it will be enough to cover the visa application and airfare to the States.

That's a costly assumption, considering I haven't heard back from Jojo. But I'm tired of waiting for our new life to begin. I can't imagine any reason Luisa would reject it.

April 17, 1989

Max stopped by my new place last night to check in on me and go over my report on Haiti.

"You look well," he said, taking in our surroundings. Though my bedroom was furnished and the kitchen clean, the rest of the house was still in shambles. There was a lot to do, and he noticed my clumsy attempt at stripping the shabby green wallpaper from the living room walls. Scraps of paper lay in small piles, and I'd hastily set aside the tools on a brown wool blanket I'd found in the hall closet.

"It's a start," I said with a half-hearted grin.

I led Max into the kitchen, offered him a seat at the pink Formica-top table, and fetched two beers from the fridge. After we'd had a few, I launched into the events leading up to my arrest. Max listened without interruption.

"I'm not giving up on Luisa and the child, though," I said.

"Child? Jesus, Ellis, what have you gotten yourself into?"

I clarified, explaining that Luisa only suspected her pregnancy when I saw her last. I said that Jojo was working on getting word to Luisa that I was trying to get her to the States. But given the political situation and Jean's aversion to me, it wasn't going be easy.

Max removed my report from his bag and placed it on the table as I opened another beer. "You have a bright future with Global, Ellis. Jojo was a brilliant suggestion, and after reviewing this report, I'd say we're ready for the next phase in Haiti. In fact, I've already called Jojo and he's on board."

For the better part of two hours, we discussed my report, Haitian politics, and the next phase for Global Vision. We dubbed it Global Healing. The new branch would take my research—the *vision*—and make recommendations for overcoming the root basis of poverty—the *healing*.

Though foreign aid workers remained banished, as a resident, Jojo could move freely, incorporating local churches and charities in cooperation with Global Healing.

"It'd be great to have someone in power there with a vision of security for the people," I said.

"You have someone in mind? Perhaps this Aristide fellow you mentioned in your report?"

I finished my beer and pushed my chair back from the table. "Avril won't step down quietly."

"Dictators never do," Max said.

We talked into the early hours. I finally put him in a spare room upstairs that Rosa had thoughtfully put in order. Before leaving today, he handed me my next assignment. Guinea. "How's your French?" he said.

"Better than my Creole." I clutched the folder, eager to bury myself in the next mission. "One thing, though," I said. "Luisa. If she—"

Max sighed. "Immigration takes time, Ellis. Be patient."

❦

I called Jojo at once when Max left. He said he'd found it difficult to get Luisa alone. Jean was her constant companion, escorting her to and from work. But he finally caught up to her at the cinderblock while Jean was away.

"She looks, well, glowing, actually. From what I could tell, pregnancy suits her."

I dropped back onto my desk chair, thinking of the moment she'd told me she might be pregnant. So, it was really happening. Jojo learned that the baby was due in September, which squares with our time at the mountain cabin.

"The baby is healthy?"

"That's anyone's guess. Luisa hasn't seen a doctor. There's no money for it."

"I've sent money. I've sent nearly everything I have. I've written too, but she hasn't replied to a single letter."

Jojo sighed. "She didn't mention it."

"You told her what happened, right?"

"I'm getting to it. I'd only just begun to tell her about your arrest when Jean shouted out from the street. A classic gatekeeper."

Gatekeeper. I wanted to cry out in frustration, angry with Jean, but angrier with myself for not having seen this coming.

We switched to talk of Global. Jojo thanked me for recommending him. He already had plans to connect Dee with the local food bank and add another program to establish St. Michel's Mission as an emergency shelter with supplies and post-storm support for citizens.

Before ending the call, I asked Jojo to keep trying to get through to Luisa.

"Of course," he said. "Be patient." Then he added, "Congratulations—papa."

Papa. Imagine that. I was more intent than ever on getting through to Luisa.

I opened the window shade and saw Oscar digging in the flowerbed outside the cottage. He wore his cap pulled low to keep out the sun. It was particularly warm for June. I watched as he planted a tray pack of something new—something I recognized from beside the cinderblock on Rue Janvier. Tiny white blossoms on woody stems. Chamomile.

A rush of memories rolled over me like an avalanche—Luisa's calm yet piercing gaze, her scent, her tender smile. "You," I said aloud, remembering how sweetly she'd said this word when referring to me.

I thought of the ring I'd bought back in January, filled with the promise of a future and a family of my own but also the memory of that horrific day. My arrest. The sickening sight of Jean with that little girl. "It's not what you think," he'd said, then silenced me by turning me over to Avril's men.

The cottage suddenly felt stifling. I walked out to the lake to clear my head, as I had when I was a boy. I imagined teaching the child to swim as Luisa spread out a picnic lunch on the sun-warmed rock jutting into the water. I recalled vividly the way Luisa moved her body while making love, tempting me with each small discovery. My fantasy was filled with laughter and love, optimism and anticipation.

On my return, though, Oscar was waiting for me in front of the cottage with a bundle of letters from Port-au-Prince. They were stamped *Return to Sender*. I lost all feeling in my hands, and my knees gave way.

Not one had been opened. I recalled the look on Jean's face when Avril's men picked me up in the street. He's to blame. I know it.

Oscar led me into Rosa's kitchen, where she brought me a cup of strong coffee and a hot scone. As if fresh pastry could fix things the way it had when I was a boy.

Mother glared at me from the other side of the kitchen, her arms crossed. "I told you she wasn't worth your trouble," she said. She meant the money I'd sent to Haiti. Her utter lack of empathy struck a nerve.

If it weren't for Oscar and Rosa, I'd feel like an orphan in this godforsaken house.

January 18, 1990

I see here that I haven't made an entry in a while. It's difficult to find the time, but honestly, it's the words I lack.

I'm in São Paulo, where it's rained nearly every week since I arrived in November and I've been holed up for days with little else to do but worry.

When Max called about this mission, I told him my concerns about Jojo, who I hadn't heard from since he'd agreed to update me about Luisa and the baby. Max hadn't heard from Jojo either, which concerned me even more. So, when Max called me on the sat phone today, I pounced on it, hoping he'd have an update.

"Jojo is in prison," Max said.

He'd been charged with espionage. It was ridiculous. Jojo's attempt to do good for his country without bribery makes Avril look bad. Though Max worked day and night to free him, he was unsuccessful. I think of Jojo's wife and daughter getting by on their own, and my heart breaks for them all. I can hardly bear it.

"I'll get word to you as soon as I have an update," Max said.

"He was checking on Luisa." I paused for a deep breath. "The baby."

"Yes, the baby," Max said. "Her name is Mia Louise. Born September 23."

"Oh, thank God. Is she—"

"She's healthy and living with her mother and uncle on Rue Janvier."

"You're a good friend, Max. I don't deserve you."

"Damn right," Max said with a subtle laugh.

I didn't tell Max about what I'd seen in the alley. Only Jojo knew. And now, after so many months, I'm beginning to doubt what I saw. The events of that day had blurred with time. "It's not what you think," Jean had said. Maybe so. And maybe it had been that fellow in the fedora who'd turned me in. Then again . . .

I wrote to Luisa in a desperate plea for her and Mia to come to the States. I told her I'd be back in Meridian in May to arrange everything. Mia will be eight months old. I've already missed so much.

May 2, 1990

When I returned from Brazil this morning, I found a stack of mail on the kitchen table. Among the credit card offers and catalogs I'd never signed up for, there was a letter from Jean.

Two full years have passed since I'd first arrived at his little cinderblock. Sixteen months since I last set eyes on him.

I took Jean's letter to my bedroom and tore it open. It was as I'd feared. He said I had no claim on Luisa or the baby. He told me to stop writing, that Luisa wanted nothing to do with me, that the child was cursed to have such a father as me. She was never to know of my existence.

I want to rip his heart out.

My rage extends to Jojo's continued incarceration, as his trial is perpetually delayed. Max found a man to keep the ball rolling in Port-au-Prince, however. His name is Billy Krieger, and he's with the US Embassy. It was a tricky negotiation that would have been a whole lot easier if Aristide had been in power.

Aristide's leadership could still happen. He's running for president in the 1991 election. The outcome will mean the difference between business as usual in Haitian politics and long-awaited democracy. I've read that Aristide was recently expelled from his church for being too political. They said he was out of line with his role as a clergyman. Aristide replied, "The crime of which I stand accused is the crime of preaching food for all men and women." I keep that quote tacked on the wall above my desk. Our goals are perfectly aligned. I'm hopeful that having such a man in power would enable me to return to Haiti.

I called Billy Krieger, introduced myself, and welcomed him to the team. We warmed to one another quickly, and by the end of our conversation, I felt comfortable enough to confide my painful history with Haiti, my separation from Luisa, and the child I'd been cut off from.

Billy knew that without Luisa's written agreement toward shared custody, I'd never know my daughter. The prospect broke my heart. He offered to look in on them from time to time and check with the Embassy to see if there might be another way. I arranged to send him money each month to be used as he saw fit to help Luisa and the child.

Spirits lifted, I walked out to the lake as I often had in my youth, stretching out on the warm rock with my sweet spaniel, Ezra. The lake was a sanctuary from my childhood—a place of comfort where I felt, at last, like myself, and where I fantasized about my future.

Staring up at the passing clouds, I fought to grab hold of that youthful optimism. I wanted it close as I wondered what life had in store for me now.

CHAPTER 23
The Green Notebook

August 9, 1993

I'm melting in this August heat and nearly suffocating with the humidity. It reminds me of the long hot days and longer nights in Port-au-Prince. They're as unforgettable as the day I met Luisa Bacri and the day I asked her to marry me. And in all the years since I'm in no better position to move on. Whenever the subject of moving on, or even marrying, has come up, I've returned to the same question: What have I to offer a future Mrs. Theodore Ellis other than my emotional baggage, a heart that still belongs to another, and a daughter I've never met?

Despite these obvious demerits, Mother continued to parade prospects through the house whenever I was home, as if to tempt me with the life she imagined for me.

Last winter, she invited Francis Turner to her table. This woman arrived partway through the meal, rosy-cheeked and hair flecked with melting snow.

I recalled her father, Lawrence Turner—Father's business partner when I was a boy. I'd only heard about Francis. A passing remark that inferred we'd be well suited. I was nine. How could they have had any idea?

Francis worked in the mayor's office in Indianapolis and was visiting Meridian on that mayor's behalf as part of a program the governor was pulling together.

After dinner, Mother left us alone on the sunporch. I explained what I did for a living—the travel, the people, and the satisfaction I got from my job. Francis nodded and smiled politely, saying that governments were vital to the well-being of their communities.

Maybe we're well-suited after all.

❧

I like Francis, but while we've been seeing one another on and off for the past year and a half, I don't love her, and I doubt I ever could. Marriage is the farthest thing from my mind. The commitment does not lend itself to my life, constantly on the go. Who in their right mind would tie themselves down to that?

Then, last week, I took Francis back to the cottage after dinner, drinks, and stares from the restaurant staff for lingering too long at our table.

We were already tipsy, not yet staggering, when I led her from the front door to the kitchen, where I grabbed a bottle of wine and a couple of glasses. Then we went down the hall to my bedroom.

I flung the window open to a warm, subtle breeze and the luminescent glow of a full moon.

Watching Francis undress in the silver-blue moonlight reminded me so vividly of Luisa, the night we lost ourselves on a balmy Haitian evening. Luisa had stood in the moonlight then, just as Francis did now. The women were nothing alike, yet I took Francis to me, thirsty for Luisa and the unbridled passion of that night.

I woke early the following day with Francis stretched out beside me. I'd long since closed the shade, and we lay in relative darkness despite the sunrise sneaking through the gaps on either side.

"I have a daughter," I said.

"Hm?" She swiped a stray hair from her face. "You . . . *what?*"

"Her name is Mia, and she lives in Haiti."

"Haiti? God, Ellis, what time is it?" I wondered if she'd heard me as she added, "What are you going on about? A daughter?"

"Yes. She's four."

"All right."

"I wanted you to know."

"All right."

This morning over coffee, Francis invited me to move into her tiny two-bedroom apartment in Indianapolis. It's closer to Global headquarters for me and right around the corner from her office. It wasn't out of the blue, I've entertained moving in together as well, but wasn't sure if we were ready for that level of commitment.

And this is where I went totally off my rocker. I went one step further and asked Francis to marry me. She's a busy woman who seems to understand the demands on my time, and I need to move on from my happy family fantasy with Luisa and Mia.

But considering Luisa's face is still the last thing I see when I shut my eyes at night, that, too, might be a fantasy.

November 12, 1994

I thought Francis was going to wring my neck yesterday when I accepted an assignment to the Dominican Republic two weeks after our son, TJ, had arrived.

In a matter of hours, I was outside the Numero Uno Cantina, sipping a warm Coca-Cola from a chipped glass in a dusty little town called Neyba. The forbidden Haitian border was merely 116 kilometers away. So close, and yet so far.

Aristide's October victory remains front-page news. It validated his popularity after the last attempt, in 1991. Though he won that election in a landslide, with 67% of the vote, he was ousted a few months later in an ugly coup. This time, to ensure a smooth transition, President Clinton sent a contingent of US soldiers into Haiti to maintain order while they restored Aristide to power. *Operation Uphold Democracy*, they call it.

I was thinking about Francis and the steely glare with which she'd assaulted me before I left for the airport, when church bells from the center of town began to clang. Two men at the next table looked at their watches, then up at the sky.

"*Alerta de tormenta*," said one of the men. I followed their gaze to a growing bank of clouds along the rim of the south-facing mountains. The bells continued ringing as the cafe owner came out to shoo us away.

I'd been waiting for the host Max lined up for me. They were late, and I wasn't sure where to go. A jeep rolled up to the curb, and three American soldiers hopped out.

"Forget the wind," one said in a thick western accent. "It's the flooding. I remember a storm back in Texas where—"

"Enough, Tex," said a dark-skinned soldier.

But Tex went on, over the clanging bells. "Three inches of silt. Plumbing shot to hell. No electricity for weeks. And don't get me started on the mosquitos. Fucking hell, it was."

"Shut it!" said the third soldier, a blond, reaching for the cafe door. "What's with those fucking bells?"

"Alerta de tormenta," I said, merely repeating what I'd heard.

Tex looked at me wide-eyed. "Exactly what I just said." He turned to his friends. "Didn't I just say that? Don't mock a hurricane, is what I always say."

Once the blond discovered the cantina was closed, he looked around, perplexed. Then he moaned that the three-hour drive back to Port-au-Prince would be unthinkable without coffee.

I thought he should be more concerned by the storm. The clouds were rolling in fast. A patio umbrella somersaulted down the street and snapped when it hit the stop sign. I thought of the cinderblock on Rue Janvier and wondered how storm-worthy it was. I'd repaired the roof myself after Hurricane Gilbert, but how well had my amateur handiwork held up? Would Mia be safe? Luisa?

I flipped open my cell phone and dialed Billy. The call went directly to voicemail.

Tex laughed and said not to bother. Nothing was going to get through in that weather.

The nearest cell tower was ten miles away. I was lucky to have a signal at all. The only way to know if Mia and Luisa were safe was to see them for myself. When I quickly explained the situation to the soldiers, they were happy to give me a lift.

I knew I was taking a terrible risk. If I were caught, I'd be turned away. If I made it across, I could be arrested. I said nothing of my fears to my companions.

The rain hadn't begun yet, but the sky was black with thick clouds. When we finally reached the border crossing, we discovered the small terminal abandoned. They'd likely taken shelter. This signaled the danger we were in. The shoddy roads of the DR joined the shoddy roads of Haiti. Dips in the road flooded as heavy gusts rocked the jeep like rolling swells at sea.

The first drops of rain began to fall when we arrived in Port-au-Prince. The soldiers asked if I'd like to shelter with them. I shook my head. The jeep stopped, and I reached anxiously for the door handle, focused on my goal.

"Wait." Tex scribbled an address on a scrap of paper. "We'll be here if your plans don't pan out."

I thanked him, took the address, and made a dash for St. Michel's. If that failed, I'd head for Rue Janvier.

The streets were madness. Men, women, and children rushed through the driving rain for safety as trash whipped about. A terrified dog ran into me and set off again. I feared I'd never find Luisa and Mia in this pandemonium and considered heading for the house instead. But just as I turned to go, I caught a glimpse of Luisa, panic-stricken, crying out into the chaos with her head pivoting left to right.

A child's shrill scream punctured the air.

"Mama!"

I noticed Luisa running toward the child before being pushed back further by the crowd.

The child. Mia? It had to be!

I broke through the throng and caught the child in my arms. I couldn't hold her tight enough to express the love I felt. But she flailed in a terror-stricken attempt to free herself. My heart sank. Who was I to her? No more than a stranger.

I threw her over my shoulder, holding tightly to her legs as I scanned the street for Luisa. "Quiet," I said. "You're safe." My Creole was rusty, but I think she understood me. A second later, I saw Luisa bearing down on us, her face and skin dampened by the rain. She looked as stunning as the day I'd first laid eyes on her. Then she recognized me.

"You can't have her!" she screamed. "You can't!"

Luisa clawed at me, desperately prying Mia from my arms as if I'd intended harm.

"Stop, Luisa!" I said. "I only want to help."

Mia—my daughter—fixed her gaze on me as the two vanished into the crowd. I pressed on toward Rue Janvier and saw them just as they were entering the house, then heard the brace fall into place. My knocks went ignored, so I turned back with one last glance at the roof, praying it would hold, and joined the soldiers at the address they'd given me.

Tex laid a bedroll out for me at the far end of a hotel banquet room with the other soldiers. Storm updates broke through the static of a cheap radio. I translated what I could with what Creole I could understand. I recalled the last hurricane I'd lived through, and how I woke up with Luisa in my arms and Jean's warning in my ears.

Leave her be.

November 13, 1994

I'll make this quick as I'm exhausted from this harrowing day. The hurricane did its worst. With the rising death toll and the extent of the damage inflicted, the soldiers enlisted to aid Aristide were redeployed to a humanitarian mission. I met up with Billy, and we did what we could to help them. I used what little influence I had with the soldiers, asking if we could check the damage on Rue Janvier. They didn't bat an eye but said it had to be quick.

As we walked down the street, I spied Jean outside the house. More importantly, I noticed little Mia peeking through the window. My heart skipped a beat. I was desperate to see her, speak to her. "I'm your papa," I wanted to say.

I broke from my companions as they continued down the road, then pinned on a smile and approached the house. Jean met me before I'd reached the porch. As much as I pleaded to see Luisa and the girl, he refused. I insisted, which infuriated him.

"She hates you, understand?" Jean said. "You abandoned them."

"You know I didn't," I said. "I saw you there—in the street. You'd turned me in." Jean smirked, so I added, "It's because of what I saw that day."

"You saw nothing," he hissed. I wanted to spit in his face.

"I have a right to see her," I said. I glanced at the child in the window, watching our every move. She was wide-eyed and curious. I looked for a resemblance to me but saw only Luisa.

"You have no rights here," Jean said, finally. I thought of the many letters I'd sent and the preliminary documents regarding custody. My suspicion was right. Luisa didn't know. She hadn't seen the letters. She'd never received the money. My message had never reached her. Jean was controlling the situation. I had lost the battle for Mia before it had begun.

I looked into Jean's twisted face and grabbed his shirt collar, pulling him close. "Don't you *ever* lay a finger on her," I said. Jean jerked away, but I recognized the flicker of hatred I'd seen that day at JC's. The horror in the young girl's eyes is still imprinted on my mind.

The soldiers were long out of sight, and my time was running out. Desperately, I lifted my camera and locked the lens on the sweet young face in the window, then snapped a picture.

❧

An hour later, I caught up with Billy in an empty lot behind a liquor store. The clatter of hammer against nail filled the air as a group of men repaired the storm damage, intent on a common goal and blind to the two white men occupying the only spot of shade on the lot.

Billy held out a hand, and I grasped it firmly, feeling his bent fingers and swollen, arthritic knuckles. I relaxed my grip promptly and stepped back as Billy passed me a brown letter-sized envelope.

"Just a few pictures. I can't get much without drawing too much attention, so—apologies in advance that they're mostly blurred. But you'll get the gist. They're doing all right. Sissy moved in two years ago. Jean took over the shop when they married, and it's doing good business. Luisa is ferociously protective of Mia. You should take comfort in that, especially nowadays."

The gangs were ruthless, there was no stopping them. Together with the Tonton Macoutes, the average civilian had to be ever-vigilant to avoid trouble.

"Certainly Aristide doesn't support these militia."

"Of course not, but they're too entrenched in the old regime. Aristide has no loyalty among them."

"Clinton has brought in some security," I said.

Billy said the soldiers weren't welcome and that Jimmy Carter, Senator Sam Nunn, and a few others were trying to work something out to keep the military out of it.

On another note, Billy had a message for me from Max. I'd been AWOL, and he hated that. It seemed I hadn't eluded him after all.

I left the hotel this morning believing I'd finally have my moment with Luisa to explain my sudden absence six years ago. To tell her I'd never stopped loving her.

I had hoped to return to Rue Janvier tomorrow with the fantasy of seeing Luisa and holding my daughter for more than thirty seconds.

Instead, I'm on a plane bound for Indianapolis after Max called me in. I pushed back, knowing I'd not get another chance, but Max said that if I didn't leave immediately, he couldn't guarantee my safety.

I regret returning to Meridian with nothing to show for my efforts in Haiti but Billy's packet and the single photograph of Mia I'd taken.

I must find a way to get through to Luisa. Otherwise, I fear that I will never know my daughter.

February 23, 1997

It has been years since I've opened this journal. Time in the field took its toll on me, and on my marriage. Two months here. Five months there. The trip to Peru last year was the one that finished things between us. Francis told me before leaving that if I didn't insist on a non-traveling role with Global or leave the organization altogether, I shouldn't return. I'd deliberately used the trip to get some distance from her petty digs at my career and my "obsession" with Haiti.

Obsession?

Like Mother, Francis never understood the importance of Mia's welfare.

She certainly seemed to understand my responsibilities with Global Vision when we were dating. I'd hoped, naively, that Francis would weather our time apart. Though that seemed to be true, it was young TJ she was trying to protect. He needs consistency.

In the meantime, I've moved back to the cottage in Meridian. Returning to the quiet house hasn't been good for me mentally. My mind, when idle, goes to my time spent in Haiti, the good and the bad.

Thankfully, Max has come to my rescue with a year-long mission to the Indonesian Archipelago. Francis assures me that two-year-old TJ will never know the difference.

The divorce was final last month. I see the legal sized envelope sticking out from my books, too big to be tucked out of sight. Irreconcilable differences. It sounds so pathetic.

Thank God for Global.

February 20, 2001

It's been four years now since my last entry, but recent events leave me with nowhere else to express the depth of my emotions. There is no one in my life who could possibly understand.

Billy called with news that shook me right down to my bones. He'd discovered Jean attempting to violate Mia.

Billy said that Mia insisted he keep quiet, and he stupidly agreed to let her tell her mother in her own time.

"I've failed you, Ellis," he said, his voice cracking with emotion, "and I've failed poor Mia."

The blame lay with *me*, though, for never challenging Jean the way I should have. I should have tried harder. I should have fought for Mia and Luisa before it came to this.

My heart ached for all involved. All but Jean, of course. I gazed at Mia's photo on my desk. So young then, but on the cusp of adolescence now.

Billy urged me to allow him to reveal his involvement to Luisa. "Once she understands, we can make a sensible plan to get Mia and her out of that house."

But after so many years, I feared how that could jeopardize his access to them. I couldn't risk it. Instead, I contacted my lawyer to double down on gaining custody. He said since Mia resides with her mother in Haiti and I have no proof of paternity, it's all up to Luisa. Without her signature on the paternity filing, I'm stuck.

Unless . . . there is another option. Now that Aristide has been re-elected, I'm hopeful that if I apply for re-entry, his administration will see the unjustness of my expulsion from Haiti and lift it.

Billy recommended patience. "There are hundreds more applications just like yours," he said, warning me of resistance within Aristide's administration.

And now I wait. Always waiting.

March 12, 2001

I'm riding an emotional rollercoaster. This morning Billy emailed with news about Jean. "The devil has been vanquished," read the subject line. Jean had been sent packing from the cinderblock after Mia finally told Luisa what he'd done that night Billy intervened.

Knowing that Jean was no longer in the house, I felt it was safe to write, explaining (for the umpteenth time) the events leading to my removal from Haiti. I wrote, too, of my current life, imperfect as it is. But I said that I have a safe and comfortable home where I hope she and Mia will come to live. This was a bold request. Until now, Jean had been successfully censoring the mail, and the letter would catch her off guard.

Still awaiting approval on my re-entry application, I mentioned in the letter that I'd begun proceedings to prove my paternity as well, but that I'd need her cooperation and consent. Should she agree, this would pave the way for their visa applications. Should she agree, I'll be one step closer to custody. And now I'm more hopeful than ever that I'll be allowed to come for her and Mia myself.

I poured my heart out in the letter—reminding her about the engagement ring I've held onto for all these years.

"I love you," I wrote. "I've never stopped loving you."

For years, I've been sending Billy money to assist Luisa how he saw fit. But now, without Jean's contribution from JC's, she'd need more help. What about Mia's school? What about the gangs? I told him now that I could cover these expenses, too.

❧

Since I cannot be there for Mia, I've decided to make more of an effort with TJ. My travel schedule prevents me from seeing him as often as either of us would like. But I asked Francis to bring him around to the cottage, and she graciously agreed.

He's a shy boy. He's tall for a six-year-old, giving the impression that he's older and wiser. Many—teachers, especially, but peers, too—expect more from him than he's capable of. So, I brought TJ into the stable and introduced him to the two horses I'd recently adopted. I hoped that one of the horses—probably Freddy, the gentlest of the two—would help TJ with his confidence the way my Ezra had helped me when I was young. But TJ was indifferent to the horses and had no interest in anything beyond his Game Boy.

We were strangers.

This happens in divorce. This happens when a child is alienated from their parent. It makes me wonder what Mia must think of me.

Still no word from Luisa. Still no word on my application.

My hands are tied.

CHAPTER 24

Partway through the green notebook, Mia skimmed what remained, uninterested in the details of life on the move and Francis's whining about—everything. Then she snapped the notebook closed and scanned the floor at the mess she'd made, before setting it aside. She didn't have time to read all the notebooks. She flipped through the first few pages of a midnight blue spiral one and was debating whether to continue when she noticed a significant date.

August 4, 2004.

A day she'd fought to forget. The day Uncle Jean had raped her.

"Mia?" TJ stood at the open door with two steaming cups of coffee.

"What time is it?" she asked, looking up from the clutter.

TJ stepped into the room and handed her a cup. She blew on it and watched the steam swirling dizzily like the thoughts in her head.

"Quarter to five," TJ said. "I couldn't sleep."

Mia pushed the notebooks into two piles: those she'd read and those she hadn't.

TJ knelt beside her and opened another scrapbook, laying it on the floor between them. Mia saw a picture of Ezra on a flier from the Nelson County animal shelter. The caption read, Four-year-old German Shepard mix. Male. Fully vaccinated. Good with children. Behind that were his adoption papers, with Ellis's distinctive signature—an elaborate E—on the dotted line. A vision of the German shepherd bounding out of Ellis's car passed through Mia's mind.

"I thought he was a stray," TJ said.

"Me too." This, together with the revelation that Billy wasn't just some good Samaritan, made her wonder about other seeming coincidences in her life.

The tuition for St. Michel's that materialized as a scholarship after Mama pushed Uncle Jean from the house on Rue Janvier, or the mysterious absence of the gangs who'd regularly demanded payment when Uncle Jean lived with them. That was Ellis, too.

She turned to the next page and noticed a report card from her first year at Meridian High School as well as newspaper photos of her from when she'd arrived. The caption read, Meridian celebrates Haitian immigrant with open arms and open hearts.

Mia winced.

"Fuck that," said TJ.

"It wasn't so bad," said Mia, recalling the French teacher and Natalie.

"Right. You just took off and never came back 'cause everything was so good. Like I said: fuck that."

Mia hadn't come back for many reasons, and the way the town had treated her was the least of them. She'd been more impacted by her history with Ellis and the way she'd left things with TJ. It was time to face the subject they'd been dancing around since she came home.

"TJ, about that night," she said.

"What night?" TJ said.

"That night you called from jail."

TJ sighed. "Really? You want to dig that up?"

Mia stared at him, open mouthed. *Really?* It seemed to her that from the tone of his phone call the other day, he'd been chomping at the bit to "dig that up."

"Okay," he said, leaning back against the bed. "Okay, well, I waited, Mia. I waited a week until Ellis bailed me out. *Ellis!*" TJ's eyes bored into her. "I told you—"

Mia frowned. "You were *waiting* for me? But I said I couldn't come. That whole situation—it was so far out of my depth. I *had* to call Ellis."

TJ shook his head. "Is *that* why you stayed away for so long? You thought I was *mad* at you?"

"I left so many messages, trying to apologize, but—nothing." She still felt the pain of rejection like it had been yesterday. "You blew me off after that."

"Blew *you* off?" TJ chuckled in disbelief. "Ellis took my phone, then sent me to my mom's. I thought you blew *me* off."

Mia's heart sank. The years she'd spent detached from her brother. All because of a misunderstanding.

"That's not why I stayed away, though," Mia said. "Not completely."

"Why, then?" TJ asked. Mia thought about her graduation and her absent family. It seemed silly now. Petulant, even. But it was more than that. It was something that had been building up since childhood, resulting in what she now saw as a massive chip on her shoulder.

I always hated you.

How could she explain to TJ what she still struggled to understand, especially after reading Ellis's first-hand account of how wrong she'd been?

"It wasn't because of you," she said. She closed the scrapbook and pushed it aside, thinking of the man who'd swept her up in his arms when she was five and how Mama had ripped her from him. How Uncle Jean had assumed himself into the father role, while her real father pined for her.

TJ sighed. "I was never mad at you, Mia."

"I understand that now. I'm sorry." It felt good to apologize, but that didn't change the fact that she'd missed the last seven years with her brother.

Mia crossed her arms and looked over at TJ, wondering what life at the Ellis estate would have been like without him.

"GG called last night, TJ said.

"I heard the phone. You spoke with her?"

"No, just the message. No change in Ellis's condition. That's why I couldn't sleep."

"I didn't realize you and Ellis were close," Mia said.

"I don't know that we were. He wasn't the best father in the world—but I think he tried, you know, a little." He flipped the scrapbook back open to a string of photos of Mia from volleyball, field hockey, and a picture of Mia grooming Freddy. Ellis had kept a copy of her acceptance letter from Northwestern University with her SAT score. There was a picture of her standing outside her dorm, a heavy backpack slung over her shoulder. Chrissy stood nearby, distracted by something out of the frame. Had Ellis taken that photo?

TJ grinned as if to tease. "Looks like you had a secret admirer," he said, taking a sip of his coffee.

Admirer? Yes. In a way, Mia supposed. Much of what she'd read rang contrary to everything she'd believed. He'd loved Mama and wanted her and Mia to live with him. He'd tracked her life in Haiti and the States. He'd known he was a poor communicator but showed his love in so many other ways. Why hadn't she seen it? How could she have been so blind? What else lay hidden in this trove of memories?

TJ flipped through the remaining pages until he reached the end. The Northwestern graduation invitation was taped to the last page. Her heart skipped a beat. She wasn't sure what it meant. He'd either seen it and ignored it, or he'd gone to the ceremony only to find that she'd skipped it.

Why, she wondered, *given Ellis's obvious love for me as expressed in the scrapbook and his journals, couldn't he have been nicer to me in person? Or was that just what I wanted to see?*

TJ gulped the last of his coffee and yawned. "What's in the notebooks?"

"They're journals. Some go way back."

"Anything about me?" He started combing through the notebooks without selecting any.

"Some. I'm only up to 2004."

"Ah, the year you came on the scene." TJ smiled sweetly.

Mia smiled back. "You were good to me."

"Yes, I was." He winked and stood to go. "More coffee?"

Mia glanced at the remaining notebooks, wondering if she really wanted to read any more. Maybe later, though. She was running on fumes, and she still had that healthcare directive to find.

"Yeah, thanks," she said.

She followed him out to the kitchen. Her legs and back ached as if she'd been riding her motorcycle all night.

She sat at the table thinking how the notebooks revealed more than she'd ever hoped to know, but Ellis wasn't prepared to say.

Mia hadn't made it easy for him, either. A teenager with a chip on her shoulder. It wasn't how she saw the situation at the time, but it was clear as day now. She'd pushed him away long before she'd arrived, and his quiet nature couldn't get through that wall.

TJ hummed as he fixed the coffee, oblivious to Mia's mounting self-blame. She wished she could be more like him, going with the flow, living in the moment. When she'd arrived at the cottage years after turning her back on the Ellis family, she'd expected a cold reception. But Oscar, Rosa, and TJ had all welcomed her as if no time had passed. She gazed up at TJ, who'd just set out two freshly cleaned cups.

"What," he said. "What are you grinning at?"

Her grin widened. "You."

"Oh, you like me now, do you?" He glanced at the pot, seemingly dissatisfied with its progress.

"I never told you how glad I was to learn I had a brother."

TJ nodded. "Your actions told me."

After Mia finished her coffee, she returned to Ellis's room and the blue notebook, unsure if her trembling hands had more to do with the caffeine or the date she'd seen in the notebook's first few pages. Either way, she knew she was about to reopen some old wounds. Taking a deep breath, she sat at the desk and lifted the cover.

CHAPTER 25
The Blue Notebook

August 4, 2004

I'm not being overly dramatic when I say this truly is a godless world. Rage boils in my blood, and I'm at my wit's end.

Billy called this morning, sobbing, his words tumbling out incoherently, but for one.

Mia.

My whole body began to tremble.

I had to ask him to repeat himself. He gasped as if he hadn't taken a full breath in days. "M-Mia . . . raped."

The air in my room, hot and humid, closed in on me. Then the earth beneath my feet seemed to tilt, and I fell against the desk.

"It can't be true," I said. It was a lifeline, something to grasp onto. Billy moaned as if he shared my agony.

The police arrested the neighbor, Jonas, but when Mia finally spoke up, she revealed it was Jean. He'd caught her in town during the protests outside the courthouse.

Jean took her to the shop. She didn't have a chance.

"I have to get them out of there!" I said, my mind jumping from one ill-conceived idea to the next—including sneaking into Haiti and slipping out again with Mia. That was a ridiculous plan. I'd be risking another prison sentence for entering the country illegally and for kidnapping.

The coup d'état in February dashed any hope that my expulsion from Haiti would be removed. Aristide promptly resigned his fragile grasp on power and fled the country. I am heartbroken for Haiti and the unrelenting power struggle it has suffered under, and I rage against the circumstances I find myself in.

"What about custody?"

I knew it was a nonstarter the moment the words passed my lips. No paternity equals no custody. Billy said he'd already spoken with Luisa. She wasn't on board. Mia's life was with her in Haiti.

I've been a fool—such a damn fool to think Luisa would come around on her own. Now, of course, there was no choice. I said I'd resend the paternity documents directly to Billy. He'd see to it that she signs them.

And if she still refuses? I cannot entertain the idea.

What is her objection at this point? A life without constant fear? There's no logic to it. Of course, if she refuses to speak with me, I cannot turn her around.

Before ending the call, Billy assured me he would try again but would wait for the dust to settle. If he pushed too hard, she'd resist. He begged me to be patient.

Patient? I'd love nothing more than to strike that word from the dictionary.

❦

I needed an outlet equal to my emotions—an escape to an isolated village in India, maybe, or Somalia. Anywhere I could replace my pain with work.

I wasted no time calling Max, who told me to take a breath.

"I'll go anywhere. Just find me a post."

"We're putting something together in Burundi," Max said. He'd need a week or so to line it up. But "a week or so" in Max-speak could be much longer. Global had a feast-or-famine budget, and their dependence on donations could mean the difference between one week and eight.

"Be patient," Max said.

He and Billy should have known by now that patience was not my strong suit.

September 28, 2004

It's been nearly two months since I wrote about Mia's rape. Even now, I find it difficult to print the word. My heartbreak grew heavier two weeks later when Billy informed me that Luisa had received a devastating diagnosis - she had a terminal form of cancer, which had spread. Billy said she refused treatment. REFUSED TREATMENT!

To make matters worse, I was powerless to help. If only she'd been here! And, of course, there was Mia to consider. Poor Mia.

I'm rambling, but I have good reason.

Today, I learned Luisa succumbed to the very disease that ended her own mother's life.

I'm devastated. When Billy first told me of her diagnosis, I'd held on to a sliver of hope that he was wrong. That the doctors had no idea what they were talking about. Sadly, no, but I'm consoled that, before her death, she'd agreed to send Mia to the States. To me. It's not the fantasy I'd imagined, but I'll gladly take it and hold it as a gift close to my heart.

She'd given Billy power of attorney along with signing the paternity papers. That settled, I needed to pull myself together and lay the foundation for Mia's arrival. There was no time to lose.

Days after Luisa passed, a hurricane swept the island. Since then, securing safe passage for Mia has proved challenging. I don't want to take risks, but the few boats allowed to leave the island will be booked if we wait.

Billy found an independent captain who agreed to take Mia to Florida, even in rough seas.

"Do you trust this man?" I asked. The last thing I want is to hear my daughter had been lost at sea or violated—again. We'd planned to have Billy accompany her, but his obligations in Port-au-Prince were too great, especially after the recent storm.

Billy reassured me that the captain had a stellar reputation. His boat was small but seaworthy.

I frequently returned to Billy's email for updates. He masterfully secured a visa, a provisional passport, and a spot for Mia on the boat, but I won't be ready to relax until she's in my custody.

Billy warned me that Mia was in a fragile state after everything she's been through. I was a stranger to her, and Billy said she'd confided her fear of me.

Right. Of course. While I'd had eyes and ears on her life, she knew nothing about me. I will heed Billy's advice and wait for Mia to warm to me.

I hope it won't take long.

October 2, 2004

I am thrilled that, after a lifetime of waiting, my beloved Mia has arrived and is resting peacefully upstairs. The long, exhausting events of the day went like this.

I left the cottage at dawn this morning and drove all day to the small Florida port where Billy said the boat would tie up. The storm, though no longer a hurricane, had ravaged much of the Florida coast. Its residual wind and rain shadowed me through the state like my personal black cloud.

I waited in my car for hours with no boat in sight and feared I was in the wrong place—or worse, that the boat had been lost to the storm. A dull ache nested in my chest as I stared out to sea.

A guilty pang gripped me as I recalled the last and only time I'd seen Mia. It was on the heels of Hurricane Gordon in 1994.

I'm sickened by my ignorance now as I think how simple it would have been to fly to the DR and have Billy take her to meet me at the border. She would already be with me, and neither of us would be in this predicament.

Please, let her be safe.

I ignored my hunger, refusing to leave my post as I kept my eyes peeled for the boat carrying my beloved girl. Dusk fell, and daylight was lost. I noticed a commotion further down the harbor. A port official stepped out from the little terminal and jogged toward an open dock. I followed, barely able to breathe.

A boat appeared on the horizon, its lights shining red one moment, then green, as it pitched in the wind and waves. Finally, it entered the calmer waters of the harbor.

As the boat puttered closer, I saw how small it was. It wasn't much more than a fishing boat. The nets were bound tightly to booms tucked up and out of the way. I found it hard to believe it could have come all the way from Haiti.

Two men lowered fat white fenders over the side as the boat sidled up to the dock. Then, a weary, dark-skinned man stepped onto the deck and called out in Creole. "We have arrived!" Relieved, I took a full breath.

The captain went below deck while his crew busily tied up. When he emerged with Mia, I nearly collapsed from relief.

She was safe, though she looked terrified and confused, hugging her backpack to her chest, her eyes focused on her feet as she stepped cautiously across the deck. I stared up at her face, which resembled Luisa's so vividly that I felt as if I'd entered the little cinderblock house all over again.

I realized the official was an immigration agent and hoped there would be no trouble as the captain disembarked and approached him, papers in hand. Mia followed. Her chin-length braids swung in the steady wind. She was ashen-faced and stooped over her backpack. *Look at me*, I begged with my eyes as the official looked over the documents. Finally, she looked up into my face, her own eyes wide and fearful.

"*You*," I said, entranced by her resemblance to Luisa. Mia looked away sharply. Then I realized I'd been staring—how could I not? Yet Billy had warned me that Mia was not a willing emigrant and that I'd have to be cautious with her.

The agent suggested she'd have to be detained unless someone could take custody. I removed my identification from my breast pocket.

"I'm her father," I said, my heart soaring with pride.

Mia shivered. The captain draped a protective arm across her shoulder. By the look in her eyes, he'd only frightened her more.

"Step away from the girl," I said in Creole.

A woman dashed from the office and draped Mia in a blanket, then led her back to the building.

The immigration agent held a clipboard out to the captain for his signature. Proof of delivery? The captain reached into his shirt pocket and removed a silver Montblanc like the one I'd left behind in Haiti.

"Where did you get that?" I asked. The captain examined the pen and smirked.

"It belongs to the girl," he said. He signed the document with it and, after a moment's thought, handed it to me.

The next couple of hours were a nightmare as I fought to prove my custody—signatures that didn't match and dates that were out of order. My passport photo didn't look like my driver's license. It felt like 1988 Haiti all over again.

The agent explained they were being extra cautious because most Haitians arrived without documents, with some seeking asylum and almost all denied entry. But thanks to Billy, Mia had a legal visa, and her citizenship status was pending. We went around in circles, but I won out in the end. Two hours after her arrival, they finally released her.

I watched her emerge cautiously from the office, head bent as she put one foot in front of the other, closing the gap between us. A van pulled up beside her and threw open the door. A man wearing a black raincoat jumped out. Mia lurched and vomited on the pavement. I rushed toward her, gripping her by the hand, and hurried her toward my car before they could take her. But the man stepped in front of us.

"Get out of our way," I said.

He shoved a clipboard in my face. "Your signature," he said. I took the clipboard and scrawled my signature on the page.

Finally, she was mine.

An hour from Meridian, Max called with my next post. The timing couldn't have been worse.

"I *can't*," I said.

"You begged for this, Ellis," Max said. I glanced at Mia, curled into a ball in the backseat, my jacket draped over her.

"Things are different," I said, trying to keep my voice down. I pleaded my case, but Mia stirred, so I hung up, knowing I'd have to drive to Indianapolis to confront Max in person. It wasn't ideal. Mia would arrive at her new home only to have the one familiar face leave her with strangers. But it will only be for a few hours, and Rosa will know how to handle it, which is probably for the best.

We arrived in Meridian early this afternoon. I felt anxious about having to leave Mia, but Rosa and Oscar were waiting with open arms. Any fears I'd had regarding her transition were put to rest. It's not perfect, but I think it will work out.

The single most difficult moment, though, was when Mia called me *Papa*. How my heart soared to hear that word from her lips. But Billy had advised me to take it slow with her, and the look on her face told me she wasn't ready. I hope I wasn't mistaken.

I think now to my greeting on the dock. "*You*," I'd said, and wonder now if Luisa had told her of this endearment. It seemed not, but I thought nothing of it at the time and now I see how she might have found it a strange thing to say. Perhaps, over time, she'll understand.

Just as I hope there will be a time when she can call me *Papa* without fear in her eyes.

I eagerly await that day.

PART FOUR
Unity Makes Strength

CHAPTER 26

Mia closed the blue notebook and squeezed her eyes shut tight against the memory of her arrival to Meridian. To top it off, she was forced to confront the memory of Uncle Jean pinning her to the floor of his shop and of the anguish that followed. Mama's illness, death. The forms signed to facilitate Mia's departure from Haiti. It had all happened so fast.

Papa, she'd called him. By his account, she hadn't been ready for that. His sensitivity only alienated her. And magnified any fear she'd had of him before leaving Haiti.

You, the endearment reserved for Mama, also hit Mia hard. She'd believed it was his lack of connection to her. She hadn't known then that it was *because* of his connection, not because he was trying to avoid it. But how was she to know? And why had he kept up with the practice of referring to her this way when she'd pushed back?

"You will call me Ellis," he'd said when she arrived. No, that wasn't it. Mia searched her early memories of her arrival to Meridian. "You *may* call me Ellis." It wasn't a command. He'd given her a choice, but she hadn't understood.

Mia glanced at the photo on the desk. "Papa," she said, remembering the first time he was there for her. His strong arms wrapped around her as the hurricane grew.

He'd been able to document the history of their family from the moment he'd met Mama to the moment they'd fallen into one another's arms. The account felt raw and personal. *This* was Ellis. In his writing, he was a romantic. Completely unlike the stern, quiet, and emotionally stunted man she knew.

Not having changed her position on the floor in hours, Mia tried to stand. *Emotionally stunted.* That's what Kali had called *her*. She shook out the pins and needles and reached for her toes in a deep stretch, then walked away from the mess and trudged upstairs for a shower to bring herself to life.

She passed TJ in the hall, hair damp from his own shower.

"Did you find what you were looking for?" he asked.

"Not yet." She realized she'd stopped looking for the health directive the moment she'd opened the red notebook.

Instead of answering the questions that had plagued her all her life, the notebooks produced more.

Why did he risk arrest during the hurricane but not when Uncle Jean assaulted her? Why hadn't Billy told Mama of his association with Ellis? Why was Ellis able to pour his heart out on paper but never to Mia's face?

The final straw for Mia had been when he hadn't replied to the graduation invitation. Yet he'd kept it all these years. Why?

Only Ellis could answer. She *had* to find that directive.

Mia remembered the shoe boxes and countless folders among the spoils from the file cabinet. The directive must be there somewhere.

The shower failed to remove the sting of regret over Mia's hateful words. Instead, she fixated on all the ways she'd tested Ellis over the years, expecting him to fail while subconsciously hoping he wouldn't. What she'd learned from the journals was that she never knew him.

That was at the center of everything.

She'd been wrong about him in every possible way.

Mia returned to Ellis's room and kicked aside the scrapbooks, wondering what she was going to say when she saw him. How could she possibly make it up to him?

A mottled yellow composition book caught her eye. It lay in a shaft of sunlight slipping through the closed window shade. Mia couldn't resist picking it up.

Though she knew she was running out of time, she leafed through the first few pages and stopped cold when she came across a passage about her emotional exit the day she'd left for college.

She'd told Oscar to stop the car and charged into the cottage in a rage.

"I'm a broken man," he'd written. "She thinks I'm cruel, that I don't know her and that it's too late. I do know her. She says I'm a stranger. I guess I am. But that will change."

Mia read on to where he'd decided to collect his journals and the facts about his life that he'd never been capable of saying aloud and open up to Mia without the guilt or shame that haunted him for his inability to free her from the difficult life she led in Haiti.

He'd intended to box up the journals, scrapbooks, and memorabilia, and hand them over as a Christmas gift, telling her how much he loved her, what she and Mama meant to him, imagining the moment as something beautiful and sacred. But he lost his nerve and locked it all away in the old file cabinet.

Mia held back brimming tears as she flipped to the part where he'd told her about the cabinet, failing again to say what he'd intended, instead choosing to leave her to discover the contents on her own should something happen to him. He feared his next mission could be his last, yet foolishly took the risk.

Mia skimmed the pages that followed and saw the entry for Afghanistan. When the village was attacked, he'd been trapped in a mountainside hut. The hut was bombed, and he'd been taken prisoner and beaten before being freed by a team of British soldiers.

Mia looked for details of his injuries, wondering if they had led to his strokes.

I always hated you.

Mia was about to dive into the pile of "project" folders to see if, by chance, one contained his health directive, when she spotted one of the shoeboxes lying on its side with the lid open.

With a quick look at her watch, she pushed the lid aside and found a bundle of letters—all addressed to her little house in Port-au-Prince and all stamped Return to Sender.

Her hands began to tremble as she lifted the corner of the first unopened envelope. Then drew her hand away. It felt like a violation. Yet wasn't this why Ellis had told her about the file cabinet? Hadn't he *wanted* her to know everything?

Mia tucked her finger under the flap again and slid it down the side. She removed the letter and delicately unfolded it. It was written in French. The butterflies in her chest made it difficult to breathe as she read the first words.

Chère Vous,

Je t'aime beaucoup.

For the first time in her life, she saw her parents as two people who'd loved one another—once. Mia dabbed welling tears with her shirt sleeve and returned to the letter.

Ellis described in detail his trip to the jewelry store, the ring he'd purchased for her, and his subsequent arrest, imprisonment, and expulsion from Haiti. He begged Luisa to join him in the States, gushing at the prospect of becoming a family and the countless opportunities awaiting her and their child.

Mia gently folded the letter, returned it to its envelope, and opened the next. This one sounded hopeful but hinted at desperation.

Why haven't you written? I can only guess that you're in trouble. If only there was something I could do from here . . .

Mia dropped that letter and opened the next one, which suggested he'd wired money. One after the other, the letters grew increasingly dark.

But she realized the blame for so much of Ellis's heartbreak was Uncle Jean. Their shared nemesis.

She was placing the lid back on the box when she heard a car door slam. She peeked out the window surprised to see Kali standing beside her car, looking from the stable to the big house.

Mia thought of her text warning Kali off from coming and felt a rush of relief that it went ignored.

After everything she'd just read—everything she'd just learned— Mia needed Kali to help her understand the emotions colliding within her. To reconcile her toxic guilt against her new and deep-abiding love for her father.

She thought of his inability to show the affection he felt so deeply and her own inability to do the same. Father and daughter, muddling through life along parallel lines.

Mia rushed through the living room and threw open the front door.

"Kali!" she called, her heart racing.

Kali spun on her heels. Her long dark hair, usually pulled back in a French braid, hung free about her shoulders, as if she'd just rolled out of bed. Mia wanted to bury her face in it, knowing how soft it would be, how sweet it would smell.

Kali's eyes locked on Mia, and she smiled. A beaming smile that instantly disarmed her. Mia took a deep breath and held the door wide open.

Kali rushed to Mia's side, and when the door closed behind them, Mia felt as if they were alone in the world. Kali examined Mia's face and frowned.

"What did you do to your beautiful hair?"

"Um, right. I did this for the interview. Don't you like it?"

Kali ran her hand over Mia's head. "I do. It's classy. Now tell me what's going on. How are you? How's Ellis?"

Mia didn't have an answer. Instead, she led the way to Ellis's room and fanned out her arms toward the messy desk, the bed with the stinky blanket, and the journals, scrapbooks, and debris from the busted cabinet strewn across the floor.

"Oh, my God!" Kali said, turning to Mia. "What happened?"

Mia reached for the photograph of her as a small child in Haiti, looking out the window at the stranger in the yard. At the man who was much less of a stranger now.

Kali took the photograph and examined it. "Is this you?"

Mia nodded, and Kali turned to the mess again. "I don't understand."

"Do you remember what I said about Ellis?" Mia said.

Kali nodded. "He's not like other dads."

"I've learned something since then." She glanced at the mess strewn across the floor.

They settled onto Ellis's unmade bed, and Mia began to tell her story. The abuse at the hands of her Uncle Jean. The rape. The storms. Her mother's death. The terrifying journey to the United States. And the socially awkward man who'd brought her back to the little cottage where she was now drowning in the sea of his truth that had been scattered across the floor.

Kali listened intently as Mia spoke. The story had been buried so deeply that even Mia was moved to tears in the retelling. She described her Uncle Jean's demon loa. How she'd be cursed if she ever told a soul.

"But the curse was a figment of a young girl's imagination," said Kali. She wrapped an arm across Mia's shoulders, drawing her closer. Mia felt her warm breath on her neck.

"No," Mia said. "It was very real—just not how I'd thought. I'd cursed myself to a life of silence, unable to confide my most private thoughts and unable to break down the silent barrier between me and the people I loved. I kept this secret to protect Mama and Auntie Sis, and because I was terrified that Uncle Jean would retaliate, which he did when he raped me then took the house after Mama died. I maintained my silence when I arrived in the States, terrified that if anyone knew the truth of it, judgment would follow. And pity." Mia put her hand against Kali's cheek. "I see pity in your face now."

"Not pity," Kali said. "You see gratitude. You see trust. You see love."

Mia searched Kali's face—her dark eyes, flushed cheeks, and quivering lower lip. They held one another close. One mind and one heart.

Kali twitched her nose. "What in God's name is that smell?"

"What smell?"

"Like—wet dog," Kali said. Mia reached for the wool blanket and brought it to her nose. She'd thought it was mildew, but Kali was right. Dog. On closer inspection, she saw dark hairs, which she hadn't noticed earlier. Ezra. Mia remembered TJ saying that Ellis had taken in the dog when she'd left for college. Maybe to feel closer to Mia. Or maybe because he, too, needed a friend.

"May I read the journals?" Kali asked, shyly. But when Mia hesitated, she added, "It's fine. You don't have to—"

"No," Mia said. "It's not that. I want to share them—need to, really." She checked her watch. "It's the directive. I still haven't found it and I'm running out of time."

"How can I help?"

Mia pointed to a bundle of old files on the floor beside the desk. Kali knelt and got to work.

Mia returned to Ellis's desk to sort through the files she'd set aside earlier in her search for the key. She flipped through the tabs—each one a "project," named for whatever mission they applied to. Halfway through, she found one that had nothing to do with a country, or political unrest.

Project Mia. She swallowed hard.

Inside the folder were two rejected applications for custody. Both included an attached form letter stating there had not been enough evidence provided. The missing article was Mama's official statement for the proof of paternity certificate.

Uncle Jean undoubtedly intercepted the first request, but the second was after he'd moved out. Mama had ignored the request on her own. However, the next sheet in the file was a signed certificate of paternity dated shortly before she died.

There was a birth certificate, though. Mia still had it from when Billy showed it to her before she'd left Haiti. Father: Theodore Michael Ellis, III. They didn't *need* the paternity forms.

Tell him I'm sorry, Mama said at the end. Was this why? She had had the opportunity for years and had done nothing. It wasn't Ellis who had denied Mia a better life. It was Mama.

Up was down. Down was up.

But how could she be angry with Mama when Ellis hadn't been? And how could she ignore her own reluctance to leave Haiti when the time came?

Mia swallowed hard and set the form aside, then, checking her watch, focused on the last two documents in the folder, a copy of Mia's visa application signed by Billy, who'd been granted power of attorney, and a photocopy of her provisional passport. This was what Ellis had fought for. Everything he'd collected over the years to bring her home.

Home. At the time, she'd had only one home—Haiti.

But now?

Home was here in this little house. Ellis's house. Her house.

"Kali? Come look at this."

Kali stood, stretched, and placed a hand on Mia's shoulder. Mia took the ring from its box and held it out. "He'd meant it for Mama."

"Oh, Mia," Kali said, taking the ring from Mia. "After all these years, how could he never have told you?"

Mia sighed and buried her face in Kali's shoulder, the sweet smell of her hair filling her senses. "I'm just like him."

"No. I don't believe that, and neither should you," said Kali, holding Mia closer.

"It's true. I'm sorry I never told you any of this sooner. I'm just so—so—emotionally stunted." Just as the words left her mouth, Mia began sobbing.

Kali laughed gently. "Not with tears like that!"

Mia grinned half-heartedly. After years of reining in her emotions, she was ready to let them go. "You know it's true. I did shut you out. I never told you how much you mean to me—to my life."

"And I never should have made you feel guilty about that," Kali said. "I know how you feel about me. It's in your eyes. I see it whenever you look at me."

Their embrace was interrupted by Mia's phone. A text from TJ telling her to hurry. "They're talking about removing the breathing tube."

Was that a good thing? A sign he was recovering? Or a sign they'd given up?

Ellis had given her a comfortable life and people to love, like

Rosa, Oscar, and TJ. He'd also given her Freddy, Ezra, and the space and freedom to explore. Mia stared at the frame on Ellis's desk. She'd believed the man who'd taken that photograph had abandoned her, but the opposite was true. He was there for her the whole time.

Another text came in. An urgent request from TJ.

"We have to go," Mia said, slipping the ring onto her finger.

"But the directive . . ."

"There isn't time."

CHAPTER 27

Kali drove as Mia willed the car to go faster, her head buzzing with what she'd say to Ellis if he were alive—and how she'd cope if he weren't. It was suddenly clear that although she hadn't loved him before, she loved him dearly now. She needed to apologize for not trying to get to know him, for not listening when his actions spoke louder than words, for assuming he'd abandoned her and her mother, and so much more.

I always hated you.

She especially needed to apologize for *that.*

When they arrived, Mia charged into the hospital and ran up the stairs with Kali on her heels. She held her phone in one hand and her jacket in the other. The second floor waiting room was like a scene from every hospital drama she'd ever watched. A cast of characters seated in twos and threes. Among the strangers in the room, she saw her grandmother sitting with TJ, Francis sitting beside Rosa. She caught Oscar's eye, and he bounced out of his seat, his Chicago

Cubs hat twisted in his hands. Mia saw the worry lines knitted across his brow as he came to her for a hug.

"Is there any word?" Mia asked as he wrapped her in his warm arms.

"No news yet, but—"

Mia followed his gaze, which had landed on Kali. She released him.

Kali took a couple of steps back. "I don't belong here," she murmured. But Mia reached for her hand and kissed it.

"Everyone?" she said. "This is Kali." She paused. "My girlfriend." This wasn't how Mia imagined she'd come out to them. She had never considered coming out at all.

TJ had already known. He'd been there when Natalie broke up with her, but he grinned and glanced around at the others for their reaction.

Francis looked confused at first. When the lightbulb went off, her mouth dropped open.

Rosa joined Oscar, who was already reaching out to Kali for a bear hug. Mia was thrilled by the response from everyone except GG.

GG shook her head with a *humph*. "I always knew there was something off about you."

What's that supposed to mean? Mia thought, then let it go. This wasn't the time or place.

When Oscar finally released Kali, Rosa stepped in for a hug of her own. "Welcome," she said.

"Sit down, all of you." GG scowled. "You're making a scene."

Mia tucked her phone into her jacket before draping it over

the chair across from TJ, then sat down. Kali sat beside her as she leaned forward, bridging the gulf between them. "I thought you had news," she murmured.

TJ shrugged. "He's off the ventilator. It's all I know."

"Is he talking yet?" When TJ didn't answer, Mia prodded. "TJ?"

He stared at her, hands gripping his knees. "They're holding him for more tests. Last I heard, he was waiting for an MRI. It's taking ages."

Mia wondered if they'd found another blood clot.

An announcement from an overhead speaker grabbed their attention. "Dr. Patel. Room 216. Dr. Patel. Room 216."

"That's Ellis's room!" TJ said.

Mia clutched Kali's hand as Becky—the nurse Mia had seen during her first visit—took off running, her squeaky shoes marking her progress down the hall.

Mia approached the desk, where one nurse remained focused on a computer screen. Kali joined her.

"Theodore Ellis," Kali said. "What's his status?"

"I have to see him," Mia insisted. "It's urgent." The nurse looked at her, then at Kali.

"You're family?" she asked Kali.

"Yes," Mia answered. The nurse blinked.

"That's his *daughter*," Nurse Becky said, returning to the desk. "The doctor is on his way. Please, take a seat."

Mia and Kali exchanged worried glances and went back to their chairs.

"What's happening?" TJ asked.

"Hush," GG said. "Here he comes."

Dr. Patel arrived, looking harried. He found an empty chair and moved it closer to the group. Mia held her breath. Would Ellis live? Would she get to say what she'd come to say? *He needs to know how I feel. He needs to know that I love him.*

"Hello, all," Dr. Patel said, nodding at Mia. "Thank you for your patience."

"Is he all right?" Mia said impatiently. "What was all that commotion?"

Dr. Patel's frown reflected confusion rather than concern as he followed Mia's gaze.

Then, with a look of recognition, he shook his head. "That?"

"Room 216," Francis said.

"We were mistaken, ma'am. The call was for a patient in 215."

Mia felt a surge of relief flow through the group as Dr. Patel folded his hands on his lap. "I have encouraging news about Mr. Ellis, though. The last MRI scan came up negative, so the physical therapist has given him the green light to be admitted to a rehabilitation unit."

"Rehab?" Mia asked.

"Yes," he continued. "He's already showing signs of voluntary movement in his arm. His legs have not responded yet, but it's only a matter of time."

Mia sighed. "How much time?"

"Hard to tell. Every patient is different." He cleared his throat. "The first three to six months will be the most telling. I don't want to give any of you the idea that this will be fast or easy. But there are ways to measure his progress, and he's already on the path to recovery."

"Meaning?" Francis said, leaning in.

"The first sign we look for is spasticity. His arm was limp when he came. Now, you'll notice that his hands are taut. His muscles are seizing up." Dr. Patel glanced down at his own hands demonstrating what Ellis's hands looked like. One was crumpled, as if he was clenching something small. "It will look painful, but it's the first sign that his brain is making new connections."

"He'll make a full recovery, then?" asked GG, literally on the edge of her seat. For the first time, Mia realized that GG loved him—in her own way. Like Ellis and herself, she didn't know how to show it or say it. Still, this personality trait would never excuse how cruel she'd been to Mia.

"The truth is, he's got a ten percent shot at a full recovery," said the doctor. "A twenty-five percent of recovering with only minor impairments. There's a much higher chance of little to no recovery. I have no idea where he is on that scale at this point. But as I said, he's already healing, and that gives me hope. It should give you hope, too."

"Can we see him?" Mia asked. But immediately, she regretted saying "we." She'd wanted to see him alone. The insight she had now, after reading his journals, told her he'd want to see her alone, too. They had so much to say to one another.

Dr. Patel checked his watch and nodded. "Visiting hours are until eight tonight. I recommend you stagger your visits, though. You can work out how you want to handle that. He'll be moved to the rehab center in the morning."

GG reached out a feeble hand as the doctor stood to go. "Thank you," she said. He shook it gingerly and smiled.

"He's going to need your support," he said, looking around at the others. "That's paramount to recovery."

"Of course," GG said.

GG was the first to enter Ellis's room. Mia accepted it, begrudgingly. His mother. It only made sense. She held back in the hall, arms linked with Kali, feeling awkward and in the way as nurses and patients sped past. After ten minutes, Francis pushed by them, with TJ following apologetically in her wake. They barged into Ellis's room to stand with GG.

"There will be therapy," Kali said. "Lots of it. Physical, occupational, and psychological therapy for months. He'll probably get Prozac or something, too."

Mia frowned. "Prozac?"

"Depression is common in stroke patients. Recovery is tough, and even in the best cases, the victims lose a part of themselves. That's why the doctor said Ellis would need everyone's support." She looked pointedly into Mia's eyes. "It's impossible to get through trauma on one's own. Everyone needs a little help."

Mia smiled. "Right." She felt the truth of Kali's words now. Having shared the suffering in her past, she felt she was beginning to feel . . . lighter. "A little help."

From where Mia stood outside the room, she could see the base of Ellis's bed and the tented peak of his feet. He had huge feet, she noted for the first time. What else hadn't she noticed? She had a sense of his bearded face and commanding presence, but she couldn't recall the color of his eyes or the slope of his nose. What would he look like without the beard? Would he be as formidable? Was he handsome?

A cough from Ellis's open door alerted them to Francis's approach. Francis looked Kali up and down, then turned to Mia.

"They're wrapping up. I don't think I've ever seen your grandmother like that. She actually *kissed* him."

Kali reached for her phone, checked the screen, and put it back in her pocket.

"Who is it?" Mia asked.

"Nothing that can't wait," said Kali.

TJ emerged from the room next. Mia stepped to the side, hoping she'd eventually get to see more than Ellis's feet.

"He asked about you," TJ told her, leaning against the wall across the way. "We thought he was saying *Mommy* at first. GG loved that. But I'm sure he was saying *my Mia*."

Mia narrowed her eyes at him. "My Mia?"

"What else is he supposed to call you?"

Mia pictured Ellis on the Florida dock, his face blank as if he'd seen a ghost. He'd seen Mama. "You," he'd said. But Mia read it all wrong. Things would be different now that she understood where that odd term of endearment had sprung from.

GG stood in the open door. Her red-rimmed eyes betrayed her emotions. Mia felt a tug at her heart for the only grandmother she'd ever known. She didn't expect much from the old woman, but her feelings had softened some.

Rosa and Oscar were hanging back in the waiting room. Francis and TJ were already halfway down the hall.

Kali's phone rang again. "Answer that," Mia said. "It's probably important."

"Not as important as this," Kali said, reaching out for a hug.

Mia held her tight. "I'm nervous."

"You can do this," Kali said.

Mia felt each thump of her heart as she stepped into the room. The last words she'd said to her father lay on her chest like a ton of bricks. Her mouth was dry. Her hands felt damp. But when she saw his face, she could only smile.

He'd shaved. Or someone had shaved him. He looked like a boy rather than the bigger-than-life man she'd known.

"Am I in the right room?" she said, smiling. Ellis's mouth twisted as it had before, but now she saw it was a grin.

He mumbled something that sounded like "right room," though barely. Mia stepped closer, studying the new face. Blue eyes. Long, crooked nose. Pale, pink lips. He had a dimple on his chin and a mole under his right eye that she'd never noticed before. She felt like she was meeting the man for the first time. Perhaps she was.

Ellis's knuckles showed white on his gnarled fingers, reminding her of Billy. Mia pulled the chair close to the bed and reached for the fisted hand. He noticed the ring on her finger.

"*Papa*," Mia said. "You don't have to talk." He nodded, and she continued. "I have so much to say. The journals. The scrapbooks. This—this ring. May I keep it?"

Ellis nodded again, and Mia found the courage to come clean.

"I've been a blind fool," she began. "It was in front of me the whole time—your love for me and Mama. And the crazy thing is, I'm just like you."

Mia told him about the time she'd read her full name for the first time in Billy's apartment. *Mia Luise Ellis-Bacri.* She'd rejected it. But now she *wanted* the Ellis name. She was proud of his humanitarianism, and proud of his fight for her despite insurmountable obstacles.

The emotion of the moment was so powerful that despite Mia's smile, tears leaked from her eyes and dripped down her cheeks, and her nose started running uncontrollably. She gently pulled her hand away and sought out the tissue box beside the bed.

Ellis gazed at her with tearful eyes and his cockeyed grin. "I love you." The words were as clear as if there had been no impediment. He loved her. He always had. But she'd been just as lousy at expressing herself as he was. And now? What was it? Had the stroke brought him so close to death that he saw what she did? The wasted years of unspoken words that only found their outlet on the pages of his journals. It wasn't too late, though, for either of them. Mia laid a hand on his arm.

"I love you too, Papa," she said, and it felt wonderful.

Mia left the hospital with a light spirit, bolstered by having taken steps to resolve her emotional struggle with Ellis, and by the doctor's encouraging news of recovery.

When they reached the cottage, Mia and Kali went for a walk to the lake. Unlike the previous day, the sky was overcast, and the snow from the night before was beginning to melt.

"I used to come out here all the time," Mia said, looking down the path. "It was the only place I could breathe. The only place I could think clearly." She told Kali about Ezra, the rescue dog that turned out to be one of the many silent expressions of Ellis's love.

"Ezra? Interesting," Kali said. Mia looked at her with curiosity, and Kali said, "It's Hebrew for *helper*."

Mia explained that it had been the tag on an old collar from the barn. She'd learned in the journals that it belonged to Ellis's own *helper*.

Mia spread her coat out on the rocks, then sat with Kali nestled beside her. They listened to the water lapping the shoreline as Mia told Kali of the many joy-filled afternoons she'd spent here, like her father before her. Swimming or relaxing. Ezra, Freddie, and Natalie.

"And now, you," Mia said, leaning into Kali, her heart filled with contentment.

Mia gazed out at the vibrant red and burnt orange leaves on the far shore of the lake. In a week or so, they would drop. Then more snow would fall, and the lake would freeze. In the spring, there would be a new flush of color from foxglove, iris, and yarrow. The calls of red-winged blackbirds, blue jays, and brilliant cardinals would fill the air while the hot summer sun warmed the rocks underfoot. Embracing nature's cycle, Mia felt as alive as she'd ever been. She turned to Kali with a swell of emotion.

"I love you," she said.

Kali grinned. "You don't have to . . ." Her voice trailed off.

"Don't have to say the words for you to know?" Mia said. "Yes, I do." She was tired of bottling it all in. That was the old Mia.

"I love you, too," Kali said.

It was the second time that day she'd heard those words. Mia leaned into Kali and smiled, grateful to have her in her life.

"Who was that who called earlier?"

"That was the Good News Fairy," Kali said, chuckling. "Eli. He didn't want to bother you but asked me to tell you the job at Moon Harvest is yours if you're still interested."

Moon Harvest? The job? It had completely slipped her mind. "Really?" she said. "You're joking. No, you're not joking. Oh my God!" Mia shrieked. "I got the job!"

She gazed across the lake and squeezed Kali's hand, thinking of how much good there was in her life when all she'd been focused on was the bad.

"It's like picking flowers in the dark."

"Excuse me?" said Kali.

"It's something Mama used to say. You need to take the good with the bad, and you never know what you've got until the light of day."

Mia spun the ring around her finger, the feel of it bringing her closer to the man she'd misunderstood and the mother she still missed with all her heart. This was just the beginning, she realized, of her own recovery.

CHAPTER 28

Ellis sat at his desk, a fresh notebook and his old silver Montblanc before him as he tried to find the words to best express himself.

Where to start? It had been six months since the stroke. The therapy had been grueling. After months of relearning to speak, eat, and walk, Ellis lifted the pen and held it between his fingers to write.

This exercise was part of the mental therapy, also grueling in its way. He was confronting his reticence in expressing his feelings. Learning to *say* what was in his heart and not simply put it on the page. Though he needed to put it in writing, too.

He tapped the tip of the pen on the fresh notebook Mia had gifted him when he'd been released from the hospital. Another red notebook. Another beginning as he and Mia built a foundation for a new relationship.

Ellis recalled seeing Mia wearing Luisa's ring when she'd visited him in the hospital. When he'd walked Luisa to the bus in Alangui, he thought she'd be part of his life always. How could he have known that would manifest in a daughter who now wore the ring he'd purchased so hopefully and lovingly for her mother?

She'd read the journals as Ellis had hoped she would, and the result was ten times what he'd expected. At sixty, he marveled at how the events of 1988 had led to where he sat today.

Though speaking remained difficult, he'd addressed her reason for never returning home. Graduation.

Ellis's own graduation had been a disappointment. His mother chose to board a cruise ship instead. Ellis had added that slight to the many others over the years, but somehow, it stung the most. Knowing how absent he'd been for Mia, Ellis made a point of attending her ceremony. He endured a sixteen-hour flight from India and took his seat among the thousands of other parents. He wanted to wrap his arms around her and tell her how proud he was. She was courageous, resilient, beautiful, and very much like her mother.

He'd looked for her in the chairs on the field, scanning the program for the seating arrangement. He'd found the name: Mia Luise Ellis-Bacri. Third row, center right. He counted out the seats, looking for her as the commencement speeches droned on, uninteresting and irrelevant.

She hadn't come.

He should have called her. He should have gone to that apartment. Rosa had the address. There was no excuse other than his pride. But he held his tongue.

So, when she appeared at the hospital after the stroke, he felt like he had the chance to say the things he'd held back for too many years. But the damned stroke robbed him of his voice.

Ellis recalled his first stroke. That night, he'd answered his phone and heard her voice on the other end. TJ had been arrested. She needed Ellis's help. Ellis never felt she'd loved him, but knowing she *needed* him was a comfort.

But as he spoke with her, Ellis noticed that something was very wrong. He couldn't breathe right, he couldn't stand, and he'd barely hung up the phone before it got worse. *911, what's your emergency?* The ambulance was there in minutes.

Mia called Ellis for his help, and he was powerless.

A TIA they'd called it. Transient Ischemic Attack. A mini stroke that came and went. A small blood clot that passed, or a blood vessel in his brain that ruptured, then healed quickly. The human body is a remarkable thing. Mild as that stroke was, he kept it from Mia and TJ. Only his mother knew. He'd seen her image in her bedroom window as the ambulance rolled down the drive. She stood beside him as they loaded him in, and they never spoke of it again. Both guarding their true feelings, a family curse that Ellis hoped he'd seen the end of.

Through the weeks and months of recovery, Ellis worked hard to repair his relationship with Mia. She'd asked to keep the ring, and Ellis said yes, gladly. He was thrilled that she intended to wear it for the rest of her life.

"It might be a wedding ring still," she'd said. Ellis was thrilled at that, too. Kali was good for her. She was patient, nurturing, bright, and beautiful. He was happy for Mia to have someone to love for the rest of her life. It was something he'd longed for for himself, pining after a woman who'd never be his.

Ellis was grateful for the hours Mia spent with him during recovery, both at the hospital and later, when she made frequent visits to the cottage. She told him stories of growing up on Rue Janvier. Not all of it was as horrific as Ellis had envisioned. With Kali's help, Mia resurrected many fond memories of Luisa, her friend Jonas, and even Billy, who'd played such a large role at Ellis's request. He lived in Australia now, with a devoted wife and twin boys.

Ellis clutched the pen and pressed it firmly to the page.

June 16, 2019

Having a stroke was the best thing that could have happened to me.

ACKNOWLEDGEMENTS

First and foremost, I'd like to thank Andrew Durkin of Yellow Bike Press—editor extraordinaire, mentor, and publisher. This will be the third book in six years Andrew has helped me launch into the world. I couldn't ask for a better writing partner.

Thank you also to Stephanie Butland, author of The Curious Heart of Ailsa Rae, who lent me her practiced ear as I explained the complicated relationship between Mia and her father, Ellis.

I'm eternally grateful to my family and dear friends for their feedback and continued support. Most notably, Willie Hartman, my husband of nearly forty years, and the incredible women in my book group who've stuck with me for sixteen years. Special thanks to my mother, Sandy Hinkes, Shelley Rotondo, my sister-in-law, and my sister, Kate Fitzpatrick, for their encouragement throughout the writing process for this and previous novels.

ABOUT THE AUTHOR

Born and raised in Wisconsin, Maureen Hartman moved to the Pacific Northwest after finishing college at the University of Wisconsin-Madison. She's always been engaged with the outdoors but finds her greatest joy trekking along a wooded trail, paddling her kayak on a clear mountain lake, or getting her hands dirty in the garden. All of which allows for quiet thought to chew on plot points and character development for her novels. Never not writing.

Dear Reader

Thank you so much for choosing this book!

You are cordially invited to leave an honest review on Goodreads, or the online store or reader website of your choice. Reader reviews are the lifeblood of independent publishing, and your opinion is valued!

For updates on the next books in this series, please join Maureen's newsletter at www.maureenhartman.com.

Authors are nothing without readers! Thank you again.